Lowell School
1640 Kalmia Road, NW
Washington, DC 20012

HEART of GLASS

ALSO BY SASHA GOULD

Cross My Heart

HEART of GLASS

Sasha Gould

DELACORTE PRESS

Text copyright © 2013 by Working Partners Limited
Jacket photographs © by C Beauty Photo Studio/AGE Fotostock (front, girl), Alan Jenkins/Trevillion Images (front, fan), and Csaba Peterdi/Shutterstock.com (back)

Visit us on the Web! randomhouse.com/teens
Educators and librarians, for a variety of teaching tools, visit us at RHTeachersLibrarians.com

Library of Congress Cataloging-in-Publication Data
Gould, Sasha.
Heart of glass / Sasha Gould. — 1st ed.   p. cm.
Companion to: Cross my heart.
Summary: In Renaissance Venice, Laura's marriage to Roberto is thrown into chaos when he is accused of murder, while the Segreta are under threat from the Doge's army, and loyalties are sorely tested.
ISBN 978-0-385-74152-1 (hc) — ISBN 978-0-375-98541-6 (ebook) — ISBN 978-0-375-99008-3 (glb)
[1. Secret societies—Fiction. 2. Sex role—Fiction. 3. Love—Fiction. 4. Venice (Italy)—History—16th century—Fiction. 5. Italy—History—16th century—Fiction. 6. Mystery and detective stories.] I. Title.
PZ7.G73585He 2013   [Fic]—dc23   2012014714

The text of this book is set in 11.75-point Cochin.
Book design by Vikki Sheatsley

Printed in the United States of America
10 9 8 7 6 5 4 3 2 1
First Edition

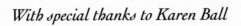

With special thanks to Karen Ball

1

I gaze down the length of the narrow blade at my enemy. His own sword is lowered, his chest heaving as a bead of sweat rolls lazily over the ridge of his collarbone and then into the dip of his sternum. It joins the others in a damp patch over his heart.

"Yield," he says.

"Make me."

Roberto sends me a smile, then attacks. I dodge across the varnished floorboards of the palace's gallery, but my silk skirts swing heavily, weighted by the lead beads sewn into the hem. They're slowing me down.

"A peacock's feathers don't help it fly," Roberto says, his eyes traveling over the shot turquoise of my dress. With a hiss of impatience I use my free hand to loosen the ribbons on my outer robe, shoving one shoulder and then the other out of the bodice until the silk slips over my limbs and lands with a sigh in a blue cloud at my feet. Neatly, I step out of it, my sword still trained on Roberto. I ignore the loud tut of disapproval from the servant who sits on one of the window seats, chaperoning us. When I first met Roberto six months ago, I might have blushed, but six moons have done more than just improve my sword skills. I'm a different person.

"You may leave us," I call out. My eyes never stray from Roberto's face.

There's a scuffle of shoes across wood and then the slam of a door shutting.

"Now there's no one to witness your humiliation," I say. My voice echoes around the long gallery.

"Or yours," Roberto replies, raising his eyebrows.

I stand before him in nothing but my linen chemise and corset. My cheeks are hot, with both the duel and my recklessness. I blow a stray lock of hair out of my face and it sticks to my temple.

Roberto slowly circles. "Are you going to use that sword or just admire it?"

I turn on the spot. Behind him shift the blurry outlines of oil paintings and—as we turn again—long windows, beyond which lies Venice. Once a prison, now my home. The days of the convent are long gone, many months ago, fading quickly into the past. My stale vows to God will always lurk in my mind, but they are nothing more than a distant chanting now, faint beneath new words of love.

Roberto dances lightly from foot to foot. One flying lunge with my sword and I'll be the victor; a single riposte from him and I taste defeat. I notice his hand tighten slightly under his bell guard, and anticipate his move. As he lunges I hop to one side, turning my back on him and bringing my own blade round in a swift movement so that it cuts up under his. Our weapons bounce apart, but with a light jump

2

I bring the buttoned point of my sword against Roberto's chest, the blade bending under the pressure. We're so close that I can feel Roberto's breath on my face.

"Disarming," he says. He fails to keep the surprise out of his voice.

I cannot help laughing, though we don't pull apart. "Does this make me the winner?" I ask.

Roberto dips his head in acknowledgment. "So it seems."

"Then I demand my prize."

He glances back up, his eyes widening a little as he leans against my blade. "Which is?"

I jerk my sword away and he staggers into me. He straightens up, cheeks flushing. "Laura—"

Before he can say another word, I bring my sword around in a wide arc until the blunt tip slides between our bodies and presses against the underside of his chin. "I demand a kiss."

We both wait. I lower my sword. Roberto is free to move. His arm is suddenly around my waist, bringing me even closer to him. As his chest presses against mine I am aware of the thin fabric of my chemise, the heat of his body. He leans over me, arching my spine backwards, and presses his lips against the hollow at the base of my throat, which I know must be salty with sweat. When he releases me, we gaze at each other, standing on either side of a long sunbeam that traces a path across the floorboards.

"Is this what love feels like?" he asks.

"I think so."

We both know how lucky we are. It might have been so different, if my father had had his way. I shudder to think

3

of the man I was to marry, one of my father's cronies from the Grand Council. Vincenzo was old, selfish and cruel, but he was rich, and that's all that matters to a man like my father. And at that time, Roberto was living in poverty as a painter, under the name Giacomo. For his past too was a prison of sorts, hiding from the vendetta that threatened his life as the Doge's son. It's a miracle our paths crossed at all.

I go to pick up my discarded dress as Roberto pours us each a tumbler of water from a glass jug with images of swans etched and gilded on its handle. He hands me the water and I gulp it down gratefully. Roberto wipes the back of his hand across his mouth, recovering his breath. Beyond his head, a row of portraits of Doges past runs across the paneled wall. Roberto's father, Alfonso, the present Doge, is last. The ancient faces that look down at me are stern and unforgiving, dark shadows lurking in the corners of one painting, a fierce dog sitting at its master's feet in another. One day, Roberto's portrait will hang there too, but I can't imagine him gazing down on Venice with such ferocity.

Roberto removes his shirt and towels himself dry with it. As he moves, the muscles of his stomach contract and expand, so that the scar on his chest seems to writhe across his skin. It will always be a reminder to us of how precarious life can be in Venice. The wound, delivered when he was just a boy, has long since healed, but a few months ago the same blood feud almost claimed his life again. It was only the intervention of the Segreta that ended the cycle of violence and spared him.

The Segreta. The Secret Women. The female balance to the Doge's brute force and power. I owe everything to them. They welcomed me to their bosom when I had nowhere else to turn. They rescued me from a marriage to Vincenzo, exposing his crimes and leading to his exile. Now they are my family. We operate under cover and behind the scenes, the hidden puppeteers who see that justice is done in a city teeming with corruption.

"What are you thinking?" Roberto asks, eyeing the sudden change in my expression.

I shake my head. "I've just remembered!" I say. "My brother arrives any day now, from Bologna. I can't wait for you to meet Lysander."

Roberto throws his shirt on the floor and pours himself another glass of water. "But will Antonio approve of him becoming acquainted with a ruffian like myself?" He raises the glass at me, then takes a deep draught.

I laugh. "Do you remember Father threatening to set the dogs on you, the lowly painter?"

Roberto rolls his eyes. "Oh yes. Those imaginary dogs." He laughs too. Father has refused to have dogs in the house ever since I was a child and a pet mastiff chewed a hole in our finest rug.

A muffled sound from behind the floor-to-ceiling doors makes us both quiet abruptly. Roberto holds a finger to his lips as we listen to the sound of voices; then one of the doors is flung open and a figure falls into the room, pushing past servants.

"I'm a lady-in-waiting!" she screeches, before stopping short. Faustina blushes crimson as her gaze travels over the sight of Roberto and me. Suddenly, I am all too aware of Roberto's naked torso and my own thin undergarments.

"Never did I think I'd live to see such a thing," she

mutters. She swivels round, turning her back on us. "Get dressed, for propriety's sake!" A servant has peered around the open doorway and she shouts at him, "Get out! Leave!" She shakes a gnarled fist and his head quickly disappears from view.

Roberto and I scramble into our clothes, and I go to my maidservant's side. If she wants to call herself a lady-in-waiting, I won't object. Once my wet nurse, she's always been my closest companion. My dearest Faustina, whose soft folds and tender hugs have comforted me through many troubles.

Her eyes flicker to one side, checking that I am back in my blue dress. "We have an appointment to keep, remember?"

I hadn't forgotten—how could I? "Help me with my bodice?" I ask her. As she tugs on the ribbons, she glances over at Roberto. "Wait for me outside," I tell her gently, turning to kiss her on the cheek. "We'll be with you in a moment."

"Don't let him lead you astray," she whispers loudly, scuttling towards the open door. Her hand darts out and she slaps one of the boy servants hanging on the frame around the back of his head. "No spying!" The door shuts behind her.

Roberto watches me as I turn back to face the room. We smile at each other and I walk to his open arms, resting my face against his chest, listening to the steady beat of his heart. I offer up my face to him and he takes hold of my chin, pressing his lips to mine.

Eventually, he pulls away. "I must attend a meeting

with Massimo," he tells me. "The Admiral wants to discuss rumors of an Ottoman threat."

My skin prickles with disquiet. Ottomans or Turks — that's all the men of Venice seem to talk about these days. But I keep my thoughts to myself.

"I'll see you soon," I say.

"Not soon enough," he replies. Since he asked for my hand four months ago, the only time we've spent apart was when he visited Constantinople on behalf of his father. Those awful few days seemed to stretch into years, and we've vowed never to be away from each other for so long again.

"Laura!" calls Faustina's impatient voice from the other side of the door, dragging my thoughts back to the present. "The sun is already dipping below the spires of Saint Zachary. Are you ready?"

I giggle and give Roberto a final kiss. Then I run from the gallery. Faustina waits outside with her arms folded.

"Come on, then!" I say, grasping her hand and dragging her behind me.

2

Faustina huffs and puffs as she struggles to keep up. We make our way down a cobbled alley that stretches out from the palace, like a single strand in the spiderweb of paths and roads that crisscross Venice. Our feet turn towards the Cannaregio district. As she walks, Faustina flaps her knotted hands before her face, then reaches into a pocket and snaps open a paper fan with a scene painted across it.

"A present?" I ask, slowing my pace so that she can keep up.

"Never you mind," she retorts.

"Must be from an admirer," I say. A man passes, carrying a tray of sardines. He smiles and dips his head. I raise my eyebrow at Faustina.

"How dare you!" she says. The man looks alarmed and scurries past us, moving closer to the wall. "I'm too old for such nonsense, you know that." She looks over her shoulder as the market trader turns down another alley. "Though, once . . . Oh, never mind."

"You must tell me!" I say, grasping her hand. We walk side by side, our bodies jostling comfortably.

Faustina gives a dramatic sigh and raises her head to gaze at the towers and columns that rise above us. The sky is a clear blue this afternoon, though tinged at the edges by the sunset that will soon be upon us. We pause by a stall and I hand over a few coins for a *pan dei dosi* each, the pastries studded with hazelnuts and dried fruit. I pass one to Faustina and begin to eat my own, licking the cinnamon from my lips as we walk.

"Our families knew each other," says Faustina. "We all lived in the same courtyard. He'd never noticed me until . . ." She casts a hand across her ample bosom. "I grew up." I swallow quickly and bite my lip to stop myself from laughing. But Faustina hasn't noticed; she's lost in the memory. We pass beside a fountain with a young man's naked body holding aloft a giant scallop shell. "He was so handsome. Like that statue."

"What happened?" I ask. Faustina has never married, devoting her life to caring for me and my siblings. The death of my only sister, Beatrice, was as hard for her as it was for me.

Faustina's face colors. "It wasn't to be."

We've arrived at an arched doorway carved out of golden sandstone. Fluted columns stand on either side of it. A young girl opens the door for us. "This way, please," she murmurs.

"We're waiting for a friend," I explain, glancing up and down the cobbled street. I smile at the maid.

Faustina explodes in a fit of coughing and hastily pulls a crumpled piece of paper from inside her bodice. She shoves the note into my hand, the paper damp from her sweat.

"I'm so sorry!" she wheezes. "I forgot to give you this. It arrived this morning."

Carefully, I open the note and flatten out the paper. My eyes scan the writing quickly. It's from Paulina.

My dearest Laura,

    I can't join you today. I'm so sorry. I know you'll choose the perfect wedding dress!

                                    Paulina

I crumple the paper back up in my hand and paint a smile on my face, ignoring the stab of disappointment. Paulina knows better than most how much this wedding means to me, how much I suffered to get to this place. My mother and sister are both dead and cannot be with me today. I was looking forward to my childhood friend helping me choose the most important dress of my life. Not even a proper explanation! I push my uncharitable thoughts away. She must have a good reason.

Faustina is watching my face carefully, and the maid is drumming her nails against her folded arms.

"Please, show us the way," I say to the servant.

We follow her up the gloomy marble staircase to the grand floor where the dressmaker accepts visitors. Faustina made an appointment for us a few weeks ago.

A white-haired woman sits on a low couch, a string of coral at her throat. She wears a simple cotton dress with a pattern of flowers woven into the fabric and hems the square of gold silk on her lap, a silver thimble on the middle finger of her right hand. Seeing her work reminds me of the many hours I toiled at making lace during my time in the convent, before I was summoned home upon Beatrice's death. A moment's pain passes behind my eyes, but as the woman looks up at me and smiles, it falls away again.

"Welcome," she says, getting to her feet. Faustina goes to greet her, and waves a hand towards me. "Do you see what I mean? Beautiful, yes?"

"Yes, quite charming." The dressmaker does not have to introduce herself. Her name is famous in the streets of Venice: Gabriella da Mosto. She made the wedding dresses for Roberto's mother and, years later, for Paulina, when she married Roberto's brother, Nicolo.

The woman turns her attention to me. She holds out her hand, and the young girl who answered the door runs to place a wooden bobbin in her palm. Around it is a thin roll of waxed canvas, marks etched along its side.

"Come here, my dear," Gabriella instructs. I feel clumsy and awkward before her. Lightly, she takes my hands and lifts them away from my sides. "Stay like this," she orders. Then she brings the tape around my waist and holds it before the front of my bodice, frowning in concentration as she murmurs numbers to the girl, who scribbles them down in a ledger. I stay where I am as Gabriella moves from shoulder to neck to waist. Finally, she steps away and casts an assessing glance down the length of me. "Doria!" She snaps her fingers without looking round. "The deep rose pink."

Faustina and I share a glance, and my servant smiles encouragingly. She lowers herself slowly onto the couch, and a male servant brings two steaming glasses of mint tea and a plate of marinated shrimps, setting them on the table before her. Faustina pops a curl of tender flesh into her mouth as the girl returns, a heavy bundle of fabric balanced between her outstretched arms. Reverently, she places her load onto a varnished oak table, and Gabriella comes to stand beside her.

The dressmaker takes hold of a bolt of the pink silk and unfolds it. I can't help but draw near. This is the fabric that I am to be married in. As she works the silk loose, Gabriella talks.

"A low bodice, I think," she says, "and tight sleeves in the Spanish mode. A cap of green netting and perhaps even a sable pelt. Gathering at the waist. Of course, silk thread for hand picking the seams." She allows the thick fabric to fall back to the table in a waterfall of color.

"I'd like a secret pocket in the lining of the skirt," I tell her.

Faustina coughs uncomfortably, and Gabriella cocks her head to one side. Perhaps she isn't used to such requests.

"A secret pocket," I repeat. "I must insist." This woman will make me a beautiful dress, of that I am sure. But I want a hand in it. This is the dress that will take me into my future.

A smile spreads across the dressmaker's face. "With our seams, you could hide a dagger and the hang of the skirts would give nothing away."

From the couch, Faustina sighs with relief.

"Thank you," I say.

"Betrothed to the Doge's first son," Gabriella continues. "This will be the marriage of the year."

Coming from Gabriella da Mosto, creator of wedding

dresses for generations of Venetian women, this is high praise.

"I am blessed," I say.

"Wait here a moment." The dressmaker retreats to the back of her quarters, and I take a seat beside Faustina, who's making short work of the shrimps. I take a sip of mint tea. Doria and the male servant are bowed over the oak table, smoothing out the silk. I catch a whisper, and it sounds, though I can't be sure, like "Doge's funeral."

I feel my face stiffen, and as my eyes meet the girl's, she blushes and looks away.

Do even common servants know about the Doge's falling sickness, the ailment that places his life and reputation in peril? And if they know, where have they heard it? Despite all my happiness, all my blessings, in that moment the past tugs at my stomach. His sickness was the secret I shared in order to be accepted into the Segreta. It was a mistake, a betrayal, but at the time it seemed the only coin I had to barter for their help. Our community of women trades on secrets, but if what I shared has become common knowledge . . . Well, the Doge has plenty of enemies looking for just such an excuse to topple him.

Gabriella returns. "Your dress will be ready for a first fitting in three weeks. Until then." She nods a goodbye.

Faustina and I say our farewells and we descend the stairs, out into the fading afternoon sunshine. For a moment, I feel weary — my allegiance to the Segreta is weighing me down. But Faustina is impervious to my mood.

"Jewelry next!" she announces. "To match the glass beads of your headdress." She is already striding down the road, and I break into a modest trot. But as we turn a corner, we both stop short. A woman a little older than I am is walking towards us, wearing a black velvet dress with raised stripes of gold thread. But there is another stripe too—this one down her face—a streak of blood that runs from a deep cut on her forehead. She holds up a hand to try to hide it, but there is no disguising the swollen bruise that is forcing her left eye half shut.

"Come here," I tell the woman, going to take her by the arm. "What happened to you?" She tries to pull away from me; I can feel her body trembling. "You don't need to fear us," I tell her. "Please. Let me help."

"Who did this to you?" Faustina asks, bustling over. "The beast!"

A few people look round at Faustina's shrill cry, and the woman flinches.

"It's nothing to bother yourselves with," she says, trying her best to turn her body from us. But I reach out a hand and gently bring her back round to face me. I take a handkerchief from the folds of my skirt and dab at the blood on her temple. She doesn't pull away.

I spot a teahouse with stools ranged beneath an awning. "Come," I say gently, taking the woman by the arm. "Sit for a moment."

I lead the woman over to the wicker stools. She sits with a sigh, resting her head in her hands. Faustina calls for the tea and pours, holding out a glass to the woman. She takes it with shaking hands. We wait in silence for her to recover as she takes small sips. Eventually she offers us a watery smile.

"Thank you," she says.

"I'm Laura. What's your name?"

"Teresa," she whispers.

"What happened to you?" I ask.

She laughs bitterly. "My husband happened to me." She starts to get to her feet, but her face turns suddenly white and she's forced to sit back down.

Faustina huffs. "Men!"

"Go and buy some figs," I tell her. Anything to get her out of earshot for the moment. "Something for our friend."

Faustina nods eagerly, glad of something to do. My nurse likes to feed people. I watch her go over to a nearby market stall.

As soon as she's gone, I lean forward and grasp the woman's hands. "You shouldn't have to suffer this way," I say.

She shrugs. "It's the way things are."

I shake my head. "Only if we let it happen. I can help you."

She looks at me skeptically. "I don't think you're a match for Silvio."

Perhaps not on my own, I think. I squeeze her hand. "Meet me tonight in the disused wine cellar on the Ponte San Polo. It has a green door. A tarred barrel sits beside the doorway, and the name of the old merchant, Zenato, is painted on the door."

"What can you do?" the woman says, her eyes brimming.

"Trust me," I say. "Come, and you will find out."

She shakes her head. "My husband holds the strings of the family's purse. I wouldn't be able to pay the gondolier!"

I reach into my purse and slide a coin into the woman's

palm. "Take this. Midnight, be at Zenato's. Believe me — I really can help." Has this woman heard of the Segreta? Does she guess what I mean?

The woman nods once, and slips out of her seat just as Faustina returns with a twisted paper parcel brimming with fresh figs. One of the fruits has burst open and its seeds glow like tiny chips of gold.

"You've forgotten your figs!" Faustina calls after the woman as she turns a shady corner. I watch the ebony hem of her skirts glide out of sight.

"Where's she going?" Faustina asks, shrugging with open palms. "Not back to that husband, I hope."

"She'll be safe," I tell the woman who knows me so well, but is blind to my deepest secrets. "Venice will look after her."

3

A hired coach takes Faustina and me across the Rialto Bridge towards home. Pulling into the gated driveway, I remember when I returned here for the first time after my incarceration. Then, it looked old and tired. Father was penniless and my sister lay in a coffin. Now, Father is on Venice's Grand Council, his greatest ambitions realized, and Beatrice is gone forever.

I step out of the coach, Faustina sighing behind me as she lowers her tired old body. The della Scala home rises up before us. The cool of the hallway beckons. I walk across the marbled floor, once broken and chipped, now repaired. The walls glow with a fresh layer of whitewash, and the gilt frame of the hall mirror has been repainted.

"I'm home!" I call out, and hear an answering voice. Too youthful to be my father's, but equally recognizable, even after all these years.

"We're in the library!"

I rush into the room at the far end of the hallway, the door half hidden beneath the stairs. Pushing it open, I see a face that almost reflects mine, but not quite. The same chin, only stronger. Eyes the same color as mine, but the hair short, thick and pushed back from a widow's peak.

"Lysander!" I cry, and fall into my brother's arms. He doesn't wear the clothes of a Venetian gentleman. He sports more somber colors, having lived in Bologna for many years, training to be a physician. I heard through Beatrice's letters that his apartments are near the Botanical Gardens, where the people of Bologna grow healing herbs, but this is the first time I've seen him since the day I entered the convent.

"Let me look at you," I say, pulling back. I hold him at arm's length and turn him round on the spot. He laughs and indulges me. "You've put on weight," I declare. I prod him in the stomach.

"Hey, hey! Aren't you supposed to tell me how much you love me and how you've missed me? Who cares about my popping waistcoat!"

Of course, my dearest brother is as slender as he ever was. He strokes the back of his hand down my cheek.

"You've grown into a beautiful woman," he says. "Beatrice would have been proud of you."

I feel my eyes burn; tears are brimming, ready to fall. I dash a hand across my face. Lysander peers at me, then smiles.

"As soft as ever. Come here."

How far he is from the truth. If he only knew. He draws me to him, and it's only then — glancing over his shoulder — that I see we are not alone.

"Who's this?" I ask, pushing myself out of my brother's

arms. A woman stands behind him. She has long auburn locks that cascade over one shoulder and a smattering of freckles against milky skin. When she smiles at me, her teeth are as white as snow and her lips blush red. As she raises a hand in greeting, there's the sparkle of gold on her finger.

"This is my wife, Emilia," Lysander tells me, turning to hold out an arm. Still smiling, the woman comes up to Lysander and slips her arm through the one he offers her. Cream organza froths at her neckline.

"I had no idea!" I cry, holding out a hand. I smile at her, and, after a moment's hesitation, she takes it.

"Love moves swiftly," she says, and laughs, the sound rolling like a bubbling stream.

A figure appears in the open doorway. "More swiftly than wisdom, it seems."

My father steps into the library, past the sweeping shelves of expensive books that just a year ago stood empty. Has he ever read any of them? A beam of light falls across his face, sending slanting shadows into the creases of his eyes and the curl of his lip. He looks as if carved from stone. "In my day, all brides came with a dowry," he says pointedly, staring at Lysander's wife so hard that her cheeks flush. He doesn't even use her name.

"Father," Lysander says stiffly. "*Emilia* and I aren't concerned by such things. We love each other."

Father lets out a hiss of disgust. "The sentiments of a young man. I hope age will bring you a better head for the business of marriage."

I roll my eyes and Lysander shrugs. "It makes no

difference now. It's not a contract I intend to alter." He gently pats Emilia's hand, which still rests on his arm. I notice that her fingers are trembling.

The elder statesman of our family stalks around the room. The floorboards creak beneath his weight. "Do you know what it's been like for me? Do you?" He swivels round to stare at Lysander.

"Oh, Father, don't make such a fuss," I say. "Our family is fine. We're in a much better situation than this time last year."

"You have no idea," he says, shifting his gaze to me. "Not a clue! The pressure I am under. Florentine ambassadors to curry favor with, delicate negotiations about the Ottoman routes. People talk of pirates! One wrong word, one misjudged conversation, and my status could be at risk. The Doge insists on diplomacy when all the Council knows that we need to come down hard. The man's a fool!"

"That's treason, Father," I say, winking at Lysander.

My father pales, then sees my hint of a smile. He glowers. "I mean . . . we are at a delicate stage. I don't need an impoverished son to add to my troubles!"

The air throbs with tension. Then Lysander's nostrils flare, and I realize he is stifling a yawn.

"How tiresome for you," my brother says, waving a hand lazily as though swatting away imaginary wasps.

Father's eyes widen in outrage. "You'll learn," he spits. He's already striding from the room, the tails of his coat flying. "A physician's wages are nothing, and a penniless son should respect his father. He clearly doesn't respect himself, marrying . . . that!"

The door slams shut behind him. I want to apologize to Emilia, but Lysander is already by her side, kissing her brow.

"Take no notice," I hear him whisper.

Emilia catches my eye and forces a smile. I walk over and take her arm, leading her to gaze out of the library windows at the panorama of Venice, lit by the moon that hangs, almost full, in the summer sky.

"I will show you my home," I say, "where Lysander and I grew up with Beatrice."

"I'd like that," my new sister-in-law tells me. She squeezes my hand as Lysander comes to stand behind us.

"He's gotten worse," he grumbles.

"Don't worry about Father," I say. "Nothing makes him happier than a dose of unhappiness, and since his success at the Grand Council, he is struggling for things to complain about."

But Lysander refuses to laugh. "It looked as though the Grand Council have been busy, judging from the harbor," he says. "Security was tighter than I've ever seen it. We had to empty our trunks to be searched."

Emilia laughs anxiously. "The guards nearly dropped my dress for the embassy ball into the water!"

"Oh, I'm glad you'll be there," I say. "It will be an important night for Venice."

Faustina has stepped into the room with a plate of olives and bread. "You can thank the Doge for the searches," she comments, setting the tray down on a small table. She looks over both of her shoulders, as though checking for strangers, and brings her face close to ours. "Spies! He's worried about spies."

Emilia's face pales and she casts my brother a glance as if to say, *What type of place have you brought me to?*

Later, we dine with Father. Success has done little to curb his drinking, and we watch in uncomfortable silence as he pours himself yet another glass of wine. A servant brings in the hazelnut pudding, but I'm fearful of being late for my appointment.

"I'm going to retire now," I announce. I push my chair back and its feet screech awkwardly against the floor.

"Already?" Father asks, his words slurred. But his eyelids are drooping, and I can tell that within the hour he will be in a deep sleep and past caring.

"I need my bed," I lie. "It's been a long day."

Emilia gives me a sympathetic look, and Lysander kisses my hand. Father reaches for the wine, and I leave the room.

While the city falls asleep, I have business to attend to.

4

I step out into the cool of the night, grasping my mask. From a nearby clock tower I can see that midnight will soon be upon us—I must make haste. I run lightly down the drive and out into the streets of Venice, following their twists and turns, glancing about for a coach to hire. I move as quietly as one of many secrets that travel through this city. The Segreta trade in the stories that no one wants to share; that's what gives the women of Venice their power. Soon, I will be with my masked friends. I hope Teresa will join us too—I know the women of the Segreta will do everything they can to help her.

The coach pulls up outside Zenato the wine merchant's. I go to the doorway and give my secret knock—not on the door itself, but on the frame, where the wool gives a duller sound, softened so that passing strangers or sleeping neighbors won't hear. The door opens silently, its hinges oiled, and there's the glint of eyes behind a mask. I slip inside and run down the stone stairs to the basement. Candles flicker like the dancing eyes of the devil. The women have gathered in a pool of light.

It's still a thrill to be welcomed by the Segreta. At first they terrified me, but I was a different girl then—caught between submitting to a marriage with cruel Vincenzo and trusting that these women could set me free. I chose the Segreta. I made the right choice. Within hours, they had exposed Vincenzo's corruption, and the betrothal was broken.

"Welcome," says a voice from behind her mask. I recognize her at once—from the mask's feline design and the husky tones. It's Grazia de Ferrara. The simple silver ring on her middle finger might look like a cheap market trinket, but for those of us initiated into the Segreta, it is the sign that someone is in the upper echelons of Venice's most exclusive club. Simple, demure—but a sign of great power. One day I hope to wear one like it, but for now I'm still in the lower ranks of this secret society. Beside Grazia is the woman who leads us, with gray-streaked hair and sharp eyes of bright green: Allegreza di Rocco. Allegreza clutches a mask, its eyeholes framed by jewels and lace, its edges sparkling with gold feathers. Allegreza's ring has a small ruby embedded in it, made for her by one of the best jewelers in the city. If the master craftsman only knew what Allegreza had commissioned from him!

"I hope you are well," I say to Grazia.

She takes the mask from her face, and her eyes, as so often, are watchful and sad. Grazia, Allegreza and I are bonded by a secret not known even to the rest of the Segreta: Grazia's daughter Carina was killed in Venice's

24

waters. Turned to spite through twisted love, it was she who killed Beatrice. When I revealed what I knew, she tried to kill me and, in the process, died herself. The image of her writhing in pain in the flames of a burning boat and the sound of her shrieks will never leave me.

"Old friends!" a voice calls softly. I recognize the tone of Paulina's whispers as she arrives, out of breath.

"So glad to see you finally," I say.

Paulina puts a hand on my arm. "I'm so sorry! My cousins were visiting and I couldn't get away. Anyway, you're a big girl now! You can choose dresses without me."

I feel a frown crease my brow, but it's hard to stay cross with Paulina for long. "No matter, Faustina came with me."

"Oh no!" she whispers. "You'll be wearing a burlap sack on your wedding day!"

I giggle, drawing a sharp glance from Grazia. Segreta business is rarely mirthful. "We'll be sisters-in-law soon," I say to Paulina.

"Not long now!" she says. "Perhaps you can spare Nicolo and me a small room in your palace."

She's smiling as she speaks, and her eyes flicker like molten gold in the candlelight. This isn't the first time she's said this, and I wonder if the repetition is intentional. It seems every time we meet she makes some comment about being disinherited or impoverished. It's true that since Roberto returned from hiding, Nicolo is no longer his father's heir, but Paulina's barbed jokes make me uncomfortable. It is not as if Paulina will ever be poor, and our friendship is worth more than money. To me, anyway.

"You know you'll always be welcome with us, don't you?" I say.

"Of course!" she replies, but still she can't seem to look me in the eye.

Allegreza walks into the center of the group and we form a tight circle of the initiated, sworn to loyalty. I wonder whether Teresa will turn up at the time I suggested.

"We have an important matter to discuss," announces Allegreza. "Word comes from our sisters abroad: a secret message written in ammonia salts. A boat will arrive here tomorrow evening. Because of the extra security at the harbor, our visitor will disembark at the island of Murano to be met by one of our representatives." She gazes around the room. "I need a volunteer."

Before I can open my mouth to speak, Paulina moves forward. "I'll go."

But Allegreza shakes her head. "You are too inexperienced." Paulina's cheeks flush, and she steps back into the circle. Allegreza's voice softens. "We would not wish any harm to befall you." Our leader's gaze drifts to me.

"Laura," she says. "You wish to say something?"

I find myself stepping forward. "I can help, if it is what you wish." Even as the words leave my mouth, I remember the grand masquerade ball that is to take place in the streets around St. Mark's tomorrow night. No wonder the rest of the group stays silent—they all want to dance and enjoy the carnival.

Allegreza bows her head in acknowledgment. "Thank you, Laura," she says. And the matter is closed. When I turn to Paulina, she is already walking away.

There's a muffled knock from the doorway, and a rush of cold air as the door is opened. Then, footsteps on the stairs, and Teresa steps into the room. She's a little early.

Quickly, everyone slides their masks over their faces. Allegreza turns into an owl, Grazia morphs into a sly black cat. I bring my own mask down to hide my expression, the swan feathers tickling my cheeks as I tie the silk ribbons around my head. As Teresa looks about, she's surrounded by a collection of hidden faces.

"Who are you, and what brings you here?" Allegreza asks, her voice stern.

Teresa clears her throat. The bruise on her eye has deepened, as dark as ripe black grapes.

"My name is Teresa," she begins, her voice shaking. "I was invited here."

Eyes dart around the room but I say nothing. Now is not the time.

"My husband is a fighting man, a soldier," she goes on. "But he has learned to love his fists too much." A hand flutters up to her face, to indicate her injuries. "I was told help might wait for me here tonight."

"That depends," says Allegreza.

The rest of the women stand as still as statues. I remember how it felt to be scrutinized by the Segreta.

"We trade favors for secrets," says Allegreza. "Do you have a secret you can share?"

"What do you mean?" asks Teresa.

Allegreza spreads her hands, and her voice is gentle. "I mean, we will help you, but there is a price."

Teresa shakes her head slowly. "I have no secrets."

This brings titters and chuckles from the room, even from me. Allegreza's eyes narrow behind her mask. "Everyone has secrets. Would you like to take a moment to think?"

Teresa stares hard at the floor, clearly trying to contain her emotions.

I step forward and put a hand on her arm. "I was the one who summoned you here," I tell her gently. "I want to make your life easier, but you must do this thing for us first. Secrets are everywhere, and what seems innocuous to you might be the difference between life and death for another. Think carefully."

When she looks back up at us, the tears finally spill from her eyes.

"Gunpowder," she says.

Hisses and whispers fly from the women, crowding in the air above our heads like a flock of birds.

"Quiet," Allegreza orders. She stares at the woman. "Go on."

"I remember my husband talking about armaments, stockpiled in the . . . I think he said the Arsenal." Teresa wrings her hands. She knows that her words put her life in danger. The contents of the Arsenal are a closely guarded secret.

"And what did your husband say?" I ask her.

"He said the gunpowder stores were tainted during the last flood. It's almost all useless now. Whole barrels of it. Admiral Massimo is furious and told him not to tell anyone. But when my husband drinks, his tongue is as loose as his fists."

This is very interesting indeed. Gunpowder is the source of our power on the seas. If our enemies were to discover this, the whole city could be in danger.

"Well done," Allegreza says, coming to place a hand on the woman's arm. "You have guaranteed your safety. In re-

turn for your secret, we can initiate you into our group."
She jerks her arm, and a small dagger emerges from her
sleeve, her hand grasping the hilt. The blade glitters.

Teresa backs away. "What is your intention?"

Allegreza smiles and turns the blade in the light. "It is
nothing, really. A small nick across your palm. Here, give
me your hand."

But Teresa is cowering against the wall now. "I don't
want to be cut! I'm a simple woman." She looks from face
to face, her eyes wild. "Please, let me go."

Allegreza makes a small movement, and her dagger disappears. "Calm yourself," she says gently. "You can leave
us. We will put your problem to rights."

A sob escapes Teresa as her eyes dart, like those of a
trapped animal, to the door. "Thank you, thank you."

She turns on her heel and walks up the stone steps out
of the cellar. She's at the top when Allegreza calls out, "Remember, Teresa, say nothing of what you've seen here."

Teresa disappears into the night. Not all are made to be
members of the Segreta, and I wonder if I'll ever see her
again.

There is a few moments' pause. "If what she tells us is
true," I say, "our ships are guard dogs without any teeth."

"And Massimo is in trouble," says another of the
women, referring to the Admiral. "The blame will fall on
him if this comes out. That must be why he's keeping this
a secret—we would have heard if he'd made an official report to the Doge on the matter."

"But how can we use the information?" says Allegreza.

Silence stretches between us. I can't think of a single
sensible theory to put forward. Paulina, her eyes wide

behind her turquoise-trimmed mask, lets out a sigh of frustration. "That woman's secret means nothing!"

But Grazia steps into the center of the circle. "Not so hasty, young one," she says. How many secrets has Grazia known? How many years has she been a member of the Society? Since before I was born, I'd vouch. "No information is without value," she says. "That woman is married to a soldier—part of a world we rarely glimpse. We should wait and watch our chess pieces. When the time is right, we'll know what move to make."

Allegreza nods slowly. "There's wisdom in your words, sister. Even a lowly pawn can achieve a checkmate. In the meantime, we must look to solve Teresa's problem. That should be easier."

"Agreed," we murmur. One by one, we climb the stairs to leave. Another secret has been shared tonight. Another mystery awaits.

5

A girl in scarlet tights walks above our heads. Emilia and I crane our necks back to watch as she balances on a taut rope stretched between two hooks high on the walls. She holds out her arms over the stiff net skirt that surrounds her hips, as satin slippers, dyed the same color as her stockings, curl with the precarious grip of her toes on the rope.

"Don't jump!" calls out a boisterous man, and his friends laugh as the girl passes over them. They stare greedily at her long limbs, encased in silk.

"Unbelievable," Emilia breathes. A group of lute players passes before us, followed by a performer wearing the familiar uniform of a colorful patched tunic and leggings. He hops nimbly and turns a cartwheel, and we are forced to leap, laughing, out of his way.

Emilia's cheeks are flushed from the heat of the ball-room, and she holds her hands to her sides. She is wearing an embroidered dress with a frilled collar at her breast. Her throat is as white as alabaster, and her hair sparkles with the gold ribbons that draw back her curls. Around us pass men and women wearing ornate masks covered in feathers and sequins, gathered scraps of lace and fluttering curtains of silk. Sinister hooked beaks, laughing clown faces and feathered hats abound. Ribbons quickly work themselves loose, and the heat of the room has people pushing their masks down to dangle around their throats.

"Good evening, Laura!" a voice calls out—one of Father's friends. People dance with dramatic flourishes, goblets are quickly drained of wine and platters of cold meats are picked clean.

"So, how do you like it?" I ask Emilia, taking two glasses of wine from a passing tray.

"It's unlike anything I've ever seen before," she replies, grasping the stem of her glass. "Do you ever grow used to this?" Her eyes shine with admiration.

"It's new to me too!" I reply. I remember listening to these long nights of celebration from my convent cell.

"When you grow used to nights like this," says Lysander, "you know it's time to rest."

I look up and see a prominent merchant leaning against a wall on the far side, smiling into the face of a younger man. The youth, in doublet and hose, leans a hand on the wall so that his face draws near the other man's. He whispers in the Councilor's ear and then nestles his face in the crook of the man's neck. As the elder statesman smiles, his glance catches mine across the crowded room. If we were out in the streets of Venice, by light of day, he would undoubtedly flinch away from his companion under the scrutiny of a stranger. Instead, he raises a hand in greeting. I send a curtsy in return.

There is the loud stamp of a staff on the parquet floor and two wide doors swing open.

"The Grand Council of Venice and the Florentine embassy!" announces a crier. A group of men in ornate ruffled shirts and deep robes walk into the room. My father is one of them, his chin raised proudly. He walks beside a man whom I recognize as Massimo, Admiral of the Fleet. They call him the Bear on account of his being so stocky and heavily bearded. Behind the Councilors come our visitors from Florence. Each wears a cloak dyed red, with what I guess is cochineal, and sewn with gold thread. Florence's wealth is on show tonight. The men arrive in the center of the ballroom and turn to greet the women who have gathered around them, in their skirts of rainbow colors. As lips brush against fingertips, it is like watching an ancient and complex ritual.

"When do I get to meet your betrothed?" Emilia whispers in my ear. She stands on tiptoe to survey the room.

"I don't know," I say, feeling momentarily embarrassed. Where *is* Roberto? I had thought he would be with the other dignitaries. "He may be on business," I murmur. "We'll see him eventually." A flash of memory recalls the image of him throwing his shirt to the floor, his torso slick with sweat, and I ache to be beside him again.

A hand grasps mine, and I am torn back to the present. "Come and dance!" A stranger pulls me onto the polished wooden floor, and I feel the suede of my shoes slip across the wax. I swirl into the waiting arms of someone in a saffron doublet and can't help laughing as we move easily into the stance of a Venetian *canario,* stamping our feet on the floor in unison. I move from one man to the other,

33

grasping arms and swinging bodies, chests pressed against each other. Candles burn on the walls and the flickering flames reflect in my partners' eyes. The sound of lutes and singers carries over the warm air to us, and I close my eyes as I sway in the embrace of the music.

"Hello, Laura," a woman's mocking voice whispers.

My eyes snap open. Despite the heat of the room, a shiver passes through me.

"Carina?" I murmur.

"Are you all right?" my dance partner asks, frowning. We've come to a stop, nearly tripping the people behind us. "Would you like a tumbler of water?"

I am led to the side of the room, pushing past bodies. I look over my shoulder, to where the voice came from. "Carina?" I ask again, louder.

It can't be her. She's dead. The last time I saw her she was aboard a blazing ship that was sinking into the sea. She drowned, if she did not first burn to death.

I find my breath coming in shallow gasps and feel a sudden urge to be out of this room, away from the excited faces that surround me. As I find my way through the open patio doors, I lean heavily on the stone balcony and gaze up at the clear Venetian sky, glittering with stars. Their reflections bob in the water of the lagoon. Carina is down there, locked in the depths.

There can be no doubt.

6

Somewhere, a clock strikes, tearing me from my reverie and reminding me that I have a job to do. I glance over my shoulder at the room, women leaning against men and strangers kissing. It's time to leave. I worry about Emilia, but then I spot her with Lysander, his arm snaked around her waist.

I check that no one is paying me any attention and head down a narrow flight of ivy-clad stairs. Even at this hour, the stale warmth of a spent day drifts up to greet me from the city's canals. I walk quickly through the streets, keeping to the shadows and darting from one tiny alley to another covered walkway. It's surprisingly easy to move unseen. Others are abroad, but they turn their faces away from me, hiding their own secrets. I spot the yellow scarf of a prostitute beneath an awning, and at another window two men are talking urgently to each other. As I pass, they slam the shutters on me.

Finally, I arrive at a concealed pier. If the Segreta had not told me how to find this place, I'd never have known that boats docked here. The entrance is disguised by heavy leather curtains, stained with blood and grease. It looks like a butcher's warehouse, a place to hang venison or pigs, and the slap of waves is concealed by the sound of singing that comes from a nearby bar. Someone has put a lot of thought and care into keeping this place hidden.

I slip between the leather curtains, carefully tucking my skirts around me, and walk down the pier. The skeleton of a boat sits across the canal, abandoned by the shipbuilders for the evening. There's a sudden splash in the water, and when I turn I see that someone has pulled up beside the pier in a low boat. On the prow is the faded mark of the Segreta, a painted key. The woman stares up at me and we give each other a sharp nod. Not a word is said until I am in the boat, having climbed down the short flight of slippery steps. I sit on the bench opposite her, holding the side to steady myself against the sway of the current.

"You know where to go?" I whisper.

"I know."

She adjusts the scarf across her face, and we begin to slice through the water. Her shoulders move strongly as she rows, and her feet are braced against the floor of the boat. I have no doubt that this woman can get me to my destination quicker than any paid gondolier.

I thought that I would resent leaving the ball, but I am glad to be out on the water, away from voices of the past. We cross the choppy lagoon in silence, cleaving into the darkness. After a short while, the glassworks of Murano stand in tall silhouettes across the island. Many of the rich men of Venice own studios here, or have shares in the factories. The island is another place of secrets—the artisans who work here are forbidden to share the details of their craft. The windows are frosted and no one can see out—or in. Perfect for our purpose tonight. So why do I glance over my shoulder, my nerves throbbing?

I climb up some steps and the woman slips her oars into the boat as it moves silently beneath the boardwalk. "I'll be back," I whisper.

Turning my back on the small pier, I step into the nearest glassworks. This one is owned by Julius, the husband of Grazia, but he has no idea of my assignation. As planned, someone has left the door unlocked for me. My feet crunch loudly on grit as I walk past the workbenches. A fine layer of glass dust covers everything in sight, and I dare not touch a thing, for fear of leaving clues. On a pedestal in the middle of the room is an unfinished urn. Half of a galloping horse is sketched into the side of the glass; the front legs are still to be completed. Beside it are a small copper drill, a bottle of linseed oil and another bottle of emery. The oil glints in the moonlight.

A sudden noise from a corner of the studio makes me scramble back behind a store cupboard, but then I hear the flap of wings and spot a pigeon resting in the eaves.

My thudding heart slows. *Calm down,* I tell myself. I've run secret errands before; I can do this. I find a low wooden stool and gather up my skirts to sit and wait. I rest my elbows on my knees and perch my chin on my fists, watching the doorway leading to the pier. When our contact arrives, I'll see her in an instant. My body shivers with anticipation. I feel honored that the Segreta have chosen me for this task, but now I'm impatient to find out what the latest secret is. Who will this person be?

∗   ∗   ∗

There is no way of telling the time here, but I know it's been hours.

My back aches and my legs have turned numb. I get to my feet and stretch my arms over my head, bringing the blood back into my limbs. Grazia didn't tell me how long I'd have to wait, but this feels too long.

After at least another half hour has passed, I begin to walk back towards my waiting boat. But as I pass beneath the roof of the studio, I hear another noise—no bird this time, of that I am sure. It's the ragged intake of a human breath.

"Who's there?" I call out. I try to keep the nerves out of my voice, but I can hear how startled I sound. There's another muffled noise—something scraping across the floor—and then a darting shadow. A woman! Her silhouette races ahead of me, and, lifting my skirts, I break out into a run. The shadow swirls round and hands slam into my chest so hard that I stagger and lose my footing, falling to the ground. I leap up immediately, but the woman is already running away from me. Not towards the pier, but towards a hidden door that I now spot behind shelves stacked with plates and vases. There's the sound of a key turning, and the woman is gone.

"Come back!" I cry. "I'm here to help!"

I follow her out of the doorway, into an open courtyard at the rear of the glass factory. Her footsteps echo on the cobblestones as she races away beneath an arch set in a low wall. I run after her, my skirts gathered in my fists. It's so dark I can hardly see what lies before me and can only

38

hope that there are no loose cobblestones waiting to twist an ankle.

As I emerge from the arch, I see dozens of shelves stacked with crates and glass products. From between two of the shelves a pair of bright eyes watches. "I'm a friend," I say, stepping towards her. She jerks away, and at once the shelf begins to lean towards me. I leap backwards as the whole tower topples with an almighty crash inches from my feet. The sound of breaking glass fills my ears.

Breathing fast with panic, I pick my way around the debris, looking for the girl, wary of any further dangers. She's nowhere to be found, and after a few more minutes I have to admit defeat.

The woman has escaped.

Pushing hair out of my face, I stumble past the glass factory and to the pier. I've failed. Whatever Allegreza sent me here to discover, it remains a secret.

I dust down my skirts, and as I climb into the boat, the woman raises her eyebrows.

"You were a long time," she says. "What was that noise?"

I shake my head and settle on the bench. "Let's go," I tell her.

7

When I return to the ball, things are very different. The glamor of a few hours ago has burned itself out. Now, empty food platters are cast aside, flagons drained of wine. The few dancers that are left lean into each other heavily, heads resting on shoulders, eyelids drooping. I wander out to the white marble balcony with its fluted columns. Beyond the balustrade, the landscape of Venice stretches across an imaginary canvas. An orange tree in flower sends out its scent from a pot beside a bench, on which my brother sits with his wife.

"Laura," he says, smiling lazily. Emilia leans into his side, a hand resting beneath her chin as she sleeps. Her curls have loosened, and the ribbons in her hair are strewn around her neck.

"She looks worn out," I say.

"Roberto was here earlier, looking for you," Lysander says, stroking a hand across his wife's cheek. She moves slightly in her sleep and then resettles. "Where have you been?"

I shrug and gaze out over Venice. Dawn mist curls off the canals. "I needed some fresh air," I say. "The streets are always interesting at this time."

"I bet they are," Lysander says, "but I'm not sure they're the right place for an unaccompanied young lady."

"Shush," I tell him. "You never used to care when we played hide-and-seek in the mariners' quarter as children."

He grins, a little sadly, and I know he too is remembering Beatrice. She used to act the damsel in distress and Lysander and I the brave soldiers come to rescue her.

"Listen," says my brother, interrupting my thoughts. "Roberto had to leave." His brow creases in a frown. "He seemed a little . . . worse for wear?"

"You mean drunk?"

"Your words, Laura. Not mine."

I laugh. "Well, it's not like Roberto to go finding himself at the bottom of a glass. But with all of the wine on offer here tonight, I'm not surprised that people are woozy."

"He was woozy, all right," Lysander comments. He glances down at Emilia and kisses the top of her head. "Come, my darling. It is time to get you home."

Emilia lets out a low murmur and smiles at some hidden detail of her dream.

"Come on." Lysander slips an arm around her waist, another beneath her thighs and in a single movement lifts her. I watch as the gray silk of her gown's hem whispers against the stone tiles.

"Are you coming with us?" Lysander asks.

"Perhaps I'll surprise someone instead."

My brother shakes his head in mock disapproval. "Don't worry. I won't tell Father—or Faustina." He shifts

Emilia's sleeping body in his arms. "I'll see you in the morning."

I wave him off as he carries his wife down the steps towards a coach. But as I watch him leave, I can't ignore the pricks of worry at the back of my neck. I've never seen Roberto drunk in all the months we've known each other.

It's not hard to find a coach to take me to Roberto's. They line up outside the palace, waiting to transport tired guests to their beds. I whisper the destination—a simple pension in the artisan quarter that Roberto keeps in secret, even though he could live in the luxury of his father's palace. When we pull up outside, I slip out of the coach, its suspension creaking, and hand over a few coins to the driver.

"Would you like me to wait?" he asks. "I can be very discreet."

I draw my cloak more tightly around my body. "No, thank you. That will be all," I say coldly, although I can hardly blame him. Trysts between unmarried couples probably account for half his fares at this time of night. Faustina would have a heart attack if she knew where I was.

I turn to the wooden door that leads to Roberto's rooms and straightaway I hear the sound of violent curses carrying down the stairs. The door, I see, is open a fraction. I step inside.

"Roberto?" I call up.

"Who's there?" demands my betrothed. His tone of voice is startled and hostile.

"It's me," I answer stiffly.

"Don't come in!" Roberto shouts down.

Something uncontrollable takes over. I run up the stairs.

"I will not be left to stand in the street," I say, my voice full of anger. Roberto rushes to position himself at the top of the stairs, his feet braced, but I dart past him and stumble into near darkness.

An image flashes before my eyes: a woman's body. I glance at Roberto, and his face is creased with anguish.

I look once more at the body on the floor. Her skin carries the faint blue stain of death. It is a color I know far too well—I saw it first on my sister Beatrice's face as she lay in her coffin. But this woman doesn't lie with her hands folded on her chest, her body cushioned by satin. Her dark limbs are flung out at awkward angles. Her face presses into the wooden floorboards. A trail of blood trickles from a corner of her mouth, and a larger wound blossoms across her corset. Her eyes look up at me, wide and accusing.

A scream worms up my throat, and I clamp my hands over my mouth as I look from the woman to Roberto.

In the gloom I see that he clutches a sword. It hangs from his fist, dripping blood onto the floor. He looks like a butcher. His shirt is torn open, and poppies of blood stain the white cotton. Red is splattered across his hose.

I find the strength to speak, backing towards the door again. "What have you done?" I whisper.

Roberto shakes his head over and over. He never stops shaking his head. His face is pale, and his hands tremble.

"I don't know," he whimpers. He takes a step towards me, and I find myself moving away. "I didn't do anything!" he cries.

A whistle pierces the air, cutting off his words; then someone shouts, "It's this one!" The sound of heavy-booted feet comes from the street outside. Roberto and I stare into each other's faces, unable to move or speak. One thought flashes through my head: it was all too good to be true. My happiness is over.

Roberto runs over to me, grips my arms so hard that it hurts. "Go, quickly! If you're found here . . ." He throws an anguished glance at the body on the floor. He need say no more. He hustles me over to a window at the back of the room. It is barely wider than my skirts, but I find myself climbing onto a chair and forcing my body through the tiny opening.

There's an angry shout from the stairs, and I let go, dropping to the street a few feet below. A low bush of bougainvillea breaks my fall, and I roll off it, cowering on the cobbles beneath the window. The last thing I see is Roberto's terrified face at the window.

"Murderer!" cries a voice, thick with disgust. Then Roberto's eyes widen as an arm comes around his throat and drags him away. I rock my body, shoving a fist into my mouth, forcing myself not to cry out. Squatting on the ground, among the scented petals, I stare at the moon high in the sky above Venice. My whole body shakes as I listen to the sounds of angry voices, until a door is slammed, and everything turns to quiet once more. In the far distance, a lute is being played by a lone musician in the night. But I don't follow the tune. Instead, I listen to the sound of my own heart breaking.

8

I don't take a coach home. I couldn't face a driver—any
person at all—the way I feel. I run across the Rialto
Bridge, towards the wealthiest part of Venice. I barely notice the wide arches of the bridge or the market stalls, the
banking houses or clock towers. I have only one thing in
mind.

As I race up the marble steps of Allegreza's home, the
great oak doors stand firmly shut. I throw myself on them,
banging my fists against the varnished wood and crying
out. I don't care who hears.

"Help—let me in!"

Will she hear my voice, from one of the many arched
windows that gaze down over the canal? I grasp the door
knocker, shaped like a writhing sea serpent, and bring the
brass down again and again. But the noise seems muffled
by the dawn air, and with a gasp of exhaustion I crumple to
the ground, my skirts rising up around me like soft clouds.
I hide my face in my hands and weep, kneeling on the steps
of the grandest house in the district.

"Get up, child!"

I peer between my fingers at the timeworn face of an old woman wearing a huge white apron. She stands in the crack of the door, resting a hand on the bolt, ready to slam it shut again at any moment.

"Please," I beg, scrambling to my feet. "Please let me in. Allegreza, she knows me. I need to see her!"

The woman's whiskered face hardens. "Venice will sink into the sea before I let you in here at this hour." She drags a hand across tired, puffy eyes. "You've woken half the household. How dare you show such—"

"That will be all," says a voice.

The servant woman's eyes widen in recognition, and I feel a small flicker of hope as she turns. Now I can see into the hallway. There stands Allegreza.

"Come in," she says, throwing a glance to the servant who stands cowed, her gaze firmly on the tiled floor. "You may leave. Tell Effie to bring our guest a warming drink. We'll be in the parlor."

"But the fires aren't lit yet—" begins the old woman. Allegreza silences her with a raised hand. "Of course, my lady," the servant murmurs. "Right away."

I step inside, and we wait for her to leave. I feel suddenly aware of my appearance—the dress stained from hiding in the street, locks of hair torn free from their pins, my eyes that surely must be red from crying. I try to smooth my skirt, but Allegreza holds out a hand to me.

"Come."

She opens a tall mahogany door, and we let ourselves into the parlor. Rugs are scattered across the floor, and light blossoms through the unlined silk of the curtains.

Allegreza strides over to a window and throws it open. Cool, fresh air snakes across the room, drying the tears on my cheeks.

The leader of the Segreta turns to look at me. Even in her nightwear, she looks magnificent. Her gray-streaked hair is tinged silver in the weak dawn sunlight. She wears a linen night smock but has draped over it a velvet shawl embroidered with turquoise thread and heavy with tassels. On her feet are light kid slippers. She notices me looking at the shawl and casts a hand over it.

"We have an embroiderer in our household. This took her two years to make." Her green eyes spark. "But I don't suppose you came here to talk about clothes. Wipe the dirt from your cheeks. We have appearances to keep up. I think my servants are loyal, but I wouldn't stake my life on it."

Hastily, I rub my palms over my face. When I take them away, Allegreza gives me a curt nod of approval. She leads me towards a low couch, and the two of us sit down. "We'll talk in a moment." Then, in a louder voice: "Ah, Effie has brought your hot chocolate."

A young servant girl comes into the room, carrying a silver tray. I watch as she takes a silver jug of steaming milk and pours it through a muslin sieve that contains vanilla pods. Then she adds brown crumbs of cocoa and sugar and stirs vigorously, finally passing the warmed glass to me. I raise the creamy liquid to my lips and sip. The sweetness takes my breath away, but immediately I feel calmer.

Allegreza watches me carefully. Then she orders the girl to leave and leans back against the couch.

"So, I assume you are here to tell me about last night's meeting. Isn't that right, Laura? I can't think of anything else—anything!—that would be important enough to disturb me for at this hour and in my own home."

Her voice sounds dangerously low. This isn't an invitation to speak, it is an order.

"No one came," I say. "Or rather, there was someone but she ran away. I waited an age."

The other woman's face clouds. "What do you mean, ran away? Why would—"

"Roberto's been dragged away, accused of murder!"

Normally, I would never interrupt Allegreza, but I can't keep it inside any longer. Who cares about Murano now?

"I went to his quarters and there was a woman's body lying on the floor." My words spill out in a rush. "I don't know what to do. This can't happen, it just can't!" I grasp Allegreza's hands in my own and hold them to my chest. "Forgive me," I mumble. "I don't have anyone else to turn to."

"Let me get this right," Allegreza says, her eyes flitting over to the drawing room door. She brings her head close to mine. "Our contact ran out on you last night, and hours later you found a dead woman in Roberto's apartment."

I nod.

Allegreza rises from her seat and paces across the woven rug. She crosses her arms, drumming her fingers. Then she stops and whirls round to face me, the tassels of her shawl flying out as it slips from her shoulder.

"Tell me everything you remember about the dead woman," she says.

My mind casts back. A dark room, blood on the floor, Roberto's face . . . everything merges into everything else. "I don't know. I can barely think. . . ."

"Well, you had better start." The blood has risen to Allegreza's face and throat, covering her skin in mottled patches of emotion.

It feels as though I've been slapped. But Allegreza's anger works to jolt something in my brain. A memory glimmers behind my eyes. "She wore a plain shift dress, pale in color. It was torn at the shoulder and . . ." I force down the choke that rises in my throat. "And stained with blood. Her skin, it was dark. I remember that."

"Good, good. Now, Laura. This is the most important question of all, so answer honestly." Allegreza comes to stand before me. "Did you tell anyone about your mission to Murano? And I mean anyone. Did you tell Roberto?"

I shake my head, rising to my feet to look Allegreza in the eye. "No," I say firmly. "I would never do that. Why do you ask?"

Without answering my question, Allegreza turns and wanders over to the open window, gazing across the canal.

"Then the Segreta has a traitor," she says, her back to me. "If the dead woman you saw is who I think it is, there will be severe consequences. She was part of . . ." Her eyes flicker over to me; then she sets her lips as though coming to a decision. "She was part of a contingency to spread our movement beyond the limits of this city. We were so close to establishing another chapter."

I bite my lip. "More of us? Abroad?"

Allegreza turns to face me. "Yes. Don't you see — someone is determined to foil our plans. Do you think it's a coincidence that no woman met you on Murano, and now there's a dead woman on Roberto's floor? A woman who was in our confidences?"

"Who was she?"

A bell rings from somewhere deep among the bowels of the house.

"That I will not say," says Allegreza, walking towards the door. "I must be sure first."

I understand that my interview with her is over.

"We must convene the Segreta at the earliest convenience." She is talking to herself now, planning. She opens the door, and as I step through, I realize that I have one last chance to appeal.

"Will you help me with Roberto?" I stare at the ground. "I would be forever in your debt."

"All in good time." Her voice is suddenly soft. "Wheels turn at their own rate. Be patient."

These few words must be enough for now. I dare not show any ingratitude.

"Go home and get some sleep." She takes up a shawl that was lying on the arm of the couch and throws it over my shoulders to cover my soiled dress. "There is much you will need to be strong for."

The door to the drawing room closes behind me. The old woman is waiting to see me out, smiling victoriously now that my time in the house is at an end.

When I emerge onto the streets of Venice, men are setting up their stalls. Another day has begun.

9

I wander through the streets, barely hearing the conversation that passes among the stallholders. A woman selling lace sets out her skeins of ivories and creams, while a man carrying a wicker basket of fresh sardines teases her.

"That would make a nice hem for a wedding dress," he comments, pointing at a roll of lace. He gives her a fat wink. The woman throws me a smile, rolling her eyes, but I duck my head and hurry past. It galls me that they should talk of weddings, when the prospect of mine has vanished in an instant.

Arriving home, I hear the sound of raucous singing mixed in with the dawn chorus of the birds. Are people still up? I feel a jolt of alarm, but then realize that Father won't question where I've been. He'll be too drunk.

I find them in the dining room. Father has dragged Lysander in here to carry on where the ball left off. The two of them crouch around a bottle of port and two small glasses on a silver tray. Father's singing an old naval song, as though remembering the ribald youth at sea that he never actually experienced. He throws his head back, his arms spread wide as he uses language that a daughter should never hear.

I stand in the doorway and wait. On the last verse, he notices me. "The lady of the household joins us," he says. "Where the devil have you been?"

"Laura!" Lysander cries out. "Leave her be, Father. She's young and in love." He smiles knowingly, though what he imagines the past few hours have brought my way could not be further from the truth. He waves me into the room.

It's clear my brother has been drinking too. Well, at least he and Father are no longer quarreling.

"Where's Emilia?" I ask as I settle into a chair opposite them.

"Gone to sea!" Father shouts, then laughs uproariously at his own joke. Lysander and I share a glance.

"Which is more than we can say for you," I reply. I mustn't let either of them know what I have seen tonight. I must smile and pretend.

Father's laughter dries up. "I beg your pardon? I am a member of the Grand Council. I'll ask you not to forget that."

"Yes, but you've never climbed a rope in your life," Lysander teases, miming a sailor's shimmying hands behind Father's back. "You get seasick in a gondola."

Father looks over his shoulder, and Lysander quickly drops his hands, painting an innocent expression on his face.

"You two!" calls a gentle voice from the hallway. "Stop teasing an old man."

Emilia steps into the room. She must have fallen asleep

in her gown. The silk is crumpled, and there are other creases in her cheek from where it's been pressed against a pillow. No matter—she still looks beautiful.

"My darling," Lysander calls with an exaggerated flourish of the hand. "Come to me!"

Emilia ignores him and pads over to plant a kiss on my temple.

"Old man!" Father protests. "I'm not old!"

Emilia must have noticed the look on my face, because her brow furrows with concern. "What is it, sister?"

I feel privileged that Emilia already feels close enough to address me so. The strain of the past night weighs down on me and suddenly I feel my whole body shaking.

Emilia draws me to her. "Shush now, shush . . ."

"What is it? What's wrong?" Lysander reaches across the table to take my hand. Father pours himself another drink.

"It's nothing. Too much excitement." I wave a dismissive hand through the air. "I'm tired, that's all." I wipe my eyes with the hem of my sleeve.

There's a loud tutting noise, and Faustina hurries into the dining room, mopping spilt port from the table. "You should all get yourselves to bed," she chides. "The servants will be up and at their duties soon. Do you want them to see you like this?" She throws me a pointed glance as if to say, *What ails you, child?* But I cannot answer any more questions and, weak as a lamb, I allow Emilia to lead me up the steps to my room, careful to keep Allegreza's shawl wrapped tightly round my shoulders, its length covering the stains on my dress. I will have to hide it and dispose of it when I can.

Lost in a deep slumber, I find myself dreaming of Carina. I'm kneeling beside the water's edge, gazing down at my reflection as it bobs and shifts with gentle waves. I can't seem to look away, no matter how hard I try. Then the water parts and a hand thrusts up towards me, fingers clawing the air.

"Get away!" I try to yell, but my mouth won't work. Then the hand's around my throat, grasping my collar, trying to drag me down into the water. I struggle and fight back, but my body tips over, over. . . . With a rushed intake of breath I sit up in the bed, pushing the sheets back and scrambling up against the pillows. I gaze around me, failing to recognize my room until sense settles and I understand that it's all been a bad dream. My nightdress is damp with sweat.

"Just a dream," I tell myself. "Only a dream."

I wait for my breathing to calm down; then I ease myself out of bed. I hear voices from the courtyard and quickly dress. I've slept late. Then the reality of the previous night hits me like a blow to the stomach. Roberto. The dead girl. It cannot be as it seems.

I wander outside and find our young maidservant Bianca is on the steps, weaving straw into hanging decorations for the garden. Lysander is sitting with Father. They're both pale, and Lysander's hair is not as neatly combed as usual. "Drink this," he says to our father, pressing a tumbler into his hand.

"What is it?" I ask, drawing near.

Lysander smiles up at me. "Good morning, sister!"

"Don't be so cheerful," Father grumbles, "it hurts my ears." He downs the concoction, and grimaces.

"It's a mixture of milk, honey and lavender," Lysander explains, crushing more lavender between the palms of his hands for a second drink. "It can soothe the soul of the devil himself." Father is too busy rubbing his temples to pick up on the joke.

A messenger boy rushes into the courtyard, shielding his eyes against the sunshine. He clearly doesn't see us grouped beneath the olive tree, for he goes to where Bianca sits on the steps. She puts aside her work and smiles up at him.

"Have you heard?" he asks. Immediately my senses jolt awake and I listen intently. Lysander has fallen silent also.

"What, you silly boy?" Bianca asks. She doesn't even think to warn him that members of the household are close by.

"Murder!" he says.

I squeeze my eyes shut tight and put a hand to my waist. I can hardly bear to hear what comes next. "A woman's been killed in Venice. They say it was . . . it was . . . Roberto, the Doge's son!"

Now Bianca is on her feet, roughly pushing him out of the gate. "Shut up!" she hisses.

"What?" he says. "What is it?"

Father leaps to his feet and grabs a pottery tumbler, throwing it after the boy, who ducks just in time. "Get out of our house with your vile words!" he calls after him. Bianca watches us, tears brimming at her eyes. Servant girls who lose their jobs can starve on the streets of this city.

"And you, Bianca," Father says stiffly. "Never speak to that boy again."

"I'm so sorry," she gabbles. "I've no idea what he's

talking about." She disappears into the gloom of the house, her sobs carrying on the air back to us.

I sink onto the bench that circles the olive tree. So, word is out. But not just any words—evil, twisted stories. I feel the eyes of my brother and father on my face, but I cannot erase the worry that I know must crease my brow.

"It's all lies," Father says. "Isn't it, Laura?"

"Laura?" Lysander asks quietly.

"Of course it is! Roberto could never harm anyone."

"Rumors always dog Venice," Father blusters. "Half of them are nonsense."

My brother sinks to his knees before me and takes my hands. "I don't mean what that boy just repeated. But Roberto and this dead woman—do you know anything? Last night, you . . ."

I pull my hands free. "You cannot ask these things," I whisper.

Father shakes his head in disgust, and turns away. "I cannot afford my family's reputation to be tainted in this way. Association with a murderer!"

"I'm going to get that boy back here," Lysander announces, running into the house. "Find out the truth!"

I follow him into the shade, and watch from the main doorway as Lysander races down the drive after the boy. He takes him by the shoulder, and drags him back to stand before me. The boy stares hard at his feet.

"What did you hear?" Lysander asks. "Tell us."

The boy shakes his head, but Lysander gives his ear a sharp slap.

"Tell us!"

The boy's started crying, but he tells us his story. As

he talks, there is a movement beside me, and a cool hand slips into mine. It's Emilia. I give her a grateful smile as she places an arm around my shoulders. Together with Lysander, we listen. The boy tells us of the whispers about Roberto's bloodstained hands, the corpse on his floor, the running feet of the guards and the shouts of horror that emerged from Roberto's open doorway. Thankfully, there is no detail of a woman escaping from a first-floor window.

As the boy's words falter to an end, I lean heavily against the doorway. Lysander's face is serious and even Emilia looks worried. From inside the house, we can hear Father shouting.

Lysander slips a few coins to the boy and sends him on his way.

"He's just a child," Emilia says. "He's probably made the whole thing up." She tries to make her voice bright, but she doesn't fool me.

"Thank you," I whisper.

My brother is shaking his head. "No, it's impossible. He knows too many details for something he's made up."

Father has arrived to stand behind us. "Is my family ruined again?" he asks plaintively.

Lysander shrugs and attempts a smile. "If Roberto is innocent, I'm sure there'll be an explanation. . . ."

"But until then, you'll continue to believe the worst?" I say. "Is that it?"

My brother reaches for my arm, but I pull back and walk on my own into the house.

10

I dress quickly, with Faustina fussing around me and asking question after question.

"What's happened, my sweet?" she gently inquires as she draws the ribbons on my corset. "The servants are whispering the most scandalous things." She gives an extra hard tug. "To think of Roberto coming to this!"

"Roberto's come to nothing," I say. "These are all silly rumors. I *will* see Roberto and I *will* find out what's at the bottom of this."

I have grown so much braver since leaving the convent, but this is a new test I never thought to face. *I must be strong for Roberto.* I have to be.

Only one person can share the truth with me — Roberto. And to get to him, I must be granted an audience by the Doge. A lacquered black-and-gold gondola takes me to his palace. I pay with a few coins and step up onto the wide pavement. It's the exact spot where once I saw a painter at work. I was fresh out of the convent, still as innocent and naive as any of the girls brought up by nuns. The man was sketching a lagoon, his simple clothes threadbare. He introduced himself as Giacomo. Little did I know his real name was Roberto. Back then, he was a prince in hiding. How far we've both come — I a member of the Segreta, and Roberto . . . I cannot bear to think. So recently come out of hiding, and now accused of murder. It can't be true. It simply can't!

The palace rears up above me with its mosaic tiles, pale statues and balconied terrace. The stone form of a woman holding a sword aloft stands at the top of the palace, and I pray for even half of her strength before ducking inside.

The covered courtyard is surrounded by more balconies. Immediately a middle-aged man in fine clothes steps up to greet me. I recognize him from my visits here with Roberto, but his face is closed, betraying no emotion.

"Can I help you?" he asks. It's as if we were strangers.

"You know me," I say, trying to stay calm. If I show too much emotion, I will surely be refused an audience. "I am betrothed to the Doge's son Roberto." When I say his name the man winces. I straighten my shoulders and cannot help the hard edge that enters my voice. "I would like to see the Doge."

The man backs away from me, bowing ingratiatingly. "I will speak to my superiors," he says. "Please wait here." As he leaves, other men file past, casting me glances. They are dressed in the cloaks and hose of the upper classes — they must be the Doge's senior advisers, members of the Grand Council. Perhaps they're meeting to discuss how best to clear Roberto's name. Perhaps I need not panic after all.

Then the Doge walks down the marbled staircase. His

is a face I recognize all too well, first encountered in the infirmary of the convent. It was I who poured the peony root into his raging throat; it was I who pressed my weight against him to stop the rabid thrashing of his limbs. He doesn't remember me from his time of ailment—and why should he want to? If rival powers in Europe, or even Venice, knew that this man was weak, our city would lose its leader and be thrown into chaos.

But now I need the most powerful man in Venice to help me. As he walks towards me I fall to my knees and hold out my hands, ready to kiss the ring on his finger. But with a swirl of long robes, he strides past me through a doorway, where the other men wait. The door swings shut, and with a dull thud I am left alone in the echoing hall.

The servant reappears. "The Duchess Besina will see you," he says coldly as he waits for me to get back to my feet. Roberto's mother! This may be better—one woman appealing to another.

"Show me to her," I say. The man sucks in his cheeks and turns on his heel, trotting up the grand staircase. I scoop up my skirts and follow, moving beneath paintings while gilded stucco detail illuminates the ceiling above my head.

Finally, we arrive at the doorway to the Doge's private quarters.

"In there," the man says, waving a dismissive hand. Then he's gone. I gather my courage and step inside.

The Doge's wife waits for me on a rosewood bench covered in buttoned brocade. She wears a red robe with fine lace around her collar and a cloak embroidered with flowers. Two large pearls set in gold decorate her ears. We've met a few times since I became Roberto's fiancée, but only at formal occasions. Her eyes have always danced with curiosity and happiness, but we have never had the chance to confide in each other before now.

I move swiftly across the room. She takes my hands, and her fingers tremble. When I look into her face, it's clear that she shares my pain. The rims of her eyes are red.

"You have heard, then?" I whisper.

The Duchess grimaces. "The head guard brought us the news," she says. "My son is incarcerated and the citizenry call him a murderer. How dare they betray us so?" She turns her face away, and for the first time, she looks old to me.

I sit beside her on the couch. "I need to see Roberto," I say.

"You know where he is?" the Duchess asks.

I shake my head. I do not dare tell her that I watched him being dragged away.

"In the Piombi," she says, her voice breaking on the last word. I shudder. Everyone in Venice knows about this prison—the place where we send our most wicked criminals to rot. Commissioned by a former Doge, the entrance of the prison is two meters from the outskirts of the palace, but the cells rest above the palace itself, right under the leaded roof.

"Why?" I gasp. "Surely he doesn't deserve that. Nothing's been proven!"

"The Doge says he cannot intervene. The law courts must go through due process, and besides . . ." Her mouth twists in a bitter smile. "He's negotiating with the Florentine ambassador and preparing for the arrival of the Turks in a day or two. That's why he could not see you. Negotiations are at a crucial stage, and my husband cannot be seen to be meddling with the law of our city." She casts her eyes around the room, taking in the gold and marble, the countless oil paintings and lacquered surfaces. "Meanwhile, I sit in a gilt cage and go slowly mad." Her gaze suddenly turns on me and her face burns with passion. "But you! You can go and see my son. Comfort him. If I gain you access, promise a mother you will do this!" She pulls my hands to her face and rests her cheek against them.

"I promise," I say. "I will do everything I can. I love Roberto."

The Duchess's eyes brim with tears. "So do I. Tell him that for me."

I get to my feet and ask if a servant can call me a coach. The prison entrance isn't far from here, but it's best to be discreet.

"Oh, I think we can do better than that," the Duchess says, the light returning to her eyes. "Come with me."

She leads me down a warren of wood-paneled corridors. I glimpse cooks and maidservants, officials and guards, who pause in their duties to curtsy or bow their heads as we go by. I sense that we are passing through the entire length of the palace. Only once do we cross an outdoor courtyard, heading through what seems to be a part of the palace under renovation. We enter a rougher section of the building, half finished and uninhabited. We climb several flights of rickety stairs. Such are the quirks of Venetian architecture; I feel we've traveled in a circle. A rat has died in one of the dusty passages. Then ascend higher and higher, the air getting hotter and hotter. At last the Duchess pauses at a door, half hidden in the shadows. I put my hand against it and the surface is cold—it's made of metal.

"The Piombi," I murmur. The leaded prison. There is another entrance. I taste the cruel irony of Roberto's situation—locked in a jail under his own roof.

"I cannot go any farther," the Duchess explains. "It would be a scandal for the Doge. Here." She hands me the ducal seal, cast in wax. "Show this, and the warden will allow you access." Her glance drifts to the secret door. "To think my son is through there somewhere and I cannot even . . ." She turns her face away to hide her emotion, then retreats back down the corridor. I'm on my own.

The door clangs as I knock on it, then slides open. A man gives me a lecherous, gap-toothed smile, his face red and greasy. "A jewel amidst the pig swill," he comments. "What brings you here?"

I feel perspiration prickle beneath my armpits. "I am here to see Roberto, the Doge's son."

The warden laughs and spits on the floor, littered with damp and rotting straw. "Oh, that one!" he remarks. "Yes, he looks handsome enough to catch a prize such as you. But I don't think he should be allowed to look upon you now."

I show him the seal, and he nods thoughtfully before turning his back. "Follow me."

Immediately, the stench hits me. I can smell sweat and dirt, feces and blood—but, more than that, I can detect the scent of desperation.

This is it, then. I must follow.

As we climb a set of stairs, the heat increases. I am soon aware of the circles of sweat staining the fabric of my dress.

Beneath our feet, I can see rows of roofless cells with men lying or squatting on the packed dirt floor. White half crescents shine from their filthy faces as their eyes watch me, and clothes torn into rags only just cover their bodies. One man is almost naked but for a loincloth, his body writhing as he stretches across his cell, froth at his mouth.

"That man there!" I put a hand on the warden's shoulder to stop him. "He needs help."

My guide glances down. "That man needs nothing. He's spoilt with attention. He'll be well again soon enough." I am forced to continue, as the prisoner's distressed cries fill the air and a jerk of his foot sends a gruel bowl spinning.

I almost wish I'd taken the man's handkerchief; the heat and the stench are overwhelming. Bile rises in my throat and I think I'm about to be sick. The sensation passes. I wipe the sweat from my face and carry on climbing higher beneath the lead roof that gives the prison its name, the metal taking the heat of the day and doubling it. I hardly dare think about what I'll find when we reach Roberto.

Finally, we stop climbing. The man jerks his chin towards a cell in a far corner and departs back down the stairs. "A few moments only," he snarls.

I walk across the floorboards, the gray roof low over my head. The heat is unbearable now. As I come to stand before the cell, I see a shape slumped against the back wall. At first I think it is an abandoned sack, but then there's a movement and the flicker of white eyes.

"Roberto?" I whisper, throwing myself forward to grasp the bars of the cell.

A head rises and a smile spreads across my love's face. He gets to his feet, moving stiffly, and as he hobbles across the cell towards me I can see that every movement causes him pain. He leans to one side as though his ribs have been bruised.

"What are you doing here? How . . . ?"

I smile. "Your mother helped. She says to tell you that she loves you very much."

His face creases with a sort of despair, but then he gathers himself and wipes a hand over his brow. When he drops his hand again, he is grinning bravely.

"What happened?" I ask, reaching through the bars to lift his tunic. Quickly but gently, he bats me away. His hair hangs in dank locks around his face, and a purple bruise stains his left cheekbone. The skin has split, and blood is crusted in the wound.

"It's nothing," he says. "Oh, my darling." He stretches his arms through the bars and draws me to him. I try not to flinch at the smell of him, and I press my lips against his. They are hot with fever.

"Tell me what happened," I whisper, glancing over my shoulder. "How did that woman . . ."

Roberto shoves a hand through his hair, shaking his head. "I don't know," he says, moving away from me. "I've gone over it so many times in my own head, trying to remember. I felt ill at the ball . . . started to make my way home. I can't remember anything after that. The next thing I know you were banging on the door and that woman was bathed in blood on my floor! You know the accusations aren't true, don't you, Laura? Tell me you know that!"

He's been pacing his cell, and now he turns to me. I hate to admit it, but the look on his face scares me. It's furious, desperate. But is there a hint of guilt?

"Of course I know that. But if I'm to help, I have to ask. How did it come to this, Roberto?"

"I'll tell you how!" he almost shouts. "Someone set me up. Those watchmen, turning up when they did. Coincidence? Only in a fool's head! The whole thing was planned."

Roberto must be right. Those men who stormed his home were only seconds behind me.

A hand lands heavily on my shoulder. "I said a few moments only," says the warden, his breath hot against my ear. I find my grip tightening on the bars of the cell.

"Just a minute more won't hurt," I say, trying to keep my voice light—flirtatious even. The hand moves to grip my arm, and suddenly I am yanked round and flung back against a wall. Roberto calls out, "Leave her alone!" but the warden has brought his face close to mine, and I can see the spittle gathered in the corners of his mouth.

"Now do as I say," the warden growls. He begins to drag me down the stairs, and it is all I can do not to trip over my skirts and go hurtling to my death.

"I'll do everything I can for you!" I call back.

"No!" Roberto's voice is hoarse with panic. "Don't get involved. The authorities will realize their mistake. Everything will be fine!"

These are the last words I hear as the warden opens the main doors to the jail and throws me out into the street. The sunlight hurts my eyes, and I raise a hand to shield my face. A woman is walking past with her daughter, and she throws me a nervous glance, drawing the child to her as they scuttle past. She's just seen me ejected from the city's most notorious prison, after all. I smooth out my skirts, pat my hair back into place and wipe the sweat from my throat. Then I begin walking without looking back. Roberto's last words make my heart beat faster. *Everything will be fine....*

"It will be, my love," I mutter. "I'll make it so."

11

In my hand is a bouquet of lilies and white poppies tied with purple ribbon. A fresh breeze comes off the water and threatens to tug my hair from its pins. I think of Roberto alone in his stinking cell and my hands tighten around the stems. What am I doing here while he lives a nightmare?

I stand in a line of women, all gazing out across the harbor from St. Mark's Basin. To one side of me is Emilia and behind me stands Faustina. We are each dressed in our finest, at Venice's formal welcome party for the Ottomans. They have sent an ambassador to join the talks with the Doge, and as a member of the Grand Council, Father insists that his family be represented today.

"The daughters of Venice will be on hand when the Turks arrive," he explained. "And you will be among them. Is that understood?"

I tried to tell him that my grief for Roberto made public appearances impossible, but how could I ever have expected Father to understand?

"Roberto has brought shame on this family. It is up to you to retrieve some honor. You will be there," he said, his voice laden with threat.

So, here I stand. Faustina considered carefully what outfit I should wear. Finally, this morning, we settled on the cream satin embroidered with gold fleur-de-lis, with a front-laced bodice. My hair is plaited and wound around my head, and a string of iridescent shells hangs from my neck. Emilia brought out her best gown from her luggage, and Faustina steamed the peacock silk until every last crease had been smoothed out. It took her the best part of a day to prepare.

Another breeze drifts off the water. Sails flutter, and Venetian flags ripple and snap above our heads. The harbor is alive with noise — people chattering, noblemen talking in whispers. Behind us, musicians play trumpets, clarinets and drums. Ahead of us is the Turkish galley ship, surrounded by smaller vessels. The Ottoman Empire has a huge fleet; everyone in Venice knows that. Constantinople's shipyard is legendary.

Massimo, the man who commands Venice's warships, has trimmed his beard back a little, I see. He heads a detachment of soldiers who form an escort to the Grand Council. The show of might is hardly subtle. I have no doubt of the importance of these talks, for they concern the trade routes across the sea that bring silk, grain and spices to our markets, and money into our purses. But my affection for Venice cannot override my love for Roberto, and the pain I feel is like an iron cage pressing my ribs tighter and tighter. I have asked Allegreza for another interview to discuss the mysterious woman at Murano. Surely, this woman holds more clues. I was a fool to allow Allegreza's empty words about wheels turning to keep me from asking more questions. There are secrets waiting to be unearthed, and I must do the digging.

For now, though, I have no choice but to play my part in this spectacle. The lead ship of the Ottoman fleet has three masts and is squat in the water. It is an imposing object, with none of the gilded beauty of our gondolas. If ships could speak, this one would say, *I fear nothing.*

"Are you nervous?" Emilia whispers to me as the breeze plays with the curls at her temples. Her eyes are fixed on the water, eating up the scene.

"No," I tell her. I feel almost nothing. The rest of life dulls to gray beside the nightmarish color of the blood I saw on Roberto's floor. I close my eyes and try to push that image from my mind, but it is branded behind my eyelids.

"You should be nervous!" Faustina's voice protests. I dare not look round to face her; I must appear as a lady of Venice, entranced by the Ottomans' arrival. "I've heard that all Turks are goblin-faced brutes. This Halim—their prince, as they call him—I've heard he can turn people to stone with his ugliness! Whatever you do, don't gaze into his eyes, girls. I won't be answerable for what happens."

On the edge of my vision, I see Emilia's shoulders shaking with contained mirth. A smile plays around my own lips, despite myself.

"You're talking nonsense," I murmur over my shoulder.

"Don't say I didn't warn you!" is Faustina's last shot. There's no time left to speak. The ship has docked, and men are scrambling up the masts to let down the sails. A gangplank has been set against the side of the vessel. Men walk down it, gazing around them with open curiosity. I wonder how Venice appears to eyes that have never seen it before; the canals and piazzas, the colorful market stalls and soaring spires.

A sudden blast of trumpets sounds, and the crowd swells forward as a solitary figure appears at the top of the gangplank. He wears an outfit of dazzling white that almost seems to glow in the Venice sunshine. A thick silk sash circles his waist and his head is decorated with a turban, the coils of linen gleaming as they snake around his brow. On all sides of me, the crowd gasps in delight. The clean simplicity of the man's outfit is in stark contrast to the luxurious embellishments in which most Venetian men indulge. His skin shines golden, and his broad shoulders shift as he raises a hand in salutation, smiling so that his teeth sparkle white.

This is no goblin-faced brute.

He stands on the pier now, and one of the Grand Council introduces himself. Prince Halim listens politely, but his eyes travel along the formal row of Venetian ladies. As he looks at each young woman, she dips in a curtsy. Finally, his gaze comes to rest on me. His eyes are a deep brown, chestnut rich. I lower mine and bob from the knees, fingertips grasping my skirts as I curtsy. But the girl to the left of me does not move. When I straighten back up, Prince Halim is still looking right at me. The sound of giggling has broken out and my cheeks flame as I realize that I am being singled out for attention.

"Don't look into his eyes!" Faustina hisses from behind me.

Finally, thank heavens, the Doge steps forward to greet the Turkish prince, and the moment is broken.

"Have you turned to stone yet?" Emilia teases, to my right. I shake my head, to prove Faustina's theories wrong. But I can't stop watching the men as the Grand Council gather around Prince Halim, their heads close together, talking. One of the prince's servants has drawn near and seems to be eavesdropping shamelessly. The bald skin of his head gleams, and I notice a slight hunch to his shoulders. As he listens, he watches the crowd. When his glance catches mine, he turns away.

There's another trumpet call to tell the crowd to disperse. People make their way through the streets, noisily eating snacks and discussing the scene that's just played out.

"He's very handsome!" says an older woman gleefully. "Not at all what I expected."

"Did you see that ship?" a young man murmurs to his friend. "I've heard the Turkish vessels are the fastest on the seas."

"Such insolence!" mutters Faustina. "I saw the way his eyes wandered."

My father comes over to speak to us. "You did well," he says, rubbing his hands together. "Prince Halim noticed you. Good girl."

I turn my face away. He's forgotten already that while people fawn over the visitor, Roberto sits in a filthy cell. Father notices my expression and draws his lips close to whisper in my ear.

"Don't think you're too good for all this, because you're not. You were good only for the convent, until my eldest daughter's death."

Fortunately, Julius and Grazia de Ferrara draw near, before I forget myself and speak back to Father in public. Faustina has taken my hand and grips it gently, silently reassuring me.

"Ah, Julius!" Father says. He bows his head towards Grazia. "What news of Carina?" As if he cares about anyone but himself! I keep my glance firmly on the ground, unable to catch Grazia's eye.

Julius sighs. "Still nothing. She always was a wayward girl. But we live in hope that one day soon she will turn up." He tries to laugh lightheartedly, but the sound dries up in his throat. My heart goes out to him, a father's grief still so fresh.

"I know what it is to lose a daughter," my own father says. "When Beatrice died, I thought my world had ended."

"Yes, but my daughter isn't dead." Julius throws him an angry glance, and I look up to see Father's mouth open and close as he struggles to find something tactful to say.

"Let's let the men talk, my dear," Grazia murmurs to me, and the two of us draw away to one side. She turns her face from the sun, and it is almost impossible to see her expression. "The Segreta meet this evening to discuss the situation with Roberto. You will attend, of course?"

"Of course!" I say hurriedly. "It will be difficult at such short notice, but I'll be there, certainly. I want to hear more about the girl at Murano also. Do you know if . . ."

I'm about to ask Grazia if she has any morsels of information to give me when the crowd suddenly heaves to one side and I stagger. Regaining my composure, I see a group of men rushing the harbor. Their fists strike the air and one of them is shouting, spittle flying from his mouth.

"Get the foreigner out!" he cries. "Go home, heathens!"

Before he can get near the ships, soldiers rush forward on a barked command and the group of men are driven back at the points of swords. Their leader stands firm, but is dragged back by his comrades. Another is wrestled to the ground. I see a knee jerk into a stomach, fists connect with skulls. The shouts die and the men are led away. I notice Prince Halim watching the group, his face serious.

"What was that?" I ask.

Grazia's face is like stone. "Hatred, that's what." She shakes her head. "When will this city ever learn?" Then she gives a small nod. "I will see you later." As I watch her move away from me across the docks, her skirts swaying, relief blossoms inside me. Tonight I will be with the Segreta, and one step closer to getting Roberto out of his stinking prison.

12

Dear Laura,

Since we spoke, I have thrown caution to the wind. I shall not allow my boy to languish in that prison! I have requested house arrest for Roberto. I will let you know the instant he is free of that festering leaded prison. I know you love him as much as I do.

In haste,
Duchess Besina

The note was waiting for me upon our return to the villa. I hastily broke the wax seal in the privacy of the garden's new greenhouse. Now, I look at the Duchess's handwriting and hope that her impetuosity will work for Roberto, rather than against him. No other woman could earn him such a reprieve, not even one of the Segreta.

"Laura?" Faustina calls for me. "Laura!"

Hastily, I shove the note into my pocket and step out of the greenhouse. She spots me and comes bustling over, carrying a large square of linen in her arms. "A picnic!" she calls. "Come and help."

Emilia and I go to our rooms and quickly exchange our outfits for loose muslin dresses so we can work in the garden after we eat. I can't stop thinking about the note and what it might mean for Roberto, but for now I must act as if everything were normal. I hastily tuck my dress, with the note in its pocket, into a blanket box and follow Emilia to the kitchens.

It's not often that I'm allowed here—it's not a noblewoman's place—but this afternoon Faustina is more than happy to let me collect bowls of olives and take a knife to shave thin slices from the cured ham. Emilia carries out a basket of bread and a board of cheeses, and soon we are settled beneath the olive tree, enjoying a picnic for three, as Lysander is out visiting boyhood friends.

As the sun rises higher in the sky, we revel in the fresh tastes, scooping up small bunches of grapes and tearing hunks of bread to soak up glistening olive oil. For a time, I try to be cheerful for Emilia's sake, and I'm surprised by my appetite. We talk of Bologna, where she grew up, of the beauty of the Tuscan hills, and of her family. We both laugh as Faustina reaches for a third slice of cake.

"You girls, you need to follow my example—get more meat on your bones!" She casts a shameless glance at Emilia's stomach. "Who knows, soon you could be eating for two." My sister-in-law's cheeks flame, and I tut loudly, giving Faustina a firm shake of my head. She shrugs. "I'm only saying . . ."

After we've all finished eating, Emilia gets to her feet and goes to retrieve the gardening basket and shears from where they have been abandoned beside the climbing rose that dances across a trellis pinned to the wall.

"Here, let me help!" I say, jumping up to join her. Faustina grumbles as she clears away the picnic things.

"Take no notice of her," I say to Emilia as I choose a rose stem to prune back.

"It doesn't matter," she says.

"You shouldn't feel embarrassed to tell Faustina to stop her teasing," I tell her. "You're one of the family now."

We fall into companionable silence as we work, side by side. I try to concentrate on picking out dead rose heads, but I can't stop thinking about the note. I allow a flicker of hope to spark in my chest, but I won't let it become a full-blown fantasy. This won't be the nightmare's end, but it is a reprieve and may be the first decent step to clearing Roberto's name.

I move slowly around the garden, seeking out the blooms that are past their best. In a corner, I kneel beside a lattice covered in climbing flowers. I reach past an olive tree, straining to catch a wild stem of roses that has snapped at the base. My hand brushes against something smooth and cold, and, looking down, I see a dagger.

The blade is plunged into the trunk of the tree. A prickle of fear spreads over my skin, because I recognize the hilt — the mother-of-pearl inlay and the polished rosewood, the turned gold of the guard. My fingers wrap around the handle, and I pull the dagger out of the tree, turning it around so that the blade glints in the sunshine.

This is my enemy's weapon. It is the blade that Carina tried to plunge into my breast that night on the boat. I am sure of it.

"What have you got there?" Faustina has arrived behind me.

"It's a lady's dagger," I say.

Faustina calls to Bianca, who comes running. I glance towards Emilia, but she is absorbed in another part of the garden and doesn't notice the fuss.

"What's this, you silly girl?" Faustina asks, indicating the dagger. "Is it yours or any of the servants'? Have you been fooling around out here?"

Bianca shakes her head. "We don't have the money for such things," she says. "And I hate blades." She looks up at me, her eyes wide. "Have strangers been in the garden?" she whispers.

I send her a reassuring smile. "Don't be silly. One of Father's friends must have dropped it." I slip the weapon into a basket of gardening tools. "I'll find out whom it belongs to and return it. Go on, back to your work!"

Bianca dips in a curtsy, before running back to the house. Faustina's gaze hasn't left my face.

"How will you find out whom it belongs to?" she asks.

"How do I know?" I say impatiently. "Let's just forget about it."

Faustina shrugs, and goes to carry the picnic things indoors. Emilia helps her, packing our leftovers inside the empty bread basket. But I stand rigid. I can't get Bianca's words out of my head. Have strangers been in the garden? Or ghosts? Only one person could have put that dagger here. Carina, the woman who once tried to kill me. But Carina's dead, just a figure in my dreams. No one could have escaped that sinking, burning boat.

I shake myself and follow Faustina and Emilia back to

the house. A silhouette appears in the open doorway, a servant, his face flushed red from exertion.

"What is it?" I ask.

"Your father," the boy gasps. "He demands your presence at the Doge's palace. Immediately!" Emilia and I share a startled glance.

"Why?" Faustina demands, giving the boy a stern look.

He hesitates, then pulls his shoulders back, determined to deliver all of his message. "Prince Halim has personally requested you to be among the serving girls. Signor della Scala told me to say that if you don't obey, the repercussions will be serious."

Emilia looks at me, confused.

"But why me? I don't understand," I say.

"Many daughters of the nobility will be on hand," says the boy.

"That Prince Halim is trouble," Faustina mutters. "I said it from the start. What does he want with my darling?"

Prince Halim's dangerous reputation isn't what bothers me. My mind turns over as I realize that my father's orders will force me to miss my meeting with the Segreta. They won't be happy.

I draw the boy to me and lead him to my father's library, out of the earshot of Faustina and Emilia.

"Can you take a message to Grazia de Ferrara for me?" I ask, scribbling a note, then sealing it with melted wax.

The boy's eyes widen. "I can, but that will cost you my top rate."

"Top rate!" I repeat, shaking my head. I take some coins out of my pocket and drop them into his hand. I give him the note too.

The boy runs down the steps away from me. He calls a final message over his shoulder: "The banquet has a Roman theme!" A few seconds later, he has disappeared from sight, leaving clouds of dust behind his departing heels.

I turn quickly and run up the stairs, pausing halfway to call into the hall, "Faustina, come and help me. I'd better find something to wear!"

13

I stand in the entrance of the Doge's palace, surrounded by laughing young women. We are all dressed as maid-servants at a Roman banquet, despite the fact that most of us come from Venice's most well-to-do families. Faustina has done a fine job with my outfit. A sheet from the linen cupboard, as white as swan feathers, has been pleated along its length and clasped at one shoulder, leaving my arms bare. There's something unpleasant about this mas-querade. Are there political points to be scored in reducing Venice's gentlewomen to these games? Does the Grand Council want to fool the Ottomans into thinking that every-one in Venice is silly and shallow?

Looking around, I see that the other women are all enjoying the charade, carrying baskets of fruit or jugs of wine. For myself, I know all too well what it is to be truly servile, bound as I once was to the Abbess of our convent, scrubbing her floors and embroidering altar decorations until my fingers bled. There's nothing glamorous about running to the shouted orders of others. Still, I must paint a smile on my face and pretend that I too am having a pleasant time.

I put a hand to my head to make sure that the rosebuds are still firmly nestled among my curled hair—Emilia brought the flowers up from the garden as Faustina readied me. The only adornment to my simple costume.

Paulina joins the gaggle of girls and catches my eye. She takes in my outfit and the heavy bowl I am carrying, filled with pastries that are covered in crystallized rose petals.

"You make a good servant," she says. I can't judge whether she's gently teasing or if there's something more cruel in her tone of voice.

"That's what the Abbess used to tell me," I say. Paulina's smile fades.

"I'm sorry to hear about Roberto," she says. This time there's no cruelty at all.

"Come, come, ladies!" calls a slightly older woman who's in charge of us girls. I recognize her as Agnesina, the wife of one of the Grand Councilors, but not, as far as I know, a member of the Segreta. "Don't forget to circulate and ensure that all of the men have something to eat. If you spot anyone without a partner, it is your duty to go over and entertain."

She snaps her fingers and turns sharply to face the door leading towards the dining hall. Then she walks down the marble hallway. Sharing secret glances and enjoying a final whisper, the other girls trail after her. I am the last to move, bringing up the rear.

When we step inside the dining hall, even I feel a shiver of excitement. I've never seen this part of the palace before. The painted ceiling towers over us, and the room is cool, despite Venice's heat beyond the windows. Oil paintings in gilded frames decorate the walls, and thick rugs of woven silk are scattered across the floor.

But an extra effort has been made for the Roman theme. Lounging couches fill the room. There is a man in an approximation of a Roman toga reclining on each, their bodies draped against the cushions. They lean over the armrests to fill each other's goblets. Heavy bunches of grapes hang from the chandeliers, and buntings made of fresh flowers weave between the paintings on the wall. In a corner, a servant boy sits plucking at a tiny harp, and, most exceptional of all, an ice sculpture of a Roman goddess—Aphrodite, I think—stands in the center of the room, the ice melting into a silver basin in which float candles. Bottles of lemon liqueur sit cooling in the melted water.

"Have you ever seen anything like it?" a girl whispers to me. She has not yet noticed that a man to the side of us is greedily feasting upon her with his eyes. He clears his throat loudly, and she jumps, then hurries to fill the goblet that he holds out to her. As she bends over the glass, his eyes follow her chest.

Agnesina watches me sternly. I am the only girl not to have hastened to someone's side. I lower my eyes and readjust the heavy bowl against my hip. But I misjudge the balance and the bowl begins to slip from my hands, threatening to shower sugared petals over the sumptuous rugs. I almost cry out, but then I feel the grasp of fingers around my arm and a tanned hand reaches beneath the bowl to catch it. When I gather myself, I find that I'm looking into the eyes of none other than Prince Halim.

"Here. Let me take that," he says. His eyes are quite remarkable—deep pools, almost black in this light. Looking into them is like staring into a well at night. Before I can protest, the bowl has been placed on a low table, and men reach for the pastries. Prince Halim and I watch for a moment; then I feel his hand against the back of my waist and realize that he is steering me towards one of the open windows, where a long muslin curtain billows in the breeze, providing a moment's seclusion and a rare glimpse of the Doge's private gardens below. As we move towards the window, I notice Agnesina nod in approval.

"Quite beautiful, no?" Prince Halim asks. Dutifully, I glance out of the window, but when I look back at him I see that he isn't looking at the gardens at all. He's staring straight at me. There's nothing aggressive or predatory in his glance. It unnerves me because it is quite the opposite—calm, patient, enigmatic. What is he thinking? His appreciation for my looks is brazen, but too honest for me to feel insulted by it.

"Thank you for your help, Your Highness," I tell him. "I nearly humiliated myself."

Prince Halim smiles indulgently. "Half the men in this room fell in love when you stumbled. And please, simply call me Halim."

I start to back away, shaking my head, but the prince clearly realizes his compliment has been too extravagant, and he holds up a hand. "Forgive me," he says, bowing his head. "I've embarrassed you. I'm a poor student of your language, and my words are ill chosen." When he looks back up at me, the sun has moved from behind a cloud, and as light pours through the window, I watch the changing colors in his eyes. They move from black to deep chestnut to a burnished mahogany, all in an instant.

"You, girl!" calls one of the guests—a fat man with a wine stain down the front of his costume. "Those pastries won't move around the room on their own!" The other men laugh. Halim is hidden from view by the billowing curtain, and they don't realize that they're interrupting a conversation. Still, he nods his head as though to give me permission to leave his side and steps out from the window. The fat man gasps his apologies, but Halim waves his words away with an idle hand and goes to sit cross-legged on a rug. A glance of uncertainty passes through the other serving girls.

I pick up my bowl and make a circuit of the room. I'm careful not to make eye contact with any of the men and to step carefully between them. Father is watching me, his arms emerging like pale sticks of driftwood from the shoulders of his ridiculous toga. The Doge is draped over a couch at the far end of the room, dressed in a purple toga when everyone else wears white, to signify his power, I'm sure. He smiles and chats easily to those who surround him. No one would know his son languishes in a cell. He is the ultimate politician.

I'm about to leave for the kitchens to replenish my bowl, when a hand grabs at one of the two remaining pastries. Buttery crumbs fall to the floor as a Venetian nobleman stuffs the delicacy into his mouth. Opposite him sits the bald man I spotted at the harbor. His mouth is twisted in disapproval as he watches the other man eat. I offer him the last morsel in my bowl, but he shrinks away from me, his lip curling in disgust.

"I-I'm sorry," I stutter. "Have I done something to offend you?"

There it is again: the warm press of a hand on the base of my spine. I straighten up quickly. Prince Halim. He's crept beside me as quietly as a cat.

"Forgive him," he says, smiling down at the bald man, who's now turned round in his seat to show me his back. "Faruk is fasting—a personal observance of his religion. Some say that he is stricter than Mohammed himself!" Halim laughs gently at his own joke, but Faruk only hunches his shoulders like a vulture. He mutters something in his language, which I don't understand, and stiffly hobbles out of the room.

I gesture to my bowl. "I must go and find more refreshments," I say.

"Let me escort you," Prince Halim answers. I can hardly protest, and he walks with me towards the open doors of the dining hall. As we move across the room, I feel the eyes of the men watching us—curious, envious even. I am acutely aware of my bare arms and throat, my red-painted toes and the light fabric that clings to my body. It seems to take an age to arrive at the doorway.

"I know my way from here," I say hastily.

"Of course you do," he says.

"Thank you," I say, backing out of the room. For some reason, my heart is racing, and I'm sure my face must be scarlet. I turn and almost break into a run. I hardly see where I'm going, and waves roar inside my head.

When I arrive in the kitchens, a huge fire is lit beneath a steaming urn. Gleaming copper jelly molds decorate the walls, and a row of pheasants hangs from the ceiling. A leg of lamb sits on a marble stand, a silver carving fork resting beside it. At a huge wooden table, two members of the house staff with gleaming faces pour ruby liquid into glass cups. The scent of cloves sits heavy in the air.

"Are you here for the refreshments?" a woman asks, smoothing down her apron. She looks to be in charge here. Then her eyes widen and she drops into a low curtsy. Looking over my shoulder, I see the Duchess is standing behind me.

"Laura!" she cries as I set my bowl down on the kitchen table. "I've been waiting for you!"

The kitchen servant begins tipping butter biscuits into my bowl as the Duchess draws me aside. We step into the cool of the pantry, where bowls of dates and dried apricots rest under squares of muslin. She grips my hands so tightly they hurt. "My pleas worked! Roberto is to be allowed out of the Piombi tomorrow."

Her eyes widen as she watches the joy flood my face. In an instant, tears are spilling over to stain my cheeks.

"He'll be free again? Can I come to see him?"

"Soon," she tells me gently. Her own smile fades. "He must have time. A bath, a meal, a clean change of clothes — and then he'll be himself. Can you bear to wait? I know how you love him, but I'm his mother. I want to ensure that he has not suffered too greatly."

I bring the Duchess's hands up to my face and kiss them. "I understand," I whisper. "I'm just so thankful."

I step out into the kitchen, pick up my bowl and make my way back to the banqueting room. I cannot stop smiling, and there is no need to fake pleasure now. No glance that lingers too long can ruin my happiness. Roberto is waiting for me. I shall hold him again soon.

14

I stand outside the dining room, framed by the doorway. A cloud of warm air, heaving with the scent of wine, billows towards me. Things have evidently moved on in my absence. The men no longer politely take a couch each; now they encourage girls to sit beside them or they talk in groups, laughing raucously. I wonder how the Doge and his Council can have such scant regard for their daughters — they must truly want to impress their guests. But then, I suppose this is all part of the game of diplomacy. Cheeks are flushed red and eyes are alight with pleasure. One of the men standing near me has dark circles of sweat beneath the arms of his toga. It's Massimo, Admiral of the Fleet. Over the course of his lifetime he has risen through the ranks.

I step into the room, still smiling. I can't stop thinking of Roberto. I pass from group to group as fingers pick at the still-warm biscuits I carry. I hide a smile when one of the Venetian delegation rolls his eyes in disgust; the Turkish man he's talking to ignores the fork with its crystal handle, instead reaching for the platters of cold meats and eating with his right hand. This is all a long way from the usual delicate courtesies of a Venetian meal.

"Is that quite necessary?" the Florentine mutters quietly—but not quietly enough.

Prince Halim moves across the room and takes his own slice of cured ham. I watch, mesmerized, as he rolls the meat neatly between two fingers and presses it against a slice of fig. He offers the delicacy to me but I shake my head, so he shrugs and eats it himself. His eyes stay fixed upon the Florentine's face.

"Who needs knives and forks!" Nicolo says. The Doge's second son has always had an easy charm, and his arrival punctures the tension. He reaches for a piece of fried squid dripping with basil dressing. With a flourish, he drops it into his mouth. The room rings with relieved laughter, and the man from Florence, who looked appalled a moment ago, smiles awkwardly.

Prince Halim turns to gaze at the Doge, who is still sitting on his own couch. "Where is your other son? Roberto, isn't it?"

The laughter dries up. Halim looks around the room, from one face to another. Nicolo is staring hard at the floor.

"Have I said something wrong?" Halim asks quietly.

The Doge gets to his feet. "You must excuse me," he says. His politician's smile has faltered and, for just a moment, we see the man as he truly is—old and ill. He walks from the room, leaning heavily on a servant's arm, refusing to look into anyone's face. As he passes me I swear I see his lip tremble.

The doors creak shut behind his back, and noise instantly returns — sounds rolling around the room like ocean water against rock. The wine flows once more, and the guests reach for the platters of delicacies. To a newcomer, it might seem that everything is normal. But as I go about my duties with the other girls, I'm surrounded by whispers of my beloved's name. They are all talking about the rumors that fill Venice — that Roberto is a murderer. He's not here to defend himself, and I cannot be seen to react. If I scramble to protect his reputation, I know what these people will think: she protests too much.

"Can I tempt you with something?" I mutter, lowering my platter to a man sitting on a long couch. When our eyes meet, I see it is Massimo. He smiles, taking a pastry from me and popping it in his mouth. He chews with his lips open and swallows noisily. I start to move to another part of the room, when his hand darts out and gently restrains me.

I look into his face, surprised. "Yes?"

"I have an invitation for you," he says, wiping his hands on a napkin.

I feel my brow crease in a frown. "I don't understand...."

He waves a hand in the air to silence me and gets to his feet. He walks to a corner of the room and I understand that I'm expected to follow. Putting my platter down, I go to join him.

"Well?" I ask as he turns to face me.

"Prince Halim has asked to be chaperoned around the city. He requested you especially." On the last word he raises his eyebrows.

I feel blood rush to my cheeks. "I'm not sure that my father would —"

"Your father and I have already cleared it with the Doge and guards will be on hand to protect you at all times. You see? There really is no reason in the world to say no. You'll meet him at the harbor tomorrow morning?"

I find myself nodding my acquiescence. "But . . ."

"Good. That's settled, then." Massimo walks away from me and is soon laughing with a group of men. My father knew of this? Why in God's name would he say yes? There must be hundreds of people better suited to act as tour guide. Even now, after months out of the convent, I feel I barely know this city.

Once again, I feel the cogs turning, and I am powerless to stop them. I could refuse, I suppose, but sometimes it's easier to swim with the current than fight against it. Roberto is released tomorrow, and I shall see him soon after. Nothing can ruin that.

And besides, one question burns in my head as Halim flicks a glance towards me, raising his glass.

Why has he chosen me?

15

At breakfast the next morning, I can barely eat. Not only because of my excitement at Roberto's release, but because Faustina is making so much fuss that it's impossible to even pour coffee without her bustling over to take the silver pot from my hands. Scalding liquid splatters on the linen tablecloth, and I sink back in my seat, defeated.

"Oh, now look!" Faustina cries, as though this was anyone's fault other than her own. She wags a finger in my face. "You'll have to be less clumsy when you show the prince around Venice. Not that I approve in the first place. Really, can't you find an excuse to get out of it? He's so"— she waves a hand before her own chin—"hairy!"

Emilia bursts out laughing across the table. She's getting used to our servant's ways. "Oh, Faustina, only you could say something like that. He's a prince! He asked for Laura especially! You should be glowing with pride." She gives Faustina a sly look. "Think how jealous the other servants in the city will be."

Faustina's shoulders straighten. "Maybe you're right.

But you, young woman!" She's staring hard at me again. "I said a prayer for your honor and chastity last night. I just hope my prayers are heard." She waddles out of the room.

"She seems to have forgotten I'm engaged," I say.

"She means no harm," Emilia says. "She clearly loves you very much."

"And I love her," I tell my new sister.

A short while later, I'm making my way to the front door. Father emerges from his study, clutching a book. He follows me out onto the steps and pats me on the head like a small dog. My spirits are so high today, it doesn't even annoy me.

"Really, I think he's been most impudent, demanding your time like this," he grumbles. He's maintaining the illusion of the grudging father with some aplomb, I must say.

"There's nothing worse than impudence from someone so very highborn," I reply. As suspected, the reminder of Halim's royal blood makes my father puff out his chest. He kisses me lightly on the cheek.

"Try to be charming," he tells me, before disappearing into the gloom of the interior. I climb inside the coach and rap my knuckles on the roof.

"To the port!" I call.

I'm so full of thoughts about how to compose myself that the journey passes quickly. Halim is already waiting for me when I arrive. He wears Venetian fashions today: a tight-fitting doublet in black, with black boots and a black leather belt. Despite the dozen or so Ottoman guards posted around him, he is the one to step forward and help me down as I climb out of the carriage. His fingers press lightly around mine.

"A beautiful sight," he murmurs, and my glance flickers up to his face. Then he spreads his arm out to take in the city. "Don't you agree?"

"The most beautiful city in the world," I tell him. "I only hope to do it justice."

He bows his head in acknowledgment. "With you as my guide, I know I will learn to love this place even more. Shall we?"

He leads me towards a waiting gondola. I see my face in the varnished wood and I am smiling. It's partly his outfit—there's something funny about a prince dressing down—but I realize too how light my heart feels.

Halim steps into the vessel and holds out his hand to help me down. I give him my arm and scoop my skirts up in my hands, but as I step into the gondola the heel of my shoe catches and I stumble into him, knocking us both onto the velvet cushioned seat at the rear. My chest bumps against his and our faces are suddenly so close that I can feel the warmth of his breath on my cheek. I push my hands against his body to lever myself up.

"I'm so sorry, I don't know what—"

"Please don't apologize," he tells me. I smooth down my skirts and settle on the rear bench of the vessel. The guards have climbed into their own crafts. Our gondolier gazes over our heads, pretending not to notice what just happened. Halim calls to him, "You may proceed!"

The man uses his long paddle to push us off from the jetty. The gondola begins to sway lazily through the water. I gaze out at the sides of the buildings and wait for my heartbeat to slow. What a strange sight we must make—

the prince and his fleet of ships pushing into the center of the city.

Soon, we are moving between houses that rear up on either side of the water, . People lean out, their elbows resting on sills. I try not to feel awkward beneath their gaze. Halim's tour has already been publicized through the gossip channels of the city.

"Throw us a kiss, young prince!" a young woman calls from a doorway, and Halim enthusiastically responds, kissing his palm and throwing his hand out towards her. The woman mimes catching the kiss and draws her hand to her lips. Halim roars with laughter, but when he turns to look at me the smile fades.

"I'm sorry," he says, "I don't mean to embarrass you. Come. Tell me something of this city of yours."

As I point out landmarks, I begin to forget all the people watching me with this foreign prince.

"That is one of the oldest squares in Venice," I say as we pass a small square off to our left. "It's easy for people to miss. It's said that is where the Lords of the Night would gather before doing their rounds."

"The Lords of the Night?"

"Those who police the streets."

"Ah! It sounds so romantic."

I try to find something else to tell him. "Here is the church of St. Mary of the Visitation. It once hid an assassin."

Halim raises his eyebrows. "Don't you Venetians call the church *La Pietà*?"

"You know more than I realized," I say. "Perhaps you should be guiding me!"

Halim smiles and holds his open palm out to me. I hesitate, then place my hand in his. Within moments, his lips brush the skin of my wrist. I shudder and pull my hand away, hiding it in my pocket. "You shouldn't."

His eyes have not left my face. "I've offended you?" he says, looking suddenly crestfallen.

"No," I reply. "It's just that if people were to see . . ."

He breaks our gaze and looks out at the merchants' mansions we are passing. "It's said you can judge a city's character by the morals of its women. Would you agree?"

It could be a reference to the Segreta, but it's not, of course. From the smile that plays around his lips, I can see he's not serious.

"If that's the case, I hope you'll find Venice to be everything it should be—beautiful, classic and luminous. Just like its women."

Halim laughs loudly and a lemon-seller on the dock looks round, startled.

"I knew you'd be good company," he says, slapping his leg.

The gondolier is grinning too, but wipes the look off his face when he sees I'm watching him. Nothing spoken in a gondola is private. In many ways, the gondoliers' currency of secrets must rival the Segreta's.

"Do you like classical or Eastern-influenced architecture?" I ask, looking up at the church of Madonna of the Miracles. Better to keep the conversation on such matters.

"Ah, built by Lombardo," Halim murmurs, taking in the building. His hand moves through the air, tracing the geometrical patterns. "Byzantine-influenced, I believe. All very different from our mosques."

I shake my head. "Are you sure this is your first time in Venice?" Finally, I spot a building that Halim can't possibly know more about than I do—the convent that was my home for more years than I like to remember.

"This is a very special place in Venice," I say as our gondola draws near.

Halim frowns. I can understand why—the convent of Mary and the Angels looks unprepossessing with its bars and grilles. I think of my servant nun, Annalena, and the dull ache of separation lodges in my heart. I wonder what she is doing now. Does she still pray five times a day on the floor of her narrow cell? She will be *conversa* to a new sister now, of course. She's probably forgotten her Laura. Certainly, her eyes would pop out of her head if she could see me now, sharing a boat with an Ottoman prince!

"So tell me why it's special," Halim says. He has pulled a short dagger out of his sleeve. It has a golden hilt, inset with mother-of-pearl. He twirls it once in his hand, then again. I try not to be disturbed by the glitter of the metal.

"I lived there for many years, incarcerated as a nun." I wait for the words to settle, to see how he'll react. He pockets the knife in a practiced move and brings his focus back to me.

"Incarcerated?" he repeats. "You did not dedicate yourself to your God?"

I incline my head. "It's not uncommon in Venice for second daughters to be sent to convents, if they are in danger of being a financial burden on their family. I was one of many."

"But still . . ." Halim's words fade away as he glances at the small windows.

97

I point to one set high in the wall. "For five years, that small room was my home."

Halim looks at me, then back at the window, as if unbelieving. "Five years?"

"And every day the same."

We drift beneath the shadow of the monastery in silence. "But surely you received visitors. Your father? Your sister? You say you were a second daughter."

"It was forbidden," I tell him. "Visitors take away the mind's focus, or so the Abbess used to say." I won't say her full name out loud. She belongs to the past.

"My sister used to keep a pet bird in a cage," says Halim. "It was the most beautiful thing, and it used to sing every evening. I thought it very cruel that it was locked up like that."

"We were allowed to sing," I tell him, glancing upwards, "but only at prayer." I'm in danger of becoming maudlin.

Halim reaches across and places a hand on my arm. His skin has the shade of varnished olive wood and there's a scattering of dark hairs across his wrist. "How did you get out?"

"My sister died." The truth, but only a fraction of it, like a painting made up of a million brushstrokes seen only from a distance. It is so simple when said like that. My voice does nothing to betray the pain I felt, looking into her coffin. He cannot understand.

Our talk turns to other things—the love that Faustina has shown me, the return of my brother with his new wife, the happy times. Halim listens quietly, nodding, smiling. The boat drifts on. It is as if we're on our very own island of intimacy, the sun rising higher and higher above our heads.

The sounds of the city have fallen away. Only the occasional slap of paddle on water reminds me the gondola is still with us.

"What about you?" I say eventually. "What was your childhood like as a prince? No barred windows for you, I'm sure!"

Halim shakes himself as though waking from a dream. "Maybe not, but there were other . . . constraints. My father . . ." He hesitates.

"You don't have to tell me," I say.

"He was very strict," Halim continues. His dark eyes cloud over. "For many years, my life wasn't my own."

I think back to my own father, either drunk at the dinner table or ensconced in his library or toadying up to the Doge and his Council. But always, always telling me what to do for the good of the family.

"I know all about strict fathers," I say gently. "Why do you think I ended up in a convent?"

"But you escaped!" Halim says, his eyes brightening again. His hands grip the sides of the gondola. "You had it in you to forge your own path. Look at you now! That's what I want too. I've emerged from the shadow my father cast—it was a long one. But now it's time for me to make my own mark." Color has rushed to his cheeks. He looks almost feverish.

"Are you feeling well?" I ask.

"Of course!" He grins at me. "Never better. Gondolier! Moor here, please!"

16

We pull up to the side of the canal and I glance over my shoulder to ensure that our sudden stop won't cause a collision with the gondolas behind us, carrying the guards. But the other boats have disappeared down another canal.

"Your security . . . ," I manage to say. "The men have gone."

"Never mind that." Halim is already standing on the dock and reaches out a hand to me. I take it and brace my foot against the side of the canal. My corset constricts my breathing and I find myself panting slightly. I hop onto the bank and move apart from Halim, pulling my hand out of his grasp—I don't want him to see how flustered I am.

"Aren't they meant to be guarding us?"

Halim gives me a boyish smile and holds out the crook of his arm. "I dismissed them. I want to walk these streets like a normal person. All the pomp and ceremony becomes fatiguing after a while. Have no fear—I will protect you."

"That wasn't really my concern," I say. "We shouldn't be seen without a chaperone."

Halim's face takes on an exaggerated crestfallen look. "Don't you trust me?"

I don't want to hurt his feelings. I find myself slipping my arm through his. "Of course," I say weakly. I glance around one last time. I am alone with a prince.

We enter the cool of the church of St. Mary of the Friars and approach the high altar, where Titian's *Assumption* adorns the wall. The church is empty but for an old man on a ladder replacing candles.

"Isn't it beautiful?" I say.

"It is," he replies. I see his lips are slightly parted as he takes in the rich reds and golds of Mary's ascent to heaven. "Christ's mother is a sacred figure to Muslims too," he replies, "but we have nothing as beautiful as . . . I wish my sister could see this."

"Perhaps one day she will." I take his arm again and together we walk along the nave. "It could be dangerous for us to be alone together," I murmur.

"You mean, for our reputations?" he asks.

I shake my head. "No, for our lives. Venice is full of assassins. Surely you know that."

I don't have to look at Halim to know that he is smiling. I'm teasing him, just a little bit.

"Then let's live dangerously. I'll run the risk of being killed. Will you?"

"I'm taking my life in my hands, you know, just being here."

We turn to face each other, then begin to walk back down the center aisle.

"How reckless we both are," he says.

We step out into the sun and for a moment I squint into the harsh light. Out of nowhere, five shapes resolve. Five men, all looking at us with cold expressions, and spread in a fan to block our route. They aren't constables of the city; that much is clear from their ragged clothes. Two hold cudgels and two have knives. The fifth man has a sword at his side.

"What do you want?" I say.

"The heart of that dog," says the central man, pointing his blade at Halim.

He throws himself at the prince, and I don't realize what has happened until he sinks to the ground, clutching his stomach. His knife rattles on the stone as blood gurgles through his clasped fingers. Halim's blade is bloody and his eyes are wild. "Run!" he shouts, shoving me aside.

I stumble as the men advance. Halim backs off in a crouch, moving towards the steps of the church, his blade turned over so it lies against the inside of his wrist. I hardly think before snatching at the hilt of the sword in the attacker's scabbard and drawing it out.

"Hey!" he shouts, spinning around.

I level the blade. "Get away from him!" I warn.

Though he looks gobsmacked, one of his companions — the leader who spoke before — merely grins and raises his club. "Don't make me smash your skull, woman," he says. The other men have paused, suddenly unsure.

"Don't, Laura!" says Halim.

I watch the man with the cudgel moving around to my left, but I keep my sword trained on the fellow in front. "Unless you want me to run your friend through," I say, "I'd lower your weapon."

The club-wielder scoffs. "You overestimate my loyalty," he says.

He lunges to strike, but suddenly stops and clutches his throat, where a gold hilt protrudes. His legs give way and he collapses. Halim's arm is still extended from the throw and he snatches up his first victim's fallen dagger.

"Three against two," he says to the remaining men. "Do you fancy yourselves our match?"

The leader of the attackers has breathed his last at my feet. Blood runs in rivulets between the paving slabs.

The remaining thugs look at each other but the fight has left their eyes. They're scared. One makes a sudden break, heading for an alley.

"The odds get better," I say.

"Who ordered you here?" Halim asks. "Tell me and you can keep your paltry lives."

The two men are silent, so Halim tosses the blade over in his hand, ready to throw again. I press the point of the sword firmly into the ribs of my man and he gasps in pain. "Tell us!" I say.

"I can't!" says the man. "Please, don't kill me. I have children." He throws his cudgel to the ground and then his companion lets go of his own dagger. "We're unarmed."

Running footsteps sound from the alley, and four more men rush into view. Reinforcements. Halim's eyes meet mine. No point fighting now. I nod and we run.

"Catch them!" comes a shout.

We dart around the side of the church and into a small alley that twists and forks. The pounding feet of our pursuers never seem far behind. I grab Halim's arm and we switch back around a deserted sculptor's yard. Half-finished blocks of marble, faces emerging from stone, watch us impassively.

"There!" I hiss, and we run towards a pile of swollen wooden barrels, their metal rings red with rust. We duck behind them, kneeling in piles of dried leaves and cobwebs.

I can feel my heart hammering in my chest, my sides hurting from the constraints of my corset. We peer through spy holes from behind the barrels and wait. Halim pants beside me, his skin slick with sweat. The heat from his body seeps through my gown.

Shouts echo, but in the distance. No one else approaches the yard. Our breathing slows, and after a few long moments, Halim grunts.

"We've lost them," I say.

He stands and pulls me to my feet, my joints stiff. I realize I'm still holding the sword, which he pries gently from my fingers. "No need for that, now," he says, dropping it to the ground. I see his hand and wrist are covered in blood.

"You're hurt," I say, touching his arm lightly.

"It's not mine."

Neither of us says what we both must be thinking: *We could easily be dead right now.*

There's a sound of shuffling steps and I tense. But it's only an old woman, chasing a cat, her back stooped over nearly double.

"Come back here, you toothless wretch!" she calls after her pet. Halim and I laugh with relief as we watch her hobble after the ancient, skinny animal.

"Let's get back to our boat," he says, shaking his head. "I've seen enough of Venice for one day."

I follow the prince out of the square.

17

When we arrive back at the gondola, Halim's men have mysteriously reappeared. How could Halim possibly have gotten a message to them? But he ignores them and stoops to clean the drying blood from his forearm. This time, he doesn't hold his hand out to help me, and one of the guards steadies me as I climb down. Halim has thrown himself back on the velvet seat, his hand to his chin. He is deep in thought, his eyes not seeing the waters of Venice that lie before him. I sit quietly by his side.

But as the boat moves out into the canal, he speaks.

"These happy times you were telling me about earlier. Do they involve a suitor?"

I'm startled by the line of questioning, so soon after we barely escaped with our lives.

"You want to talk about love and romance at a time like this?" The question's out before I can stop it.

"Of course!" Halim says, sweeping an arm across the vista. "How could we not in a city as beautiful as this?"

I roll my eyes. "You can drop that act now. We can both

stop pretending that we're on a sightseeing tour. Those people tried to kill us!"

The Turkish prince folds his arms, the shot silk glistening. "That's not quite true, Laura. Those men tried to kill me. You just got in the way."

Is that supposed to make me feel small? As if I don't count? Is he so full of self-importance that, that . . . "How do you know that?" I ask, ashamed at how high and squeaky my voice emerges.

Halim allows his gaze to travel down my body. It feels like a scorching bolt of lightning, and my arms move protectively around my waist. "How could anyone kill a creature as beautiful as you?" he murmurs. "Now, please answer my question. Lovers? Suitors? Would-be husbands? Will one hand be enough to count them?" He holds up a hand and pretends he's about to list off my love interests.

I shake my head, more irritated than I know I should feel. "No one. There's no one," I say as we pass beneath a bridge. Thank goodness for the shadow covering my face. My cheeks flare with shame at my own lie. Why am I denying Roberto? Why don't I tell Halim about my one true love? I fall into silence and reason with myself: Halim does not deserve to know my heart. And I do not wish to share Roberto's current pain with anyone, much less a handsome prince who thinks he can charm the birds out of the trees. What Roberto and I share . . . it's worth so much more than that.

I settle back against a cushion. Roberto gets out of jail today—even now, he may be soaping the dirt from his skin in water perfumed with oil, fresh towels waiting for him.

My darling, I think, and then I wonder if I spoke the word out loud, because Halim is staring at me.

"I think there may be someone," he says, with a small nod.

Fortunately, the gondola is pulling into the port. Faruk waits there, still as a statue. His gaze bores into Halim as we climb out of the boat. He motions the prince to one side, whispering urgently. An emissary from the Grand Council in his official robes and flat hat stands by, his eyes dropped to the ground.

Halim strides over to me, his body language transformed. Gone are the smiles and warmth.

"I must go," he announces. "Thank you for your time."

I drop into a curtsy, stung by his dismissal. "I was only doing my duty," I say, returning the insult. But Halim has already turned from me and is deep in conversation with the emissary, his hands gesticulating as he speaks. I can't hear what they are saying and find myself standing alone, abandoned by prince and guards both.

At least my coach is still waiting for me. I climb inside as a church clock strikes the hour.

"To the palace," I call up to the driver.

I don't even look back at Halim as the coach pulls away. My love is waiting for me.

Servants in uniform show me to the private apartments. The corridors and galleries seem endless, but finally I arrive at the doors to Roberto's rooms. Two guards stand outside, each wearing a *schiavona* sword with a basket guard and double-edged blade. I approach them with my shoulders drawn back.

"Is Roberto here?" I ask.

The men exchange a glance.

"May I see him?" I ask.

"Who's out there?" calls Roberto's voice, faint from behind the doors.

My heart quickens. "It's me—Laura!"

One of the soldiers sighs. "Go on inside, then," he says.

I run between the guards and throw the doors open. Instantly, my smile fades. Roberto is sitting on the edge of the bed, stripped to the waist. His ribs are dark with bruises. The mark on his face has faded to a sickly yellow.

"Quite a sight, aren't I?" he says. I walk to him, and he stands stiffly to enfold me in his arms. "Careful, now!" he says.

"They can't treat you like this," I say. "You're the Doge's son!"

"The rules in the Piombi are different," he says, his voice hoarse. "I made the mistake of answering back."

He presses his face into the folds of my dress. I wait, resting my fingers in locks of his hair. I can feel his chest moving with contained emotion. After a moment, he pulls away and smiles. "I hear you've been playing the tour guide."

I blush deeply, and I'm not sure why. "It's been a bore. I've been thinking only of you."

Roberto kisses my lips, and in those few seconds, all is forgotten.

"I hear my father is playing the diplomat," he says as we break apart.

I shake my head. "Never mind that. You're out of that hellish place now. Soon, we'll be able to prove your innocence."

Roberto's smile fades. He turns away from me to shrug on a shirt. "Do you think so?" he says. I can tell that he is listening carefully for what I say next.

"Of course!" I say. "In time, all Venice will know the truth." I want to tell him that the Segreta are meeting, perhaps at this very moment—that there are people who can help. Instead, I pull him to me and press my lips against his throat. He kisses the tears from my eyelashes. I could happily stay right here forever, locked in our little room together.

A distant shout tears through our intimacy. A ragged voice of anger carries up the corridors. "Where is he?"

Roberto pulls away and stares at me. "What's that?"

Before I can respond, he's making for the doors. The shouts are close.

"You cannot enter these chambers!" one of the guards protests.

"Do not stand in my way!"

I clutch my hands to my chest, fear rolling over me. I know that voice.

"Halim," I murmur. Why is he here?

"Who?" Roberto asks, turning to look at me. I don't know how to respond. I don't have to. The doors burst open, sending Roberto staggering back, and a figure appears in the room. Dark skin, darker eyes, hands clawed and face twisted with a fury I could never have imagined.

"You will pay!" Halim screams at Roberto. The veins stand out on his neck as the guards hold him back. "My sister's blood stains your hands!"

18

Halim's men crowd around, trying to restrain him.
"Get off me!" he cries, pushing them away. He lunges towards Roberto, fingers grasping the air. Roberto stands his ground, but his face has drained of blood. Halim's chest heaves, and his eyes are wild. He doesn't even seem to have seen me. "You murdering monster! Is this what you do to women in Venice?"

He manages to free himself and his fist crashes into Roberto's face with a sickening sound. Roberto staggers back, but Halim's men are able to drag him from the room. Roberto is too shocked to do anything but watch, fingers staunching the blood from his nose.

"I'll tear your throat out!" Halim screams from outside.

I peer out of the doorway to see him being pulled down the corridor. The guards at the door keep their swords trained on him. For a moment, our eyes meet, and I see a flicker of shame.

"Unhand me!" he growls. "I won't fight any longer." As the men release him, he straightens his clothes and walks away, his retinue following.

When I turn back into the room, I see that Faruk has remained. He watches my face carefully. Though his own expression is as blank as a mask, I can't help but sense a smile lurking behind it.

"What's happening here?" I ask, swallowing hard. My mouth is so dry I can hardly get the words out. "I don't understand."

"You should," Faruk says, darting a glance at Roberto. "I have learned you are engaged to this brute. Did you forget to mention to the prince that you were going to marry a child-slayer?"

A Venetian servant would never dare speak so, but this adviser seems more like a confidante than a manservant.

"Get out," I command. His glance rolls over me as if to say, *And who are you to give orders?*

One of the remaining guards takes a step towards him. "Do as the lady asks," he warns.

Faruk turns his stooped back on us and follows his master outside. Other footsteps pound up the corridor, and the next moment Nicolo appears, swinging around the open doorway.

"I'm not too late, am I?" he gasps. He spots Roberto's bloodied nose. "Are you hurt?"

Roberto lets out a long exhalation. "I'm fine. But what did that man want?"

His brother walks farther into the room and sinks onto a stool covered in jade brocade. He shakes his head, staring at the marble floor. "You wouldn't believe it," he says, almost to himself.

"That was Halim, the Turkish prince," I say, going to take Roberto's hand.

"That much I gathered."

"He asked to see the girl's body," says Nicolo.

"The girl from my rooms?"

Nicolo nods and explains quickly that Halim was escorted to the warehouse in the harbor, where the body was being kept ready to be shipped to Lazzaretto Nuovo. The watchmen prised the coffin lid off. "We only did it to keep Prince Halim happy!" Nicolo says. "Even though we thought it very strange. He wouldn't explain what she was to him. But the girl who was lying there . . ." Nicolo shakes his head. "It wasn't good, Roberto. She hadn't been washed or cleaned up. There was dried blood all over her dress and the air stank with decomposition. The prince—he fell to his knees! Began screaming and howling. No one understood."

"Go on," I say in a low voice.

Nicolo gets to his feet and wanders over to a window to look down on the palace courtyard with its bronze wells. Behind him a bird darts from the eaves, just like the little bird I used to feed in the convent.

"Prince Halim had a pendant. He was clutching it to his chest. He seemed to . . ." Nicolo turns to face us, and his eyes are full of pain at the memory of what he saw. "He knew the girl—said it was his sister. Her name was Aysim. Next thing, that bald-headed fellow is whispering in his ear and Prince Halim curses, swearing to kill you, Roberto. I got here as fast as I could, but he'd already started running up the stairs."

"I must go to him," Roberto says quietly. "Tell him I didn't do this. He has to understand."

Before I can move to stop him, he is out of the room. I throw a glance to Nicolo, and the two of us give chase down the corridor.

"No, Roberto!" I call after him. "Give him time to calm down." I know what it is to lose a sister, and I cannot blame Halim for his rage. But by the look in Halim's eyes just now, he'd be capable of anything. I cannot lose my only love.

Roberto's marching stride does not falter. "My reputation is at stake," he says over his shoulder. "And Halim is a prince, an honorable man." Nicolo throws me a helpless glance, and there's nothing we can do but follow.

We find Halim by the sound of his shouts. He is in the Doge's apartments, appealing to him. Appealing — or demanding.

"You put her in a cheap box!" he bellows as we near the door. "A princess of the Ottomans, rotting and soiled in a pauper's grave!"

We enter, and Halim doesn't see us straightaway. The Doge sits implacably still in his high-backed chair. Some men from the Grand Council surround him. He holds up a hand.

"We didn't know," the Doge explains. "If we'd had any idea, of course we would have paid your sister the appropriate respect. But you must remember, no relatives came forward to claim her and she was an anonymous woman on the streets of our city."

"Not on the streets, in the house of a . . ." His words fade away as he notices Roberto's presence in the room.

"You! In *your* house. In a murderer's home! What was she doing there?" He strides towards Roberto, hands twitching. Roberto opens his mouth to respond, but Halim has reached to his waist and drawn a sword. One of his servants must have given it him, because he wasn't wearing it just a moment ago in Roberto's rooms, nor was it the one he had on our tour of the city. There are gasps, and people shrink back against the walls.

I have never seen a sword like Halim's before. It curves in a smooth, lethal sweep of metal. There is a cross of gold at the hilt and calligraphy engraved near the top of the blade.

"I demand my honor," Halim says in a low, thunderous voice. "I will fight you, Roberto, until one of us is dead."

A sudden clamor of voices fills the apartment. Only the Doge sits silently at the heart of it, staring at the man who would kill his son. One of the elder statesmen takes a cautious step forward.

"This cannot happen," he beseeches the Doge. "Roberto has not yet even been tried for murder."

"Let God decide," says Faruk. His thin lips are pursed into a smirk and I feel I could strike him down myself, if I only had a blade. He holds out a hand, palm up, and waits. One of the Ottoman servants scurries forward and places the hilt of a sword in his hand, and his fingers close around the metal. With a flick of his wrist, he turns the sword around so that the hilt faces Roberto.

"No!" The cry bubbles out from me as Roberto steps forward. This can't be happening.

Roberto grasps the sword, and for a moment, I feel unsteady on my feet. Nausea squirms within me. I've seen

Halim kill two men already today, each with lethal efficiency. After everything we've been through, for my beloved to be killed like this. . . .

Faruk smiles as Roberto takes the sword from him. Servants slip out of the room, and one of the women has begun crying. I feel fixed to my spot. It's as if I'm watching a play unfold, and can do nothing but witness the actors' performance. Roberto looks around the room, his gaze finally coming to rest on Halim, who rolls his wrist to flash the blade back and forth. This is nothing like our practice sessions—it's so horribly real. Sweat beads on the prince's brow. "Ready?" he says.

In reply, Roberto extends his sword. Its blade gleams beneath the chandeliers. Then something remarkable happens—I watch Roberto's fingers peel away from the hilt and the sword clatters to the floor, its blade ringing as metal meets marble. Now, even the Doge's eyes widen. A servant hurries to snatch the sword up and out of harm's way. Roberto has done the unthinkable: he has refused a duel. I want to rush to his side, but I daren't move.

"I won't risk your death because of a misunderstanding," Roberto announces.

Halim strides towards Roberto until the point of his curved sword presses against my beloved's shirt. I can hardly watch.

"Fight me," Halim demands. He looks close to tears now, his anger transformed into something else. Despite everything, I feel a wave of sympathy for him. It is grief that has brought him to this.

Roberto shakes his head. He keeps his face neutral, neither mocking nor full of pity. There's a flicker to one side and I glance over to see a woman whispering into some-one's ear. Already this scene has become gossip. Halim must notice too, and something passes behind his eyes. All of a sudden the anger has returned. He shoves Roberto hard in the chest with his hand and draws back his sword, ready to strike.

"No!" I shout. The servant who rescued Roberto's sword stands beside me and I snatch it from him. My hand slides around the hilt and my feet slap against marble as I rush forward. Ringing metal echoes as my blade parries Halim's.

"Get back!" Roberto hisses to me. I don't respond. My eyes are trained on Halim's. There's respect there, but con-fusion too, as if he doesn't understand my gesture.

"Step away," I urge him, my muscles straining as I hold back the weight of his blade.

"My sister's spirit watches," he tells me. "*You* step away!"

I shake my head. "There's been enough killing today."

"Laura," the Doge protests. It is the first time he's said anything. But it's too late.

Halim gives a sudden twist of the wrist, bringing his sword beneath mine. Another jerk and my weapon goes clattering to the floor and I stagger sideways. Halim raises his sword into the air and steps towards Roberto, his face implacable. Roberto jerks sideways to avoid a lunge. Halim swipes and just misses his throat.

"He's unarmed!" The shout comes from Nicolo, who throws himself forward, panic twisting his features. His eyes lock onto Halim's face, widening in recognition. I drop my glance to his chest and see what everyone else has al-ready witnessed: Halim's blade between his ribs.

Nicolo sinks to his knees as blood trickles down the curved metal, spattering in fat droplets on the floor. Howls of shock and sudden grief fill the room. Nicolo's mouth hangs open, and scarlet rivulets run between his fingers. I hear a scream and realize it's my own.

19

With a grunt, Halim pulls his blade free, and Nicolo tips forward to fall facedown on the marble, his blood spreading quickly in a crimson pool. The Ottoman prince stares at him, an appalled expression on his face. He looks up at Faruk, as though seeking guidance. But the older man gives nothing away. He closes his eyes and lowers his head, murmuring under his breath. A prayer, I suppose.

My first thought is for Paulina. My friend is too young to be a widow. *This will kill her.*

Roberto pushes past us and kneels beside Nicolo, gently cupping a hand behind his brother's head. A woman throws herself down beside him, murmuring reassurances. I recognize her as one of the Duchess's closest servants. The Duchess! How will she find the strength to bear this?

People are crowding round now, leaving me standing alone on the outskirts.

"Get back! Give him some air." Roberto's voice cuts through the wails.

"Leave us!" calls the Doge.

Slowly, the courtiers seep away, casting horrified glances as they retreat. Roberto turns Nicolo onto his back, and his brother's head hangs awkwardly to one side, blood frothing at his mouth. I hear a ragged breath. Nicolo gazes at his brother, eating up the sight of him as Roberto brushes a damp lock of hair out of his eyes.

"My brave brother," Roberto murmurs.

Nicolo attempts a smile but it quickly disappears in a grimace of pain. A woman muffles a sob and turns to hide her face in her companion's shoulder. Nicolo seems to be forming his mouth around a word. Roberto bends his head closer. "Paulina," Nicolo gasps. Then his head lolls back.

Carefully, Roberto lays his body flat on the floor. He brushes his palm over his brother's eyelids to close them. The Duchess's servant lifts a crucifix that hangs from her neck and kisses the tiny figure of Christ, beginning a prayer under her breath.

Halim is still watching, his sword now on the floor at his feet. He shakes his head, over and over, but doesn't utter a word. When he finally looks up, his eyes meet mine. I'm not sure what I see there. Hostility? Regret? Fear? He turns sharply on his heel and marches from the room. The rest of the Ottoman party scurries after him. Only Faruk glances over his shoulder as he leaves.

Soon, the room is empty, barring myself, Roberto and the Doge. A starling sings outside the window, breaking the silence.

"What now?" I ask.

"Now we arrest Prince Halim!" a voice calls from the doorway. We turn, and I see Julius standing there —

Carina's father and Grazia's estranged husband. How it must cut his pride, to see the Doge's son laid out, blood pouring from a sword wound.

But the Doge shakes his head. "We cannot."

"He killed your son."

"Ambassadors are protected by Venetian law," Roberto says, bending to smooth Nicolo's tunic. "Diplomacy must rule, even now." He looks up at his father, and the Doge nods in agreement.

"But surely, in circumstances such as these . . ." Julius begins to protest. "Laura, tell them!" He must be desperate, if he is appealing to me.

I can barely look at Nicolo's body—I've already seen too many corpses in my short life. "We must do as the Doge wishes," I say quietly.

Servants have started to file back into the room. The Doge speaks without looking at them. "Take my son from this place," he commands. "He must be laid out."

The servants crowd closer, uncertain how best to proceed. It takes Roberto to organize them.

"You, at the head. You, come here and take the weight of his torso. One man at each leg and arm." On Roberto's count, they lift Nicolo. He sags heavily—all that light youth turned to meat. His skin is already fading to white, and as he is raised up, we see the sticky blood pooled on the marble beneath him. It's too much to bear.

The Doge stands beside me, his face unreadable. Roberto's eyes watch vacantly as the servants turn out of the doorway, and the body is gone. We stand at the three corners of an invisible triangle. Then the inevitable comes. A screech of agony as the Duchess's voice rings out.

This morning, she celebrated the partial liberation of her eldest son. Now, she mourns the death of her youngest. My own eyes are dry as her cries fill the palace. My fingernails dig into the palms of my hands to stop the tears, and my mind turns to someone else.

Where is poor Paulina?

After a long while, I make my way back home. I've done my best to comfort the Duchess, but my words seemed empty even to me, and I left her maid giving her a sleeping draught as she lay on tear-soaked pillows. I am exhausted in body and spirit.

Faustina enters the room with none of her customary bustle. Bianca follows, clutching a pile of laundry.

"They've called a curfew from sundown," Faustina whispers. "All across the city." She sits beside me on the window seat and we look out over Venice. She places a hot hand over mine and muffles a sob. "To think it has come to this! Nicolo dead at the hand of an evil foreigner. I knew we should never have welcomed them into the city." She shakes her head bitterly.

"Prince Halim is not to blame," I say. Bianca is folding clothes over by the bed, and pauses in her work.

"That's not what they're saying on the streets," she tells me. "A rug stall was burned to the ground this afternoon — the owner wasn't even Turkish! I'm glad we have to stay housebound. It's dangerous out there." She brings a lace shawl and Faustina takes it from her to wrap around my shoulders.

"Why do you defend the prince?" Faustina asks. "He tried to kill Roberto and then slaughtered Nicolo. How does he deserve your pardon?"

"I was there," I say. "I saw the grief in his face. He wasn't thinking. . . ." I draw the shawl tighter around me. "You could say that this is all *my* fault. If I hadn't got involved in the duel, Nicolo wouldn't have come to my defense!"

The two servants watch my face with wide eyes. Bianca looks as though she could burst into tears at any moment.

"Now, now," scolds Faustina. "Enough of that. It's not your fault that angry men were holding swords."

I know she's right, of course. But it doesn't make me feel any better.

"I hear that Halim has fled Venice," Bianca says. She sits on the floor at my feet.

"I hear the same," Faustina adds. "He's taken his sister's body to the mainland for burial. Good riddance, I say!"

I jump up from the window seat. "Stop it," I say. "The poor man is mourning his sister. We all know how that is, don't we?" I glare at my servants, daring them to remember Beatrice's coffin.

Bianca's face colors, but Faustina stares back at me stubbornly. "I'm only saying . . . ," she comments, smoothing down her apron and pretending to be affronted.

A bell rings, and Bianca leans out of the window to peer down at the villa's front steps. "It's a messenger," she tells us over her shoulder. "I'll go down."

Faustina is still sulking as we listen to the sound of subdued voices. Then there's the clatter of feet and Bianca steps back into the room, holding out a note to me. I break the seal and read, aware of the others watching me.

You are needed later this evening. Come to us.

I recognize Grazia's handwriting. The Segreta are summoning me. Good—now more than ever I need answers.

I roll the note back up and hold it to a candle flame so that it catches and quickly turns into burning flakes of ash that fall into the saucer. The bitter scent of smoke fills the room.

"You may leave me," I tell Faustina and Bianca. When I look back up at them, their faces are full of questions. Questions that I won't answer. I walk down the steps and find that the messenger boy is still standing in the doorway.

"Is there a reply that you want me to carry?" he asks, hopeful of earning a few coins.

I shake my head. "No reply."

I'll go to the Segreta in person. In times like these, I need to be among my own kind—with the other women who weave Venice's tapestry of secrets.

The threads must be untangled if the bloodshed is to stop.

20

The sun sits low, just over the city's many spires. Soon, it will dip below Venice's skyline and we will all be forced to stay indoors, under the rules of the new curfew. I walk down a cobbled street with three other women — Allegreza, Grazia and a young woman called Sophia.

Four Venetian women, our faces hidden behind fans.

Four members of the Segreta, secrets hidden in our hearts.

The city is quiet — quieter than I've ever known it. A lace seller lounges on a stone bench beside her wares, looking sad and bored. Soon, I'm sure, she'll disappear indoors to eat an evening meal alone. Perhaps even she has been touched by the news of Nicolo's death.

We turn a corner and travel down a path lined on one side with a series of stone archways. Above each arch is carved a trefoil knot of three overlapping rings. They cast distorted circles of light and shade on the wall opposite. Sophia and I are honored to be among these two, selected for this private discussion, but thus far we have yet to touch upon the topic closest to my heart.

As Allegreza details the plan for dealing with Teresa's husband, Silvio—a plan simple and direct—I'm thinking about the best way of opening the subject of Roberto and Aysim, Halim's poor dead sister. For she must have been the girl I was sent to meet on Murano.

"By the time that monster leaves, he'll have sworn never to raise his hand to a woman again," Grazia says, her voice rich with satisfaction.

"Teresa's not the only person in Venice who needs help," I say. "Roberto may be out of his stinking jail cell, but he still stands accused of murder."

"Everything in due course," says Allegreza. "Are you sure you're clear on the plan for Silvio?"

"Yes, yes," I say, growing impatient. "But you said Aysim was coming here to meet us? There must be a clue, something . . ."

Allegreza raises a hand to halt my speech. "When the time is right, we will turn to these matters. Laura—you brought Teresa to us. Small plights are as important as big intrigues."

I hold back the scream that wants to come. Roberto's fate is more than an intrigue to me—my life is caught up with his. Can't these women understand that? *Are they so heartless?* I think, then immediately feel guilty. Allegreza and Grazia are two of the most important women in the Segreta, and therefore in all of Venice, and have done more than anybody to change countless lives. I should not be so ungrateful; I should remember the patience I was taught at the convent.

Allegreza gives me a sympathetic glance as though she can read every thought. She leads us to a bench inside the archways. "Let us sit."

Alleys stretch out in every direction, curving out of sight and into the unknown. This city is as convoluted as any intrigue.

After a pause to make sure no one is approaching, Allegreza begins talking. "Aysim risked a great deal coming to us."

Grazia nods. So she too knows more than I do.

"We'd been in touch for some time through . . . intermediaries," says Allegreza. "Of course, almost no one is completely trustworthy. Especially when a network starts reaching abroad." She takes a deep breath and raises a hand to her face. Startled, I realize that this older woman is close to tears. "We encouraged Aysim to join forces with us, but ultimately we let her down. I will have that woman's death on my conscience for as long as I live. But at the moment much is unclear. It would be foolish to rush in when our security is at stake. Do you understand?"

Sophia sits quietly, her profile illuminated by the setting sun. I have no idea what she's thinking.

"I'm beginning to," I say quietly, but my mind is shouting, *That's not good enough! We might not have long!*

"Good girl," Allegreza tells me, with something like fondness in her voice. "Let us deal with Silvio first and discuss Roberto after."

She leaves us, slipping beneath an archway and out of sight. The sun is setting, and the darkness summons the people of the city to their homes, and the women of the Segreta to their duties.

The heat in the small dressing closet is stifling. Grazia stands on one side of me, and Sophia on the other. We each wear heavy woolen cloaks with hoods and black felt masks that hide our faces. My mask makes it difficult to breathe, and I can feel pinpricks of sweat in my armpits. I slip my hand into the pocket of my cloak and stroke the hilt of a stiletto dagger, its blade sheathed in a leather holder. Grazia gave me this weapon before we arrived. My fingers tremble in my pocket. I've handled more weapons in the last day than in the rest of my years combined, even with my months of practice with Roberto.

A strip of light glows at the edge of the closet door, revealing a hook from which hangs an orange studded with cloves. Its scent does little to overpower the smell of mothballs tucked into the folds of garments on a shelf above our heads. Sophia's eyes shift between Grazia and me. My left foot has almost gone to sleep. Perhaps Silvio won't come at all.

I suppose it's only fair that I'm one of those chosen for tonight's task. It was I who drew the Segreta's attention to Teresa's plight. I shift my weight to the other side of my body, feeling the tingle of blood returning to my ankle.

"Wait!" a woman cries merrily. There's the sound of a grunt and a heavy, unsteady footfall. A wet noise of lips smacking against skin and a moment's silence, and then: "I said, wait!" She is laughing, the good-hearted courtesan whom I first met through the Segreta. She helps us in our work; few of the men in Venice realize that the yellow handkerchief that marks her as a woman of ill-repute

127

hides a quick wit and more secrets than anyone can possibly guess.

"I have to be home soon," slurs the man. "My shrew of a wife will burn my dinner otherwise!" His voice is thick with drink.

"Does your wife know where you are?" Bella Donna asks in a teasing voice.

"I don't care," he snarls. "Now come here."

"One moment, my Silvio." Bella Donna's voice is closer now. This means she is moving towards the doorway, ready to exit. "I just need to freshen up."

That's our cue. The bedroom door snaps shut, and we spill out from the closet. I've drawn the dagger from my pocket. Around us, candles burn low, their smoky flames flickering and casting the room in dancing shadows. An unmade bed, piled thick with blankets, stands in the center of the room. Teresa's husband scrambles back against the headboard as he sees us emerge, and we quickly move around the bed to surround him on three sides. There's no escape.

"What the . . . !" Silvio scans our faces, frowning and squinting. "Who are you?" His frown turns to a sly smile as his addled brain tries to make sense of the situation. "Are you part of the entertainment?" he asks. His face is matted with stubble, and even from a distance I can smell the drink on his breath. "Come here, my darlings," he says in a singsong voice, curling a finger.

I go to my position, guarding the door. Grazia throws back her cloak, and I understand that she is allowing Silvio to glimpse the silver dagger at her waist. His smile fades; he knows the game is over. He moves a hand towards his own waist and pulls out a leather purse. He loosens the strings and exaggeratedly tips it upside down. Nothing spills out.

"You're wasting your time," he says, his words bleeding into each other. "I don't have a penny. Not even enough to pay that whore!" He throws his head back and laughs with gusto.

"It's not your money we want," Grazia tells him quietly. The dagger is now in her hand, held out towards him.

Silvio still refuses to be scared. "A lady's dagger," he says. "Isn't it pretty? Close to useless!" He turns his back on Grazia, grunting as he shuffles towards the edge of the bed. He must be really drunk if he doesn't realize how deadly Grazia's weapon is. That slender blade could slide between a person's ribs before they've even registered the attack.

Sophia draws a sword with a snake engraved around the hilt and trains the point on Silvio. He staggers back into a bedside table.

"Where's my girl?" he asks uncertainly.

Sophia gives him an icy smile. "You won't be seeing her again," she says. She takes a step forward and slices her sword through the air, a hairsbreadth from his nose. He flinches and cries out. "In fact, you won't see anyone else ever again unless you do everything we tell you."

"What do you want?" he asks. His voice is weak, his eyes watery and yellow.

Sophia lowers the point of her sword, then jabs it beneath the oily sash that fastens his trousers.

"What are you doing?" he protests, trying to curl his body away. But with a sudden upward jerk, Sophia tears through the sash and his trousers sag around his hips.

"Take them off," Grazia orders, watching from the other side of the bed. She is smiling from behind her mask.

Silvio's eyes widen. "You're joking?"

Grazia shakes her head and tosses her dagger from one hand to the other.

"Do it," I say.

Slowly, Silvio unlaces his trousers and they shudder down his white legs to gather at his feet. He steps out of the trousers and kicks them into a corner of the room. Bella Donna can burn them later.

"Now your shirt," I say from my place at the door.

Trembling, Silvio heaves his filthy cotton tunic over his head, struggling to free his arms. For a moment, all we can see of him is his round belly, soft as dough. It sways from side to side as he tries to maneuver out of his shirt. Grazia and I share a glance while Sophia stifles a smirk.

"You heathen women," Silvio bellows from inside his shirt. With a loud tearing sound, it finally pops over his head and he throws it to the floor. "Happy now? Does my humiliation amuse you?"

"It does indeed," Grazia answers smoothly. "But it isn't over yet." She dips the point of her blade towards his undergarments. "And the rest."

Her eyes haven't left his face. He hesitates for a moment; then with a grunt of disgust he hooks his thumbs into the waistband of his stained cotton hose and pulls them down, bending at the hips. I keep my eyes fixed on the wall above him. I can hardly believe what Grazia's making him do—but after all, he has forced Teresa to endure much more than petty embarrassment.

Silvio straightens up, cupping his hands over his groin.

"Are you women or witches?" he spits, his eyes swiveling between our three masked faces.

Grazia draws near to our victim. Her smile has faded. "Now, if you ever raise a hand to your wife again, or betray or cheat her, I promise it will be more than your clothes you lose."

Silvio's face hardens in partial understanding. "Teresa is behind this? How do you know her?" I can see the anger rising inside him. He must be warned.

"If you make your wife suffer for what has happened tonight, the consequences will be severe," I tell him. "So far we have been lenient."

Silvio throws me a scornful glance. "Who do you think you are?" he asks. "No woman tells me what to do!"

Within a moment I am upon him, the tip of my dagger at his throat, drawing a bead of blood. I can feel my heart thudding and the roar of anger pushing through my veins. One thrust and I could have this man's throat cut open. Where has this taste for blood come from?

"Do you understand?" I hiss into his face.

His lip trembles, and his brow looses a bead of sweat that trails along his jawline. "I'm sorry! I didn't mean it! Whatever you want me to do, I'll do it."

I sense the other women watching.

"Careful now," Grazia's voice tells me. I press the flat of my blade against Silvio's Adam's apple. Then I pull away, taking my weapon with me.

"Then go," I say. "Take your hateful face out of our presence and thank Teresa that you still have your life. And remember, we can find you anywhere."

Silvio staggers slightly as he bends to retrieve his clothes.

"Oh no you don't," Sophia tells him, kicking his shirt under the bed, out of reach. "Those don't belong to you anymore."

"What? You . . ." He starts to protest but then thinks better of it. Holding his hands over his nakedness, he waddles out of the room, cursing under his breath. I slam the door shut behind him, then move to the window, watching as he emerges into the alley below, looking over his shoulder nervously. He's lucky. The nighttime streets of Venice will likely preserve his modesty. I almost wish we had struck during the day, so that he could be openly mocked in the busy markets. But the cover of night is always best for us.

"All clear?" asks Bella Donna, poking her head around the bedroom door. Grazia beckons her into the room, and we conceal our weapons. Bella Donna rests her hands on her thighs and guffaws. "I was watching through the keyhole. Did you see the size of that belly? I thought he would pop with outrage!"

We pull down our hoods and take off our masks, shaking out our hair. We trust Bella Donna enough to share our faces with her—a rare privilege. It's good to go back to being Laura, a woman with a face.

"Your performance was the best," Grazia says to me. "The move with your dagger was very clever—even I thought you were going to run him through."

I bow my head modestly, but only because I don't want her to see my face. She can read eyes, that one. And I know what she would see in mine—guilt. These women can't know how close I came. How my anger almost won.

21

We leave Bella Donna and go to meet the rest of the Segreta, following the best route to avoid the city's night watchmen. The appointed place is a grain store in a secluded part of Venice, near the northern shore. Four stories high with a peaked roof, it sits beside a canal where supplies can be shipped by boat. I follow the others inside, and my nose picks up the comforting scent of wheat. Burlap sacks, each printed with the supplier's mark, sit in neat rows along wooden shelves. We pass them and climb the stairs until we arrive at a wooden platform beneath the eaves of the building. Would the merchants of Venice ever guess what secrets their storehouses hide?

The other women are waiting, lit only by the moonlight streaming in from a window in the roof. One person is missing—Paulina. It's hardly a surprise. I sent a note of condolence to her home, but words are never enough. I wish I could see her and try to offer some true comfort.

Allegreza steps into the center of the circle and turns on her heel, gazing into each of our faces. The success with Silvio fades from my mind, and I remember why we are gathered here—because our city, and my love, is in crisis.

"These are testing times," Allegreza begins. The other women murmur in agreement. "But the Segreta have been tested before. Aysim put her trust in us, and we have failed her. There is no avoiding that fact." She pauses, and I can feel the attention of the women linger on me, even if their eyes do not. "Moreover," continues Allegreza, "her secrets have gone to the grave with her. What worries me more is this: Why did she die when she did? Who else knew that she would be coming?"

I remember Allegreza's words to me when I visited her at her house. *A traitor in the Segreta.* The others pick up on her meaning too. We each keep our gaze firmly fixed on our leader, not daring to look at each other in case our glances are misconstrued as accusation—or guilt. My cheeks burn nonetheless. Does anyone here believe that I'm the person giving away our secrets?

"I tell you now," Allegreza continues. "Stay alert at all times. If you see or hear anything—anything!—that is suspicious, it is your duty to report it to me. Do you understand?"

There are murmurs of assent. Allegreza's glance lands on me, and I nod quickly.

"Excellent. Now, go back to your homes. Remember all that I have told you."

The other women begin to move away, but I'm frozen. Surely our meeting can't be over already? Nothing has been said of my fiancé's plight or his brother's death. Not a word has been shared in sympathy and understanding for

Paulina. But it's my loved one's dilemma that troubles me most.

"Will you help Roberto?" The words spill from me before I can stop them.

The other women pause and share confused glances. Allegreza's face hardens.

"What do you think we can do, Laura?" she asks.

"Either get him out of Venice or work the Segreta's influence on the trial. He's an innocent man—he does not deserve what is happening to him."

Allegreza walks around the room, the floorboards creaking beneath her feet. Her shadow moves with her, stark black against the milky light of the moon.

"We must use our power carefully," she says. "A knife overused quickly becomes blunt."

This is too much for me to bear. Allegreza told me—promised me!—that in time the Segreta would turn to Roberto's plight. Now she talks of caution! I can't stop myself; I step towards her, my voice loud in the silence of the room. "You had that monster Vincenzo exiled, so why can't you help Roberto?"

Allegreza pats the air as if to calm me. "Vincenzo was guilty of spying, an agent for the Duke of Milan. We had good reason to banish him."

"And Roberto is innocent! Isn't that a good enough reason to help?"

I wait for the murmurs of agreement, but silence stretches between Allegreza and myself. I look around me at the other women and see none of them moving to speak. When I try to make eye contact with young Sophia, my accomplice such a short while ago, she looks away.

Understanding dawns. "You don't believe in his innocence, do you?" I begin to stalk from woman to woman, staring brazenly into their faces. "Do *you*?" I pause before Allegreza, my breathing labored.

She shakes her head. "Calm yourself, Laura. A woman has been wronged. We must remember that above all."

"But not by my fiancé!"

Grazia moves to Allegreza's side. "You are behaving inappropriately, Laura," she says.

I step back, trying to calm my thumping heart.

Allegreza sighs. "We understand your pain, Laura," she says. "Why don't we put it to an anonymous vote? To help Roberto or to stay out of the case? We will help only with majority assent."

I feel a flutter of hope. One of the women tears slips of paper from an old, dusty ledger, and we each cast our votes. People can vote yes or no to help Roberto in his plight. We deposit our pieces of paper facedown on the floor in front of us and one of the Segreta collects each of our slips. She goes to a corner of the room and begins counting them out into piles.

Suddenly, there is a clatter of footsteps on the wooden stairs. The Segreta scatter, slinking into the shadows or crouching behind sacks. I press myself into one of the dark corners.

A black-clad figure enters. "Paulina!" cries one of the women, rising to her feet and rushing out to meet her. But Paulina pushes past, glancing around the room. One by one, we step out of our hiding places. Paulina's eyes come to rest on my face.

"I'm so sorry," I tell my friend, holding out my arms to her.

"You!" Paulina lunges at me, her nails raking the air. She grabs my hand and drags me towards her. "Nicolo is dead. All because of you!"

Her face is close to mine, and I can feel the spittle on my cheeks. Her hand grips my hair.

"Stop!" I say. "Please!"

"It's your fault! It should be Roberto's blood staining the palace floor. Instead, instead . . ." A sob escapes her. "My love is dead! And with him, my future!"

With a sudden groan of defeat, she falls away from me.

"Roberto is innocent," I say quietly.

She scoffs. "You simply have no idea, do you? What do you think he was doing when you were in the convent? Saying his own prayers? Don't make me laugh! He knew his way around every whorehouse in Venice."

"Hush now," someone protests. But not because the words offend her — I can sense that she's trying to protect me.

"What are you talking about?" I say.

"Your one true love!" says Paulina. "A man of spotless character. Oh, please! I'm only saying what we all know."

Paulina's face is red with fury, but even as her final words melt away, I can see the guilt there too. She knows she's gone too far. All of the women's eyes are on me, and I want nothing more than to disappear.

"I see," I say stiffly. "Thank you for educating me."

Grazia reaches out for Paulina, but she turns away, defeated and sobbing. "Leave me be!" She runs from the room.

"Shall I go after her?" asks Sophia.

Grazia shakes her head. "There's nothing we can do for Paulina at the moment."

Why did my friend say such horrible things? I suddenly feel very young again. Naive and innocent as the day I left the convent. Was she speaking merely out of anger and grief, or was she venting secrets that have been kept from me? I swallow back a rising panic. Roberto is no whore-monger. He isn't capable of anything like that.

Allegreza watches from across the room. In her hands, she holds the scraps of paper from the vote.

"A decision has been made," she announces. "The Segreta have spoken."

"And?" I say.

Allegreza looks at me, but I cannot read her expression. Compassion, maybe, or pity. "I think it best for you not to know the result of the vote," she says.

I'm flabbergasted. Not tell me? "But why?"

Allegreza nods. "You are too close to this, Laura. Too emotionally involved."

"But I have to know," I say. "Will you help him?"

Allegreza shakes her head. "The meeting is over."

22

The noise greets us even before our coach arrives at the cathedral. It is the sound of mourning—wailing voices and low sobs. But nothing prepares me for the sight we come upon as we turn into St. Mark's Square. Beside me, Emilia lets out a small cry of shock, and I feel my breath catch in my lungs. So many people!

Venice is mourning Nicolo's death. Hundreds are crammed into the square and lining the surrounding streets. Rope barriers have been erected and soldiers stand before them to keep back the press of the crowds. Women dab their eyes with handkerchiefs and opportunistic stall sellers are offering black-stained flowers to throw upon the coffin when it passes. The scent of incense is heavy in the air, and a distant band of street musicians plays a lament. Agile young men climb the fountains and statues to get a better view of their dead prince when he arrives.

The funeral has been organized quickly. In this heat, no one wants to leave a body waiting for burial. Word traveled the streets, the canals and the narrow alleyways, sent out from the Doge's palace: the ceremony would take place on the second Sunday of the month, four days after Roberto bent to hear his brother's last words. I haven't seen my beloved since, and my messages have received no reply.

Now, even the Segreta are keeping secrets from me.

The coach draws to a halt, and I step out, helped by my father. The skin of his hands is papery and dry, and when I look up into his face I see nothing there but accusation. *You bring us to this,* his eyes tell me. *You and the man you insist on loving.* If I hadn't been loyal to Roberto, defending him against Halim's attacks, Nicolo would still be alive and my family would have been saved from scandal. Perhaps Paulina was right to attack me. But the moment I think this, my heart twists. How can loving Roberto be wrong? What could I have done differently?

As I move across the square, the black taffeta of my skirts swishes noisily. I wear a single string of pearls at my throat, and my hair is framed by an embroidered cap. The sky is gray above us, and the tiny pieces of jet sewn across my bodice barely glimmer.

Lysander looks up at the dense clouds threatening rain and shudders. "The perfect day for a funeral," he comments.

"Don't," Emilia reproves.

"Show some respect," Father hisses from behind us.

"Yes, show some respect!" calls a stranger's voice. I look over my shoulder and see a woman, her bosom spilling out of her corset, lunge towards me. Her eyes are wild, and I can smell the wine on her breath. "Look, everyone! It's Laura della Scala—betrothed to a murderer."

More noise erupts around us, angry shouts and curses. Lysander puts his arm around my shoulders and pulls me to him. "Ignore them," he whispers into my hair. But I can feel the blood drain from my face as the awful truth hits me with the taunts and insults that ring in my ears. The people of Venice hate me! They are filled with hate, filled and overflowing.

"Shall I try to talk to them, to explain?" I twist my neck to look up into my brother's face, but he's too intent on scanning the crowd to respond. He pulls me along now, forcing me to walk faster than my petticoats allow. I almost trip, and it's only Emilia's hand on my elbow that saves me from falling into the waste that pours down the open sewers of the street.

Thud! Something smashes into the side of my head. I stagger slightly as the sensation of warmth and moisture creeps down my cheek. I put a hand to my face. When I take it away to stare at my fingers, I frown with confusion, my thoughts struggling to keep up with what is happening. Someone has thrown a rotten fig at me, its golden seeds squelching out of the purple skin.

"You should be ashamed to be here!" shouts a man. He pulls back his head, purses his lips and then spits. Warm saliva hits my chest, and Emilia hurries to wipe it away with a handkerchief.

"Don't," I try to tell her, "don't take it away." But she can't hear me for the clamor.

"Is that your daughter, old man?" someone else cries. I glance back at Father and see him turn away. He doesn't try to defend me. I stumble onwards, looking neither right nor left.

"Your fiancé is a coward!" someone in the crowd shouts. "He deserves to die."

"Murderer's creature!"

"Harlot!"

"Roberto's head should have rolled already," a woman yells, her eyes narrowed. "Just because he's the Doge's son . . ." She stoops beneath the rope barrier and lunges towards us.

"Guards!" Father calls, his voice straining to be heard above the crowds. "Come and help!"

Men in cloaks carrying swords at their waists run over, and suddenly I am surrounded by a wall of broad shoulders. I am able to move quickly inside this cavern of safety, and our family is escorted the rest of the way to the Basilica, with its lead-covered domes and turrets. Lifting my skirts, I run up the steps. I can't believe my arrival at Nicolo's funeral is so undignified. Tears of shame swell in my eyes, and I wipe them away with a fist.

As we step inside, I'm grateful for the coolness that surrounds me. Lysander is looking at me hard.

"Why are they attacking *you*?" he asks, his voice somber. "You haven't killed anybody."

He suddenly sounds much older than the young man who sat at our table tipsily teasing his new wife, not so many days ago.

I look down at my stained skirts. "Neither has Roberto," I say coldly. "It's all such a mess."

We turn to face the rows of official mourners. I gaze up at the cathedral's high domed ceiling, which glistens with gold foil. We are surrounded by marble columns and bronze statues. Singers gaze down on us from the choir lofts, and the gilded mosaic ceiling makes my eyes dance. No wonder it's known as the Church of Gold. It's an exercise in opulence: Venice at its best—and its worst. After all, we are here because of a good man's death.

My family walks down the main nave towards a row of seats that have been saved for us. On either side, women are dressed in their finery and men sport silken cloaks, the colors denoting their status. No one looks at us—whether out of respect for Nicolo or distaste for my presence, I don't know. I spot a space farther back in the church and duck into it, leading Emilia after me.

"I don't want to be too near the front," I whisper in explanation. "For Paulina's sake."

I can see my friend, her back poker straight as she trains her face on Nicolo's coffin where it rests near the high altar.

Emilia bobs her head in understanding and I sink onto a bench as Father and Lysander move ahead to take our family's allotted place. I grasp the wooden bench in front of me, my fingers turning white. Emilia reaches over, takes my hand and holds it in her lap.

Beside Paulina sits the Duchess Besina, Nicolo's mother. She glances over her shoulder and spots me in the crowd. Standing, she moves past the Doge and walks up the aisle towards me. Others shift in their seats, and I feel a hundred staring eyes. Emilia stands to give the Duchess her place, and the older woman sits beside me.

The Duchess carries the perfume of grief with her. I smell it oozing from her skin, beneath the stronger scent of her pomade. When she gazes into my eyes, I think my heart will break. Any light that once danced there has been extinguished. I want to draw the Duchess to me, but her status as the Doge's wife makes this impossible. She is cast adrift, isolated by an advantageous marriage that robs her

143

of simple human kindness. For a moment, I wonder if I really want to enter this family, to marry Roberto. Do I wish the same fate for myself? For people to fear, more than care for, me?

"Roberto," she starts to say. She pauses and swallows hard, composing herself. "Roberto is back in the . . . in that place."

"No," I mutter. Not the Piombi.

"The house arrest was not well received. And especially after Nicolo's death, it became a scandal. The Doge had no choice. Laura, I'm sorry. You won't see Roberto again until his trial, two days from now." Her voices catches. "I wanted . . . I wanted to tell you myself. I know you love him as much as I do."

"Two days is a long time," I whisper. "In two days, this nightmare could be over."

She gives me a watery smile. "You're right. We should be pleased for the progress we've made. You're a good girl." She strokes a hand down my cheek; then with a heavy swish of skirts she returns to her place at the front of the church.

Emilia takes her seat beside me once more, and the funeral service begins.

The formality of it helps. The cathedral is huge, and Nicolo's coffin is a tiny oblong box a long way from me, pointing at the grand altar. To see it I have to strain my neck to peer above the crowd of heads. I imagine him laid inside there, as cold and still as my sister was in her own coffin. The voices of the priests barely carry to me, and I copy the movements of others in the congregation, making the sign of the cross when they do or sinking to my knees. I feel bleached of emotion, counting the moments until I can be out of this place. It's not that I don't care for Nicolo or Paulina, but life is pressing down very hard on my shoulders.

A small, almost indiscernible movement at the upper edge of my vision draws my glance to the ceiling of the church. In one of the many balconies, I spot a shadowy silhouette half hidden by a porphyry statue. The silhouette sharpens into the outline of a small waist, a curved hip—a woman. She's dressed in black and wearing a mask that glints silver beneath the gold of the church ceiling. How strange. I'm sure the mask isn't one of ours. Luxurious curls of brown hair cascade down one shoulder. Why is she in the balcony rather than among the congregation? I twist round in my seat for a better view, but as soon as I move, she slips behind the statue, disappearing out of sight.

As the incense clouds about me and bells are rung, I turn back towards Nicolo's coffin. My senses are ablaze. Grief is all around me, yet only one thought fills my head.

Someone is spying on me.

23

I wake the next morning and watch the muslin curtains billow in the warm breeze. The masked figure haunted my dreams, waiting each time I closed my eyes. Not for the first time I ask myself, *Can I trust the Segreta?*

I barely have the energy to leave my bed and get dressed. Nicolo's funeral and the hatred shown to me in the streets have left me drained.

I can hear Faustina in the courtyard below, slapping wet sheets against a washboard. Then there's a voice that makes me sit up sharply.

"Is she in?" gasps a young boy. It's the messenger who brought me the notes from Grazia. I've contracted him with a steady supply of food from the kitchen to apprise me of any interesting developments. After all, if I am to help Roberto survive the scandal that has beset him, I must know what whispers are abroad.

"Yes," answers Faustina, puffing heavily. I hear the creak as she turns a mangle, squeezing water from fabric as it passes between the wooden rolls. "I'll take you to her."

I leap out of bed and draw a dressing gown around me, tie it hastily at the waist and run towards the main stairs. Barefoot and with my hair loose, I descend into the main hallway—just as Faustina, her hands red from scorching hot water, leads the boy indoors. They stare at me in surprise.

"Aren't you dressed yet?" Faustina asks. She wipes the soapsuds from her hands onto her apron. "I've been working since dawn!"

The boy gawps at the open collar of my dressing gown, and hastily I pull it tighter. "You have a message for me?" I ask. The boy nods, his mouth still hanging open. I throw a glance at Faustina, who has folded her arms and is giving me a long, narrow-eyed look. "You may leave us," I tell her formally.

She opens her mouth to protest, then thinks better of it, turning on her heel to walk back out to the wooden washbasin that rests on the courtyard tiles.

"Well?" I ask.

The boy swallows hard. "A ship has docked in the harbor," he says.

I feel my skin prickle with anticipation. "Whose ship?"

"That Turkish prince's—Halim." The boy's face colors. "The one you fought with a sword."

"And how do you know about that?" I ask sharply.

"Everyone's talking about it."

I feel my face stiffen. "I can hardly set foot outside my own door. I rely on you to tell me what's happening in Venice—remember?" The boy looks as though he's about to burst into tears. I soften my voice. "Thank you for the message." I walk over to where my purse hangs from a wooden clothes hook and dig inside it for payment. As the coins fall into the boy's open palm, I give him one last instruction: "Tell our coachman to prepare the horses."

"Where shall I say you're going?"

I look out the open front doors of the villa. In the far distance, I can see the sparkle of water. "Where is Halim staying?" I ask.

"I know that!" the boy says proudly. "I asked around before coming here. He's taken apartments near the harbor, on Albanesi."

"Well done," I tell him, smiling. I slip him an extra coin. *That's where I'll go, then,* I tell myself.

When I emerge from my room, ready for the journey, Lysander and Emilia are standing in the hallway. They are dressed in walking clothes.

"Won't you join us?" Emilia smiles. I shake my head, glimpsing the coachman waiting patiently out on the drive. Lysander looks over his shoulder, following the direction of my gaze.

"You're going out alone?" he asks.

"Why not?" I say. "I'm not going to be a prisoner here." But as I start to walk towards the open doorway, Lysander grasps my arm.

"Are you sure you'll be all right?" he asks, drawing me to one side. "Remember what happened before the funeral."

"I have to leave this house one day."

Lysander's eyes are pained and he lowers his voice. "I've heard rumors, Laura . . . about Roberto."

"Oh yes?"

"Consider, how well do you really know this man?

He was hidden for many years, living a life free of restriction. . . ."

"Just say what you mean."

"Do I have to?" he asks. "I know what young men are like, sister."

"Really?" I say. "Well, you don't know Roberto. He's a good man. I know this from the depths of my soul."

"All women in love say this, and we both know that some are wrong," says Lysander. "Please, listen to my counsel. . . ."

I shake myself free, firmly, but I don't want to cause a scene in front of Emilia.

"I've heard the rumors too," I say. "But if I believed every rumor to take to the air in Venice, I'd be a fool indeed. Roberto. Really, brother." I force a smile onto my face. I don't want him to ask where I'm going.

Turning to the waiting coachman, he calls out, "Take care of her!"

The man nods in acknowledgment. Hastily, I go outside and climb into the coach. As the driver slams the little door shut behind me, Emilia's face appears at the window. She reaches inside the carriage and takes my hand.

"Stay safe," she tells me. "We love you, you know."

"I'll be fine," I reassure her, wondering if she too has heard this new gossip about my beloved Roberto. She steps away from the coach, and I hear the crack of a whip. Then the coach lurches and I ride out towards the harbor. To the man who can change everything.

I ask the coachman to drop me off a few streets away from Halim's apartments. I cannot risk word getting back to my family as to my whereabouts. I duck down the alleyways, keeping to the shadows. Perhaps it's the clandestine nature of my visit that makes me check frequently over my shoulder, but that masked face stays with me. Turning a corner, I glimpse a flash of purple skirt slipping out of sight. It could be anyone, but three more turnings on, I see it again, dipping behind a stall. There's a wooden bench ahead, and I pause beside it, as if trying to get my bearings. My senses are stretched taut, but I don't see the dress again.

In the Calle dei Albanesi I spot two dark-skinned guards posted at a doorway. The men are dressed in short red jackets and billowing trousers tucked inside leather boots. Swathes of green cloth bind their heads, and each carries a short sword shoved inside a leather belt. Their thick beards make it impossible to read their expressions.

"I'm here to see Halim," I say.

One of the men grins. "No one sees the prince without permission," he says in Italian. "And he hasn't said anything about a Venetian courtesan paying him a visit."

I keep a straight face. These men are not thugs, I know that. I have heard about the Ottoman army and the privileges of learning and social status that their soldiers enjoy. To call me a courtesan is not a mistake, but a well-aimed weapon. The guard's companion joins in the mocking laughter. He nods towards San Polo, where most of Venice's prostitutes live and work.

"You're a long way from home," he tells me. "Better run back to your customers."

I dip my head modestly. "There must be some mistake," I tell them. "My father sits on the Doge's Grand Council. I am sure Halim will see me if he knows I'm here. Tell him . . . tell him that Laura della Scala wishes to visit."

The men share a doubtful glance and speak to each other in their own tongue.

"That's right," calls a voice from the hallway. The prince steps out of the shadows, into the column of sunlight streaming from the open doorway. "She's the one I've been speaking of."

"My lord," I say, dipping into a curtsy.

Another figure sidles from within the apartment and stands beside the prince. Faruk.

He speaks urgently to Halim, looking at me with barely concealed disgust.

The prince waves a hand through the air. "Paper and ink can wait," he says, staring at me. "Come inside, Laura."

The guards step aside.

I take Halim's outstretched hand, feeling his fingers curl around my own.

"Thank you," I say. He has no idea how much I mean it.

Then he leads me into the hidden darkness of his rooms.

24

I've never seen a Venetian apartment like this before. It has been transformed. Clouds of incense fill the air from shallow copper bowls, and thick rugs cover the marble floor. Chairs and couches have been pushed against the walls to make room for scattered cushions. Halim lowers himself onto one of them and sits cross-legged. A length of glistening linen has been twisted around his temples in a neat turban. His trousers are made of rich silk that whispers luxuriously as he moves, and rows of tiny buttons line the edges of his collarless tunic. Over it, he wears a waistcoat of cream taffeta embroidered with gold brocade. There is a wide sash at his waist, and leather boots encase his feet. When he smiles, his teeth glitter white against golden skin.

Across the room from us are some of Halim's advisers. They kneel and sit around a low wooden table with a map spread across it. From the familiar curves of the coastline, I recognize it as the Mediterranean. Faruk goes to join them, and the men pause in their murmuring, watching as

Halim indicates a cushion to me. I tuck my skirts beneath me carefully, sitting with my legs arranged to one side. It is difficult to be a graceful Venetian lady sitting so close to the floor, but I take a tumbler of white liquid from a servant and sip it to hide my embarrassment. It's sweet and sour at the same time, and I wrinkle my nose.

Halim smiles. "It is a yogurt drink," he explains. "Traditional in our country, though I fear the Italian cows do not produce such rich milk as ours." The smile falls from his face. "But I'm sure you're not here to discuss dairy cows."

My eyes flicker over to Halim's advisers as I try to judge what I can and cannot say in front of witnesses. Halim notices my reticence and clicks his fingers above his head. "You can go," he tells the men. Led by a grumbling Faruk, they leave the room, shutting the door behind them.

Now we are alone. Now I can say anything I choose.

"You are a brave woman," Halim tells me. "Strong in spirit, too. It cannot have been easy, coming here today."

"I heard that you buried your sister on the mainland," I say.

I wonder if he knows why his sister came to Venice in the first place — why she felt the need to make contact with the Segreta. An answer to that question flashes across my mind, but I push it away for now, because it's too painful to think about.

Prince Halim leans to light another cone of incense and I guess that he is playing for time, waiting for his composure to return. Finally, he looks at me through the clouds of frankincense and juniper.

"Do you want to know about Ottoman funerals, then?"

"I want to know how you are," I tell him. If I want this

man to help me, I need to understand him. "I know what it is to lose a sister, remember."

Halim changes before my eyes. Something seems to fall from his face, and he slumps back against the cushions.

"After my sister was born, my mother gave away the — how do you say it? — the 'good-luck eyes' she'd had since girlhood. Do you know what they are, Laura?"

I shake my head.

"Glass beads that ward off ill fortune. Mother always said that her beautiful daughter was all the good luck our family needed." Halim laughs at the memory. "We all believed the same, until she ran away. . . ." His eyes cloud with darkness, and I move to sit on a cushion nearer to him. I daren't reach out and clasp his hand in sympathy, but it doesn't matter — he's lost in a scene playing out in his head. "She ran away from home a month ago, and we didn't even know why. She was the center of our family, and suddenly our heart was torn from us. When she disappeared, I truly thought . . ." He breaks off, and suddenly his eyes snap back to me, his gaze hungry for reassurance. "Why would a young woman run away like that?"

"I don't know." If she hadn't run from me on Murano, she might be alive now. But my theory continues to take shape in my head, and this time it won't be chased away. Roberto visited Constantinople. What if Aysim's coming here had something to do with him? What if that is why she was in his rooms? "The whole of Venice grieves alongside you," I say.

I realize immediately that this is the wrong thing to say. At the mention of the city, Halim's face closes up. He gets to his feet and walks around the map spread out on the table, pretending to inspect it.

"You haven't told me. Why are you here?"

"Because I need your help," I reply. There's no time to dance around the truth.

His eyebrows lift with surprise. "Go on," he says, after a moment.

The incense is thick in the air now, making my throat dry, and I struggle to say my next words out loud. "Roberto is innocent."

Funny, I used similar words not an hour ago to my brother. So why do they now carry less conviction? No! I mustn't let the rumors of this city infect me. Nothing has changed.

Halim closes his eyes, his brow creasing with pain. I know it must be difficult to hear me defend Roberto. I rise to my feet, moving to stand beside him. I place a hand on his arm and wait to see if he pulls away, but he does not.

"Whatever you believe, Roberto is not to blame for Aysim's death. He is a gentleman, and I love him."

At these words, Halim opens his eyes to stare at my hand, still resting on his arm. I take it away. My voice drops to a whisper, as I am suddenly aware of the advisers who left us and wonder if any of them are listening at the door.

"He could never have committed the crimes for which he is imprisoned," I say. "He is the most honorable man in Venice."

Silence throbs through the room. After a few seconds, Halim nods slowly, and hope flickers into life. But then he speaks.

"No."

He walks languidly over to the doors and opens them. There's no anger in his movements. *See how little I am affected by your story,* his actions say. The Ottoman prince has returned and Halim is lost to me. "There's nothing I can do to help," he says. "Simply nothing."

I walk through the door and turn back to him. But his gaze remains fixed on the stairs—my invitation to leave.

"Halim . . . ," I say, sending out one last desperate plea.

He shakes his head and, finally, looks at me. His brown eyes scorch my face. "I have proof," he says. "Proof of what Roberto has done. It's you I feel sorry for, dear Laura. You stand loyal to the wrong man."

And with that, the door shuts. I behold the varnished mahogany for a long, painful moment. Then I stumble down the stairs. The guards watch me step out into the sunshine, my eyes watering in the light.

"That was quick," one of them says. There's a sound from above our heads, and when I glance up, I see Halim standing on a balcony, watching me.

"You'll see at the trial how right I am," he calls. It's as though he's raining arrows on my head instead of words, and each one causes fresh pain.

I walk away, past the fountain and the bench.

I hardly see where I'm going.

25

"Proof?" I mutter as I walk through the streets. I don't care if people hear. Who is he to talk of proof? What does he know?

I turn the corner and realize I'm beside the public entrance of the Piombi. Through this door, up near-endless stairs and corridors and above the heads of his family Roberto lies in a cell strewn with damp straw. Have the guards been at him again? I hardly dare think. My breath comes in shallow gasps, and I lean against the wall, its bricks warmed by the sun. A passing fruit-seller pauses and throws me a concerned glance, before hurrying on.

I crane my head back to observe the swallows darting in the sky above us. The thought that wormed its way into my mind is festering there. Has Roberto lied to me? I twist around and slam my palm against the wall. It cannot be.

I try to think things through logically, linking one event with the next. Aysim should never have been in Roberto's room. She planned to meet with the Segreta. I hurry on, my skirts bunched up. A street actor calls out a joke after me and his audience laughs to see a noble lady embarrassing herself in this way. I don't care. I need answers.

A servant accompanies me into Allegreza's private quarters and announces my arrival. My mentor stands beside a gilt sideboard that supports a bird stand with two doves cooing on their perch. She indicates with an open hand towards a seat, and I settle on the damask.

"Your hair has come loose," she says. My hands dart to my temples, smoothing my curls back into place. "You must not make a habit of unsolicited calls. But as it happens, I'm glad to see you this time. I have news."

"Oh, thank goodness! Will it help Roberto?"

Allegreza reaches inside the folds of silk at her bodice and pulls out a key. She leans over to a table with an empty plate on it and unlocks a drawer. Then she places her hand inside, pulls out a roll of parchment and reads it. "You must not let that man rule all your thoughts," she says.

I feel my features twist. "I'm betrothed to be married to *that man*, and he languishes in the foulest prison in the city!"

Allegreza shakes her head. "If you want to help Roberto, you must learn patience and diplomacy. You display neither at the moment."

My insides shrivel. "Please, tell me what you know."

She watches my face. "You must move carefully, Laura. We all must. These affairs are grave and the repercussions will be felt across the city. Have I taught you nothing?"

"You have! You have!"

Allegreza's face softens. "Well, then." She reads the final lines of spidery writing on her scroll, then places it back in the drawer. With a single turn of the key, it is locked away. She slips the key back into her bodice. "Three nights ago . . ."

"The night Aysim was killed," I whisper.

Allegreza nods. "Three nights ago a dark-skinned young girl went to the convent of Saint Susanna in the early hours, begging charity from the nuns." She sees my glance darting to the locked drawer. "My correspondent tells me that the girl barely spoke a word during her time there, but yesterday she asked to be moved on. Now she resides in your former convent."

"The House of Mary and the Angels?"

Allegreza's mouth twitches. "It might just be a coincidence."

"But it might not."

Allegreza's eyes dart towards mine. "I know what you're thinking, Laura, but I forbid it. You're not to go anywhere near your old convent."

Doesn't she understand? I have the perfect alibi! "But I know a girl there called Annalena. I can call on her—I can go and find out more." I can't believe Allegreza is even thinking of stopping me.

"I said no," she says, her voice firm. "What has happened to you, Laura? Where is the measured girl I first met on San Michaele Island?"

I've changed so much since that night I pledged myself to the Segreta. I'm stronger, less innocent. But still I'm trapped. Once I was a prisoner in my convent cell, now I am constrained by the rules of the very society that freed me.

"As you wish," I mutter, dipping my head out of respect—and to hide the glint in my eyes. If Allegreza won't allow me to visit my old home under the orders of the Segreta, I'll go on my own.

Allegreza places a hand over mine. "Thank you, Laura."

I look down at our fingers curled together in my lap. Allegreza's skin is scattered with age spots and fine wrinkles; my own hands are still youthful. What can she know of love? Each decision she makes is a move in a larger game, a jostling of positions for the greater good. She would sacrifice a pawn to keep a queen, because the ends justify the means.

"I'll do everything you ask," I say.

I never would have believed that deceitful words could fall from my lips so easily. Not to Allegreza. But these are desperate times.

I won't let Roberto be a pawn. I won't take orders if my heart tells me they're wrong.

Here, in my years of torment and incarceration, I was once called La Muta—the Silent One. As I stand and regard the walls of the convent, I remember the grilles and bars, the Abbess Lucrezia and my lay sister and friend, Annalena. Will she have changed? I know that I have, from that timid girl who sat in the gardens, making lace and keeping her head bowed. What would the Abbess say if she saw me sparring with Roberto, a man at the point of my blade?

I step up to the heavy, studded door, carrying my gift for Annalena. It's a box of sugared almonds wrapped with a ribbon of pink silk. Decadent, by the convent's standards, but I'm allowed to bring gifts for my friend, surely. I rap my knuckles against the ancient wood, and a small window, cut into the door, slides open. A woman's eyes, framed by a cowl, widen in recognition.

"Laura's back!" she calls to someone. Her glance drops to take in my scarlet dress and the little window slams shut. A moment later, the door creaks open and a hand gestures for me to step inside. Looking over my shoulder, I hesitate. Then I walk into the darkness.

Annalena stands at the end of a covered walkway. She hasn't changed, and for a moment she watches me with a cold stare. Does she even know who I am? Then, as if to dispel my fears, she breaks out into a joyous run and throws herself into my arms.

"Laura, Laura! I knew you'd return, one day. Oh, my heart, are you here to say your prayers?" She laughs excitedly. But we both know I'd never enter these doors again without very good reason. I am one of the lucky ones—I escaped. The other women here, the unwanted second daughters of Venice's gentry, will spend their years watching their lives diminish as they lie in narrow beds, with only their rosaries and their matins for company. Their families don't want to pay their dowries, so instead they are banished as wives of Christ.

Annalena pulls me over to one of the many stone benches where I once sat learning scripture. Everything seems smaller than I remembered.

"For you," I say. I give her the box of sugared almonds, and she cries out with delight, before hastily hiding the gift beneath her coarse habit.

"Look at you!" she gasps. She strokes a hand over my gathered skirts and then touches one of the earrings hanging from my earlobes, marveling at the gemstones. "Sapphires?" she asks. I nod, smiling. She shakes her head in amazement. "Just look at you. You're like a lady now." Again, she laughs. "What am I saying? You *are* a lady!" Her smile suddenly fades and she takes my hands. "But I've heard . . . you know how gossip comes to us, from those we take in and shelter. . . . Is it true what they say?"

I sigh. "Don't listen to Venice's gossip, Annalena. You should know better than that—a good sister like you!"

My friend's cheeks color with embarrassment. "I'm not so very good," she says quietly.

Darling girl. Does she have any idea of the corruption that lies outside this convent? But time is pressing. "Annalena, can you take me to the Abbess?"

She looks surprised. "If that's what you want," she says, getting to her feet. I stand up too, and we walk past the rose gardens towards the Abbess's rooms. It was a walk I always dreaded, and some of the old fear creeps over me now. But I straighten my back and shrug it off. She has no power over me any longer. I can walk back into the daylight at any time.

The Abbess is sitting in her usual place, as if she's never moved in all those months since she dismissed me. Above her head hangs the painting of a lion, the Agliardi Vertova family crest. There is her Bible, the lettering picked out in gold. I clear my throat, and the older woman glances up. I wait for one of her usual chastisements, but instead her face melts into a warm smile. Most disconcerting.

"Laura," she says, getting up to move from behind her desk. "What a pleasant surprise."

Her sour mouth suggests it's anything but.

"Abbess."

"You've changed," she says as her eyes range over the curls heated and set around my temples. Her forehead creases in a frown of disapproval.

"You haven't," I say. The words tip out of me before I can stop them, and we both look at each other for a moment, shocked. Then the Abbess has the good grace to laugh.

"Don't worry," she says. "I know what you mean. Time moves more slowly inside the House of Mary and the Angels. Now, what can I do for a fellow sister?"

She smiles, and it takes me a moment to realize the meaning of her words. For she was never a sister to me here. She can only mean some other kinship that we share.

"You too?" I ask. Somehow—even now—she makes me feel small and foolish.

"That's right, Laura. I was a member of the Segreta long before you even knew it existed."

"The society's range is wide," I say. "I just didn't realize how wide."

"Come, come," the Abbess says, striding towards the door. "You want to see the girl, I presume."

Before I can respond, she is already out of the room, her footsteps ringing on the flagstones of the corridor.

We arrive at the doorway of a tiny cell, and I need to duck my head to step inside. A girl sits on the edge of a bed. She looks up at our entrance, the whites of her eyes two unearthly pools in the gloom.

"Call me if you need anything," the Abbess whispers to me. Then she is gone, closing the door behind her and shutting most of the light from the room.

163

The girl scrambles back on the bed, bunching her knees up to her chin. Her hair hangs in greasy tresses, and I can see bruises along her arms. Someone has restrained her forcefully. She's like a terrified animal, ready to run or attack. She watches my face.

I take a tentative step farther into the room, and a moan of fear erupts from the girl.

"Please don't be afraid," I tell her. No response. From the girl's dark skin and eyes, I can see that she is not Venetian. But haven't I seen a flash of those eyes before?

"Do you understand me?" I ask gently. No response. I try again in different languages—the French I've been learning since leaving the convent, and the Latin I knew too well within—asking the girl where she is from. Nothing. Her limbs are shaking. What can I do? I cannot leave here without information. I'm risking all my links with the Segreta just to be standing here now.

"Do you know anything of a woman called Aysim?" I ask, getting straight to the point.

Suddenly, there's a reaction. Her eyes blaze and she leaps up, standing on the bed, her hands balled into fists as she glares down at me. She looks fierce and proud and absolutely unwilling to tell me any of her secrets.

I push on. "Prince Halim, Aysim's brother, is distraught. His sister . . ." I hesitate, then instead ask the question that's been haunting me ever since I stepped into this room. It may just be enough to get this girl to speak. "I know you, don't I? I've seen you before—that night on Murano, at the glassworks. That was you, wasn't it?"

Something inside the girl seems to break. Her knees buckle, and she collapses back onto the bed. I rush to stand

164

over her. Her breathing is shallow, and when she speaks it's in French.

"Some water?" she asks in a cracked voice. "Please?"

"Of course."

I step out into the corridor, to the table that carries a jug of water and a pile of wooden tumblers. I pour water into one, and take it back to the girl's room.

"Here," I say, holding the glass out as I duck my head beneath the doorway. But my word echoes back at me from the empty room. I rush to the open shutters, but the girl is already at ground level ten feet below, limping along the street. "Come back!" I shout.

She doesn't even turn around.

26

I race out of the cell and down the walkway, past two
panicked-looking nuns in conversation. Heaving open
the main door to the convent, I spill out into the street,
then follow the perimeter wall to where I guess the cell's
window looks out. Wisteria clings to the wall here, sturdy
enough for a slight woman to climb down. I reach the corner where I last saw her and look up and down a street
thick with Venetians going about their business.

"Have you seen a girl with dark skin, about this tall?" I
ask a passing man.

He sends me a lascivious smile. "I see many girls," he
jokes. "I can see you too, if you like."

I turn my back on him, walking a few more paces. But
it's no good. The roads and alleys are labyrinthine here,
and she could have taken any of them. I turn and march
back into the convent. What a fool I've been! I lied in order to meet this girl, and now she has fled. I've scared her
away, and when news gets back to Allegreza . . . I dread
to think.

"Put a message out!" I say as I enter the Abbess's rooms. "Our bird has flown." The Abbess's glance darts towards me from the pages of her Bible.

"I don't take orders from you," she says.

"This isn't about rank," I snap. "You are one of us. Help, or suffer the consequences. A missionary post in the Far East, perhaps? A woman of your experience would surely be able to work wonders out there." I hate myself for the satisfaction I feel in seeing that my bluff has worked—a flicker of horror passes over the Abbess's features.

"Of course I'll help," she says, lowering her voice.

My muscles relax. "Tell all the convents in Venice. If that girl turns up, I want to hear about it. Bring a message to me specifically. The convents are not to give her sanctuary. Understood?"

The Abbess bows her head. "Happy now?"

"This isn't personal."

"Of course it isn't." Her face twists in a smile full of bitterness. "It never was."

As I leave the convent, I hear a scuffle behind me and then I feel a hand tugging at the sleeve of my dress. It's Annalena.

"Weren't you going to say goodbye?" she asks.

I pull her to me in an embrace. I had again forgotten my old friend. I kiss her eyes and brush a hand down a cheek. My insides twist with guilt. I have been dancing, sword-fighting, dressing in fine robes. And all the time, my lay sister has been locked inside these four walls. I should have thought about her before now.

She walks me to the main doors and kisses my hands. "It has been good to see you again," she tells me.

"And you will see more of me," I reassure her, though I wonder if I am deceiving us both.

Annalena smiles sadly. "We'll see."

It hasn't been a happy visit, and all the sugared almonds in the world won't make up for the wretchedness of my friend's fate.

I head straight back to Allegreza's apartments. I must be the first to tell her, and I can feel my heart palpitating as though it wants to jump out of my chest. I can hardly think.

So there were two girls that night on Murano. Of course Aysim wouldn't travel alone. This stray must be her servant, or her friend. She must have answers.

At Allegreza's house, the old servant lets me in again, and my skin prickles with anxiety.

"They're in the parlor," she says.

And then I'm at the doors, and my thumping heart almost stops. For it isn't only Allegreza in the room. Others from the Segreta, at least ten, including Grazia, are ranged about. To anyone else, it would look like a gathering of well-to-do ladies taking tea. But my eyes travel among the aging faces, and see they all wear the silver rings on their middle fingers. These are the most senior of our number.

"Well?" Allegreza says. "What brings you here?"

I bite my lip. "I went to the convent."

Women exchange startled glances. The temperature of the room seems to drop. "What?" Allegreza's fury is not far from the surface of her face.

"Forgive me, please. I wanted to find out her secret! Roberto, his reputation—his life!—depend on it. I was just trying to do the right thing."

Allegreza nods to her servant, who closes the doors.

"She wouldn't speak to me at first," I continue, "but when I mentioned Aysim she became angry and defensive. I told her about Halim's distress and I also told her that . . . that I knew her." Several of the women frown in confusion. "When I was disturbed at the meeting on Murano . . . it was her, I'm sure of it. I'm sorry I went against your orders, but . . ."

Allegreza's lips are pale, her eyes dark and deadly. "And what did you learn, Laura?"

And so we come to it. In a halting voice, I tell her of the escape, and with each word my shame grows. The glares I receive tell the same story. None of these women would have made the same foolish mistake.

Our leader turns her back on me and addresses the other women in a trembling voice. "You've heard what happened. It is of primary importance that this woman be found again. I ask you all to do what you can. You have contacts, you know the city's secrets. Talk, persuade, bribe—whatever it takes. But find out where this girl is!"

The women nod and begin to filter from the room, leaving me with Allegreza. She still has her face turned away from me.

"I specifically forbade you to go to that place," she says, her voice cold. I don't know what to say in response. Finally, she turns and the curl of disgust at her mouth makes the blood drain from my face. "You can go now."

I think about speaking once more, but what can I offer but pleading and excuses? I leave, back into the harsh daylight of a city that no longer seems to be my friend.

I've failed Allegreza, and I've failed the Segreta.

But worst of all, I've failed Roberto.

27

"Chaos," Father grumbles. His eyes dart over to see if I'm listening—clearly he has something on his mind. "Nothing but chaos."

We're dining, just the two of us, as Lysander and Emilia are visiting friends. The food turns to mush in my mouth, and I struggle to swallow. I cannot stop thinking about how badly I performed today. But I must humor my father.

"What do you mean?"

He pours himself a glass of wine and drinks it down greedily, wiping the back of his hand across his mouth. Then he shrugs. "People are talking."

"People are always talking in Venice," I say.

He watches my face carefully. "Yes, but this is different. There are men who . . ." He allows his words to hang in the air.

"Men who what?" My nerves are suddenly alert. "Is this about the Grand Council? What have they been saying?"

Father twists a napkin round and round between his knuckles. He hangs his head to one side, as though unsure about what to share with a simple woman.

"There's a faction," he says eventually. "I think I see their side of things."

"What side of things?" Venice doesn't need more intrigue, not at a time like this.

"They think that the Doge is handling the city's affairs badly, that he is too compromised by everything that is happening in his family—one son dead and another a murderer."

I flinch at his words. "How can you talk about Roberto like that—your future son-in-law?" I ask.

"Do you blame me?" he replies. "All of Venice says the same thing."

"What else do they say?" Father pushes his chair away from the table, as though preparing to leave. "Tell me!" I say, my voice dark with warning. "You've started, so you may as well finish."

Father throws his napkin down on the table. "The Doge's position is becoming untenable," he says, staring me brazenly in the face. "There are plans. . . ."

"What plans?" He shakes his head, but I repeat myself, my voice louder. "What plans?"

He glances uneasily at the doors, beyond which servants will be waiting—and overhearing. "All right, all right. Be quiet, and I'll tell you. Massimo, the Admiral of the Fleet—he thinks he could take command."

"Depose the Doge?" I ask.

Father leans back in his chair. "You sound surprised,

Laura. Don't you think it would be best if Venice was rid of such a family of monsters?" He waits for me to protest, but I manage to control myself. I won't leap to Roberto's defense in front of Father. Strong emotions make weak tacticians. I'm learning that. If I'm to protect Roberto, I need to compose myself. Stiffly, I get to my feet and begin to walk out of the dining room.

"Don't worry, daughter," my father calls after me. "It will all be for the best. You'll see. Then we can start piecing our lives back together again."

I leave the room and pause by the veranda doors. I glimpse the jasmine in the courtyard beyond, its small white flowers glowing in the moonlight. Their scent carries to me on the air and draws me out. I go to sit on the bench beneath the olive tree and lean against the gnarled wood, my head tipped back, my eyes half closed as I watch a bat dart through the shadows.

How did it come to this? How can the city I love have become such a prison? Not just for Roberto, but for myself also.

I hear the scuff of leather on stone, and when I glance over, Emilia is standing in the doorway, her dress shining in the candlelight. A shawl droops from one hand, its silken tassels whispering across the flagstones as she comes to sit beside me.

"Lysander's gone to bed," she says, reaching to tuck a lock of hair behind my ear. "You look tired, too. What are you doing out here?"

I shrug. Any explanation suddenly feels exhausting. More lies on top of too many others.

Emilia wraps her arms around her waist, hugging herself. She follows my glance up to the fat orb of the moon.

"It shines on us, wherever we are," she says with a smile. She looks back at me. "Lysander and I are thinking of going home soon. Perhaps you . . . perhaps you'd come with us?"

I'm suddenly wide awake. "Leave Venice?" I ask.

Emilia grins. "That's not such a very extraordinary idea, is it? You're a young woman who has had a heavy weight on her shoulders these past days. A trip away could work wonders for you. Or perhaps something more permanent." Her hand grasps mine and her skin is warm.

"Without Roberto? How could I?" I ask, too sharply. I immediately regret my tone and squeeze her hand. "You know I couldn't leave him."

"He could join you!" she says. "When all this is over, the two of you will be free to travel wherever you please. Away from all this intrigue and gossip!"

Emilia has a point. Listening to Father this evening, I felt heavy with fatigue. How much longer do I have to defend my fiancé against the rumor mills of this city?

I get to my feet, and Emilia rises beside me. "Thank you," I say, "but . . ."

"Just think about it," says Emilia.

I promise that I will and we walk back indoors.

Bidding her good night, I take the stairs to my room.

I kneel beside the window. I haven't prayed properly since my days in the convent, and I wonder if anyone will be listening now.

But I ask anyway. I pray that Roberto will walk away a

free man. That we will then be free together. That we can leave this place and all its worries.

I stand and lean out of the window, looking in the direction of the Doge's palace.

The Segreta can keep their secrets, if only I can get my beloved back.

28

The crowd jostles me as I stand before the temporary wooden stage that's been built in St. Mark's Square. My fingertips grip its edge, my face level with the rough-hewn planks. I'm surrounded by men and women who have been up half the night in anticipation of today's events. The smell of stale sweat hangs heavy in the air, but above us the sky is blue and clear. The Basilica of St. Mark's stands at the eastern side of the square, and the clock tower looms over the scene, marking out each passing second as I wait to see Roberto's face. We're hemmed in on the other three sides of the square by rows of archways and columns, three stories high.

One thought swirled around my head last night as I tried to sleep: could I be wrong about Roberto? It makes me sway on my feet to even consider such a possibility.

A man laughs beside me, his breath ripe with the smell of beer. A flagon dangles from his hand despite the early hour. "I hope we see his innards slither to the ground!" he cries, before belching loudly.

I close my eyes and force my expression to stay blank. I cannot risk these people sensing my disgust; they must believe I'm one of them. The Venetian nobles are watching from above, in the buildings surrounding the square. No lady would lower herself to stand at the front of a boorish crowd eager for a spectacle, and I've taken some of Bianca's clothes to conceal my status. The fabric of the dress is dyed a simple dark blue. My curls are scraped back severely, and I wear a bonnet with a deep brim to hide my face.

"You won't see his innards," a woman says, prodding the drunk man in the ribs. She jerks her chin towards the stage. "He's too good for that." She spits vigorously on the floor, and I only just manage to pull the hem of my skirts out of the way in time. "Son of a Doge? He'll get a nice, tidy execution. It's not right, if you ask me. Should be . . ."

Whatever she says next gets drowned out by a sudden, vicious roar from the crowd. I stand up on tiptoes to see. It's Roberto! A guard leads him out onto the stage. He looks much better than last time, thank goodness. He's wearing clean clothes, his hair is washed and his bruises are almost healed. He's thin, though—the veins stand out on his arms, and he holds his body slightly to one side as he walks, as though protecting an injury. His hands are manacled in front of him.

"My love," I whisper.

As he passes the edge of the stage, I reach forward, my fingers trembling.

"He won't have any coins for you!" the man beside me guffaws. "Son of the Doge or no."

I snatch my hand back, but not before I hear Roberto

176

gasp in recognition. His eyes widen and he slows. A guard shoves him roughly in the back and he stumbles forward, his eyes flickering over to me one last time. Then he has moved away, going to stand in the center of the stage.

Three men step onto the wooden boards. These are the judges, three senior members of the Council. They're wearing ceremonial robes and sit themselves on high seats at the back of the stage, staring out at the onlookers. Their faces look carved from stone, expressions unreadable.

There's no sign of the Doge or his wife. Perhaps they're hiding behind one of the hundreds of windows in the palace that rears over us. Roberto is so fully alone that it makes my heart ache.

A figure in a cloak steps up onto the stage and brings a wooden staff down against the floorboards.

"Silence!" he calls. His voice carries easily across the square, and the people around me stop their gossiping, their eyes trained on the stage.

A second figure comes forward: Faruk. His stooped shoulders are hidden beneath a luxurious robe, and his face is clean-shaven. He is invited by one of the Council to begin the prosecution, and he turns to face the crowd, sending them a winning smile. It makes my blood run cold.

"The Ottoman Empire sends out its thanks to you, Venetians, for allowing us to plead our case today. My countrymen have heard much of your fair-minded and educated legal system, and we are privileged to be part of it . . ."

He's transformed himself for today's performance, and even I am amazed. His Italian is faultless as he walks confidently across the stage.

". . . but there can be no denying that the Ottoman kingdom has been maligned by a son of Venice." At this, he flings out an arm, motioning to Roberto.

My fiancé simply stares at his feet, his face hidden from the crowd. A flash of frustration passes through me. Can't he see that standing like that makes him look defeated already? Guilty, even?

"The case is clear-cut. Princess Aysim was found dead in this monster's rooms. We have watchmen who will swear to it. The motive for murder? Frustrated lust! Our dear princess would not fulfill his wishes and so he brutally killed her." Faruk shakes his head in disgust. "Do you want this stain on your society?"

"No!" the people around me chorus. "Never!" They are like baying dogs. How can they allow themselves to be so easily deceived?

Faruk gives a solemn nod, as though confirming how very wise they are, and retires to the side of the stage.

"And now for the defense," announces the man with the staff. There are crows and hoots of anticipation, and Roberto is led forward by a chain to the front of the stage.

His eyes scan the crowd, though I notice he avoids looking at me. I mustn't feel hurt; he is doing what he can to get through the next moments.

"I am proud to be a son of Venice," he begins, his voice cracking. He straightens his shoulders. "I would die rather than dishonor this city."

"Die, then, dog!" someone shouts from the back of the crowd, and ugly laughter fills my ears. Roberto waits for the insults to die away. His expression is strong and proud;

this is not a man who will cower before them. Hope flutters in my heart. Finally, quiet descends.

"This much I can tell you: I have never met the woman, Aysim. On the night she was so foully killed, I was drugged and my apartments arranged to look like the scene of murder. Whoever committed this crime, it wasn't me."

Now there are hisses of disapproval from onlookers.

"I am an innocent man," says Roberto. He lowers his head again.

He allows himself to be brought back to the center of the stage, and I feel my hands ball into fists at my sides.

"Is that all he has to say?" The words are out of my mouth before I can stop myself.

"I could have done better myself," says the man beside me, taking a long gulp of beer.

Anyone could have done better than that. Roberto has betrayed his fate with a few paltry words and a story that not even a child would believe. I want to sink to my knees, to weep. What hope is left to us now?

Halim steps up. Handsome, powerful Halim. His hair is freshly oiled and his robes are pristine. He looks every inch the prince he is. He talks quietly with the judges, and I guess that he is requesting permission to speak. Then he turns to face the crowds.

"I'd hoped that the Doge's son would show his noble birth, and admit his guilt, but it seems that is not to be. So my hand has been forced." My glance darts towards Roberto. The blood drains from his face as he watches Halim intensely. "My poor sister was the most virtuous of women. When she first disappeared," Halim continues, "our lives fell apart. We didn't know whether she had been kidnapped, or worse. We searched high and low for clues that might help us find her." From the sash of his robe, Halim pulls out a roll of parchment. "Then we found this letter."

Halim slowly unrolls the parchment, which bears a broken ducal seal. Though no one can read the writing from their vantage point, the crowd seems to press forward as one. I can see the prince's hand shaking a little. He looks upwards to the sky.

"Forgive me, sister," he mutters. "I betray your secrets to save your honor." Now he turns his face to the parchment and begins to read.

"My Darling,

"Since we met in Constantinople last month, I have not been able to put you from my thoughts. Even when I close my eyes, your face does not leave me. Each day since seems a year in length. That night, you gave me a hundred reasons why we should not be together, but my single reason trumps them all. I love you, and cannot live while we're apart. Come to Venice at once, and I promise our life together will be a paradise. I think of you whether the sun or the moon rules the sky."

Halim's voice cracks on the words, and he holds the letter up for all to see. "I ask you to bear witness to the signature."

"Roberto."

The crowd boos and hisses in fury. Halim holds the letter towards Roberto, and the ugly sounds cease.

"Do you deny this handwriting is yours?" The last word is almost spat.

Roberto looks at the letter for what seems a long time. His face grows pale and his brow creases with . . . what? "I don't understand," he says. "The handwriting is mine, but the letter is not."

Halim shakes his head. "Even now, you damn yourself with lies. I would have expected better." He throws the parchment on the table in front of the judges.

My vision blurs as my eyes fill with tears.

"Are you all right?" the woman beside me asks as she takes my elbow and holds me upright.

I manage to nod. "Yes, I'm sorry," I gasp. "It's the heat."

Up onstage, the judges are passing the letter among them.

"Do you have anything more to say?" one of them asks Roberto. "I taught you to read and write as a child. I would know your handwriting anywhere."

Roberto looks bereft. "I've told the truth," he says.

"Were you in Constantinople?" another judge demands, his face cold with fury.

Roberto nods. "You know I was. I supported the trade delegation but two months ago."

The crowd erupts in roars and the judges exchange glances. They don't even need to speak to one another; they already know what they're going to say.

"No!" I cry out.

"Shush, child," the woman tells me. "Don't excite yourself."

Roberto is looking at me now. My own eyes are fixed on his, unable to break our shared gaze across the stage that

181

stretches out between us. He is so close, yet totally out of reach. Tears are running down my cheeks. Roberto shakes his head, and I read the words that he mouths to me: "I'm sorry."

The cloaked man steps forward again and the blow of his staff against the stage floor rings out. "The judges have come to a decision," he announces. Low whispers travel through the crowd, but his eyes stay fixed on the balconies at the back of the square. "Silence!"

The voices fade away, and one of the judges stands up from his seat, clearing his throat. My fingernails cut into the palms of my hands.

"The prisoner is found guilty of the crime of heinous murder," announces the judge. "He will be executed an hour after dawn tomorrow."

The crowd erupts in a roar of thirst for blood.

I turn and push through them. I can hardly breathe. "Let me out, let me out!"

Everyone is shouting, and I keep running, pushing people aside. My bonnet is torn from my head, but I don't stop to retrieve it. A voice rings in my ears, calling over the heads of the crowd. Unmistakable. It's Roberto.

"Laura!"

But I don't stop and I don't call back. I plunge down a narrow street leading from the square, until I'm quite alone in a courtyard. Everyone else is at the trial, and I hear their distant hoots and catcalls. I pause for a moment, leaning against a wall to catch my breath. The sun beats down on my head, and white stars dance behind my eyes. My hopes, the prayers and sureties that had supported me, seem to have crumpled like some cheap stage trick. Judgment has been passed. There's nothing I can do. Nothing the Segreta can do. Nor the Doge. Roberto's guilt has been signed by his own hand. He is to be executed tomorrow, at sunrise. The law has the final say.

I manage to walk on. Even the *words* of the letter sounded like Roberto's. Like the words he used to speak to me.

I hear quick steps behind me. As I turn, before my eyes even take in the figure, a burlap bag is brought down over my head. I stumble and scream. It's suffocating, and I can see only tiny squares of light seeping through the sacking. I hear the sound of feet scuffling against wood, and I am dragged inside a doorway. I kick out, but it's hopeless. The arms that grip me are strong, and it's all I can do to stay upright. We move farther into darkness and a cool interior. There's another set of arms, a muttering voice I can't make out. Then my legs are kicked away, and my rear lands on a wooden seat.

Someone pinions my hands behind my back, and I feel ropes on my wrists. I hear heavy panting beside my ear as a body leans over me.

"Who are you? What do you want?" I ask.

Nothing but a low chuckle of laughter. Rough fingers grip my wrists, and the ropes are pulled painfully tight. Footsteps move away from me, growing faint, and there's the slam of a door.

Am I alone? My chest heaves as I struggle to draw in air through the coarse cloth. I feel myself gagging as panic rises within me.

Then there's a soft noise from somewhere to my left. The pad of leather against wood. Someone else is in the room, approaching me.

I want to call out, *Who are you?* But all that comes out is a strangled sob.

Suddenly, I sense the warmth of another body beside my cheek. Someone is very close, I can tell. The panic is almost overwhelming now. I wait for the sensation of cold metal against my throat.

"Hello, Laura." No blade, just a voice. But a voice I know all too well, even if the words are slurred.

A ghost from my past has returned.

"Carina?" I gasp.

29

The hood is ripped from my head, and I stare around. An anonymous room; I could be in any apartment in Venice. Empty flagons are piled in a corner, and the fireplace is stacked with logs, waiting to be lit. The chair I sit on is in the center of the room. There's no other furniture, barring a low wooden sideboard.

Carina stands behind me, the evil of her presence filling the room. I crane round to try to get a glimpse of her, but the ropes cut into me. She kicks the back legs of my chair, and I nearly tip onto the floor, but she catches the chair and rights it. To my shame, I cry out in fear.

My old enemy laughs. "What a sniveling fool you are," she says. A corner of her cloak swishes out to one side of me, then I spot the hem of a skirt, and finally she comes to stand before me. The cloak's hood hides her face, but there's a dull flash of silver from deep inside its folds.

"Show yourself," I say, sounding bolder than I feel.

"Gladly." She tears back the hood. Before me stands the person I thought was dead. Carina, my sister's oldest friend and the woman who betrayed me. She's wearing a silver mask, behind which flow red locks of hair. The mask seems to be made of some kind of filigree, light enough to wear, but sparkling with curling threads of silver on which are threaded tiny jewels. How long has she been following me around the city, watching from behind her mask?

"You were in the church, weren't you?" I ask.

She dips her head in acknowledgment. "You made such a beautiful mourner," she says, her tone of voice mocking. "Almost worth Nicolo dying, to see you looking so wan and pale."

My lip curls in disgust.

"What would your father say?" she teases. "To see you like this?" She once asked me the same question when she caught me talking to a lowly painter. That was before I knew he was the Doge's son, and before I realized how deeply evil ran in Carina's veins. Now, I know better. She reaches out a gloved hand, and I flinch away. But she doesn't strike me. Instead, she strokes my cheek gently. "Such beautiful skin," she says.

"I thought you were dead," I say.

Carina walks around my chair in a tight circle, her skirts brushing against my legs.

"Sometimes I wish I were," she says. Her voice is light. "It would suit many people if that were the case. Wouldn't you agree?" I daren't respond, but it doesn't matter—she barely catches a breath before continuing. "After the accident on the boat, I often begged God for my pulse to still. The pain . . . You can hardly imagine. I yearned for death!" Now her voice turns darker. "But no one was listening."

She smacks a hand against the back of my chair, and I

can't help jumping. Carina bursts out laughing. She leans over to whisper in my ear. "Calm yourself, little bird."

I shudder to feel the warmth of her breath on my neck. "How did you survive?"

She straightens up again. "God saw fit to spare me," she says.

I think about screaming, but with every other able-bodied Venetian at the scene of the trial, would anyone hear? I flex my hands. The knots don't budge. It was a man, perhaps two, that brought me here. They could be waiting outside.

"What do you do with yourself?" I ask.

She casts out a hand to indicate the window looking over the bay. "I watch! People come and go. You wouldn't believe the gossip that takes place beneath my windowsill. I watch from afar and laugh at Venice's pride. Your petty longings for wealth and beauty. Following around hand-some fiancés in the hope that they'll bring you happiness." She stares at me, her head cocked. "Don't feel sorry for me. My life has new purpose, now that my face counts for nothing. Would you like to see?"

She reaches up, and, in a single, shocking movement, the red locks fall to the floor. The candlelight plays over a shining, scarred scalp. The skin seems stretched and rip-pled with channels like the sand of a beach when the tide has receded. A few wisps of her old hair grow in short, crinkled tufts.

"You like it?" she asks in a mocking voice. I force myself not to look away, even when she raises her hands to the mask that covers her face. My throat goes dry as she care-fully pulls it away.

Now I cannot look, and lower my eyes.

"You don't want to see your handiwork?"

I take a breath and raise my gaze. Carina's brow appears half melted, the skin drooping at the corner of one eye. Her mouth twists in an unnatural grin, and the skin across one cheek blossoms with scars and broken veins. This face, once so beautiful, is now a distorted version of what Carina once was.

"More to your taste?" she asks.

Pity plunges through me. How could it not? Carina is still a young woman, trapped behind the face of a corpse. One of her eyes is weeping, and she lifts a square of linen to wipe away the tears that flow from the red swollen rim. But as I remember glimpses of the past, my feelings quickly disappear. This woman lunged at me with a dagger on the boat. If she'd had her way, I would have died that night. Roberto too.

"You tried to kill us," I say. "Whatever happened to you, it's your own doing."

I expect her to lash out, but instead Carina titters. "My dear Roberto," she says. "I hear he too will suffer for his deeds tomorrow."

She reaches into the deep pocket of her skirts and pulls out a stiletto knife. Involuntarily, my hands strain again. The narrow blade makes it perfect for sliding between ribs, puncturing deep into the flesh. One movement, one twist, and a heart can be stopped in seconds. The handle is made of mother-of-pearl, and there's a golden guard and pommel. They glint in the weak light as Carina brings the knife closer, closer to my throat. I catch my breath and wait for whatever comes next, not daring to move.

She draws the blade through the air, a hairsbreadth away from my neck, in a slow, luxurious movement.

"Tomorrow the executioner will take Roberto's head and place it on a lance," she says. Then the twisted smile drops from her face, and her voice turns low and angry. "You wouldn't remember the execution of Grand Councilor Luciano Braccia, I suppose? You were in the convent still. Well, I remember. I held my mother's hand as the old fool put his head to the block, his lips muttering a useless prayer. Some say he hadn't bribed the executioner to make it quick. Others that the axman was drunk. Anyway, it took half a dozen blows before he was dead, and the ax handle broke after the third. It was almost funny as they hunted for a replacement, and all that time he lay there twitching."

I feel the bile rise in my throat, and my chest heaves as I struggle to contain the gagging sensation. Carina claps her hands in delight, turning around on the spot like a child at a party.

"Oh, good! The great Laura is human after all. Have I turned your stomach, dear heart?"

"What kind of animal are you?" I spit. Any sense of treading carefully has evaporated. "What is it you want?"

Carina places the knife in my lap, tantalizingly out of reach of my bound hands, then bends down to retrieve her mask and wig. She places the red locks on top of her head, tugging at them until they sit in place. She looks laughable, like a gaudy puppet. Then she ties the mask in place and straightens her shoulders, as though retrieving what little dignity she has left.

Finally, she answers me. "I want nothing more than to see you and the Segreta suffer."

She snatches up the knife again, and moves behind me. Every sense seems on fire as I wait for what must surely come. Will it be quick, or will she leave me to bleed to death in this lonely room? I close my eyes and try to think of Roberto's face, but even that offers me no comfort now. I think instead of Lysander, the brother only recently returned to me. I think of Emilia, and hope their life together is a happy one. I even feel a long-forgotten fondness for my foolish old father. *Beatrice, I shall be with you soon.*

The knife is cold as she places it along the top of my ear. "Do you know how it feels to be disfigured?" she whispers.

I feel a sharp tug, and pain. Then there's a pressure on my wrists, and suddenly they're free. My hand goes at once to the side of my head, but I can't find any blood. I climb from the chair. Carina stands by the doorway. In her hand she trails a few locks of long, curled hair. "I could have killed you, Laura, or I could have made your face like mine. Perhaps one day I will. But for now, I want to see you suffer. I want you to wake each morning and feel the pain I do, never knowing when your end will come, when I will appear to you again."

She places her knife back in the hidden pocket of her skirt and turns away from me, striding from the room. After catching my breath, I follow. I wouldn't put a final trick past Carina. But the corridor is empty, and daylight glows from the far end. I walk out into an empty street.

I go straight home, walking rather than hailing a coach, with my hood pulled up. I need time to think. When I arrive back at the house, Father is in his study, and I can hear raised voices through the studded door. I can only catch the odd phrase, but enough to tell me the men inside are arguing about the Doge. Is this the faction of which he spoke? Members of the Grand Council, planning to usurp him? I creep closer and rest my ear against the leather-paneled door.

". . . his infirmity . . . ," a voice says.

Another joins in—Father's. ". . . need a strong leader, one who isn't compromised by personal problems . . ."

There's no place for loyalty in the circles among which my father moves.

I check my head in the hall mirror. By rearranging my hair a little, those missing locks are hardly noticeable.

The voices are getting louder. "But who can possibly take over?" says one man. Other voices clamor to be heard, and now I can't make out anything other than a general sense of anger filling the room. I step away. Is this what Venice has become? Full of hatred, deceit and politics. Or perhaps it has always been like that, and the shroud is only now being torn away from my eyes.

It doesn't have to be like this, I tell myself, remembering Emilia's offer. I could leave. Perhaps if the ruling class left, Venice could become a better place again.

I start to ascend to my room, when the door is flung open and men stride out into the hallway. As I pause on the stairs, one of them throws me a surprised look and I bend my head deferentially. The others are grim faced and leave without casting me a glance. My father emerges last.

"Happy now?" he says, glaring at me. "You still want to marry that fiend?"

Then he walks back into his study and slams the door shut behind him.

"You're back," says a voice.

Lysander appears at the door to his chamber. He comes to take my arm and leads me farther up the stairs towards my own room.

"You must have been at the trial, I think." He casts a wry glance at my outfit, and I remember for the first time how I must look.

"I had to go," I say.

"Then you know about the Doge?"

I shake my head. "I couldn't stay," I tell him. "I couldn't watch them take Roberto away."

Lysander's face is grim. "Forget that man," he says. "His life is over, and it's all he deserves."

Each word cuts me. "How do you know that?" I say.

"The Doge had a fit after you left, Laura. He and the Duchess came onto the stage to speak with the Council. She tried to conceal it, leading him away, but everyone could see how he wasn't in control of his own body. It was awful." Lysander gathers himself. "It's clear that something is seriously wrong. The Doge's days are numbered, one way or another. Venice will be in turmoil."

I realize I no longer care.

30

I climb out of my simple clothes and pack them away, back in Bianca's chest. Brushing a hand over the rough linen, I think, for the hundredth time since my visit to the convent, of the simple girl who lived in seclusion. Were things better then? My days were long and empty, yes, but the slow burn of that existence hardly compares to the pain of this. I knew nothing of love and its joys, but nothing of its disappointments either.

I close the chest and rest my forehead against its lid. I consider saying a prayer for Roberto, but then my body sags with exhaustion. They would be empty words sent up to a God I no longer know.

I hear voices in the courtyard. More visitors? I rush over to a window and lean out, momentarily forgetting that I am wearing nothing more than my linen undergarments. Raising a hand to shield my eyes from the sun, I spot a group of six soldiers in Turkish uniform waiting at the front gates and a carriage behind them. A moment later Faustina bustles in.

"That brute is here!" she says. "Hide the jewelry!"

Bianca enters next, equally flustered. "There's a visitor for you," she says. "I told him your father and brother are out in the city, but he insisted. He waits for you in the library."

Why has he come? What could he possibly want now, after the last time he showed me from his quarters with so little ceremony?

"Don't go to him!" says Faustina. "He can't be trusted."

"I'll be down in a moment," I tell Bianca. I fetch out the first dress I find—my lemon silk. My hands twist around behind me, struggling to tighten the strings of my bodice and fumbling with the tiny satin-covered buttons of the dress.

"What are you thinking?" asks Faustina. "People will talk!"

"Then perhaps you should practice silence," I tell her.

I hastily plump out my skirts and brush the hair off my face, while loosening my curls. Taking a few deep breaths to compose myself, I descend the stairs. The double doors to the library are open a crack, and I see Halim gazing at the books on the shelves.

As I step inside the room, he trains his eyes on me. I close the doors on Faustina.

"What are you doing here?" I ask. I don't have the energy for polite conversation.

"I'm sorry for your deep suffering," he says.

I will not break down now. Not in front of him.

He reaches out and takes my hand, raising it to his face. The gesture so takes me by surprise, I don't stop him. His lips brush against my fingertips and I feel goose bumps tighten. "I never wished to cause you harm."

Now I pull my hand away from his as the tears well in my eyes. Before I can brush them away, Halim offers a handkerchief to me. I hesitate — this man has sealed Roberto's death — before taking it.

"I know what you must be thinking," he says. His face creases in pain. "But I've acted the only way I can."

"Roberto wouldn't murder an innocent woman. He simply *couldn't*. Venice is a brutal city, but he is the gentlest soul I've ever met."

I could say more. I could tell him that I cried daily when Roberto was away in Constantinople, and of the longing in his eyes when he returned. Those lips, when I kissed them, were not lying to me. I would stake my life on it.

Halim's look is one of heartfelt pity. He's stood up for what he believes to be true. What is the truth — his version or mine? Is it possible that we're both in the right? I saw the strength of his feeling when he learned of his sister's death. We're each fighting for what we believe in.

I'm unable to break his gaze, and now I see there's something else there whom I barely dare acknowledge. I feel the heat emanating from his body and realize that we haven't pulled apart since he wiped away my tears. With a sudden, awkward movement, I go to sit down and indicate another chair at a fair distance from me. "Please, take a seat."

Halim shakes his head and casts a despairing glance around him. "This place — this city — you deserve better."

"It is my home."

"Then I hope you can find happiness again — somehow."

"Happiness?"

He must see the wretched look of shock on my face. "Your soul is too good to be trapped in grief."

As he hurries to the door, I follow. I don't want us to part like this. Our differences are great, but we share something greater I don't yet wish to relinquish. He turns in the doorway, and we collide.

"Oh," I murmur.

His hand is on the small of my back.

"You mustn't . . . ," I begin to say.

"Mustn't what?" Halim asks. His breath smells like cinnamon.

Our faces are so close, our bodies too. His eyes are all I see.

"Mustn't grieve too much for your sister."

There's a sudden movement and the door is pushed open wider. Emilia stands there, staring at the two of us, her mouth hanging open. "I'm sorry. I . . ."

Halim draws away, but slowly—as though we have nothing for which to apologize. As for myself, I can feel my cheeks flaming.

"I should go," he says, looking past Emilia and into the hallway for his servants. He walks past her without a backwards glance. I retreat into the room and curse silently as I hear Emilia follow me.

"What just happened?" she asks.

I shake my head. "I need to rest," I murmur.

It's the grief, I think, sinking onto a couch. *That's all. I need to rest.*

31

Even in my wretchedness, sleep took me, and now a bleak new morning has arrived.

I force myself to get up and go through the motions of preparing for the day. Bianca fills my copper bath and I am grateful for the clouds of steam that hide me from the world.

Outside, everything is christened by morning dew. Emilia is waiting for me by the gates; she has promised to come with me for support today. The two of us greet each other silently and move over to a canal, where we summon a gondolier.

"Take us to St. Mark's," Emilia says in a soft voice.

I can't speak. I'm going to watch my beloved die. To watch him die.

The gondolier must see the look on my face, as he doesn't try to engage me in conversation. Instead, he whistles softly, a plaintive tune that fits my mood well. Mist seeps off the canals, and the houses of Venice look more beautiful than ever in the morning light. For once the streets are clean and empty of people. They'll all be gathering in the square.

Emilia's fingers rest beside mine on the velvet cushion. I suddenly feel the need to explain yesterday's encounter, when she interrupted me with Halim. If I cannot clear my conscience to Roberto, I must to someone, before he is gone.

I clear my throat. "What you saw yesterday—" I begin.

"You don't have to tell me anything," she interrupts. "I realize I should never have asked. It's none of my business."

"It's no one's business because nothing happened," I say. I can hear how high and tight my voice is and I force myself to calm down. *Think of Roberto. Always Roberto.* But that's the wrong thing to tell myself—my throat constricts and I don't know how I'll get the next words out. "I would never betray . . ." I can't finish.

Emilia pulls my hand into her lap. "Don't worry. You don't have to tell me. I understand."

My shoulders shake with suppressed sobs. The gondolier's whistling has stopped. Please, God, let today be over.

We reach the canal that runs parallel with the square, cluttered with other boats. As we climb out of the gondola, supported by the pilot's hand, a column of smoke streaks the sky.

"What's that?" I ask.

He shakes his head and tuts. "Did you not hear? Arson! During the night someone set fire to part of the palace. Rebels, they say. The Doge is losing his hold, that's for sure. Did you see his performance on the stage yesterday? Kicking and jerking like an invalid." He nods at the thick black clouds that drift above our city. "No one has faith in him anymore." Then he climbs back into his gondola and pushes off, the stern of his boat parting the water.

Emilia and I share a glance.

"What is happening to this city?" she murmurs. "Lysander always had such good things to say about his home. And now . . ." She doesn't need to say anything else; I feel certain we're both thinking the same thing.

We make our way towards the square. As we approach, we see youths scrambling up statues and sitting in rows along high stone walls, craning to see the stage. Food-sellers with trays are weaving among the spectators.

"Imagine!" a woman walking beside me says. "Executed before all of Venice." She holds a linen handkerchief to her mouth. Emilia shakes her head at me, warning me not to take any notice.

As we draw nearer the stage, jostled by other people, I spot the wooden planks covered with straw to soak up the blood. My empty stomach squirms. Roberto's life will draw to an end up there. The heart I've loved will beat no more. I rest against a pillar, feeling faint, struggling to compose myself.

I've heard tales of previous executions in Venice. The man who was suspended in an iron cage, surviving on bread and wine, until he was brought down and hung. A criminal whose body was stripped and dragged through the streets behind a cart. How one man was cut into four pieces and his head stuck on a lance-point for all to see.

The executioner, a giant of a man, already wears his canvas hood and cloak. He sits on a stool and has a whetstone braced between his feet, against which he sharpens the blade of his ax. It's all a performance, designed to get the crowd in the mood. The ax glistens. Carina will be disappointed today. Not a blunt blade in sight.

Emilia leads me through the gathering crowds towards the front of the stage. Today, I don't care that a noblewoman should not be amid the throng. Now that I no longer wear the disguise of a servant, people recognize me as Roberto's betrothed and step away, lowering their eyes in respect. Justice is about to be done; no one need hate me anymore. Soldiers line the front of the stage, wearing cloaks and carrying leather shields. Executions can become animated, and these men will stop the baying crowds from climbing the stage and attacking the prisoner. They'll also stop the condemned from escaping their fate, I think bitterly. I haven't eaten in who knows how long and feel light-headed. But I must stay strong. I won't let him down.

A drumroll sounds from a young drummer at the side of the stage. The executioner takes his place beside the block, and a herald steps forward. "Bring forth the prisoner!" he shouts. At my side, I hear Emilia's breath catch.

The drummer takes up a slow rhythm. I close my eyes for an instant, but when I open them again the boy is looking uncertainly at the herald. He gives the drummer a quick nod, and the drumroll continues as the older man darts from the stage. Murmurs pass through the crowd.

"What's happening?" Emilia whispers. I shake my head; I have no idea.

After slow, agonizing seconds, the herald appears back on the stage, his face flushed. He goes to talk to the commanding officer of the soldiers. Beside him I notice for the first time the Doge, cloaked in black robes, sitting in a low chair at the side of the stage. The Duchess Besina is absent, presumably unable to bear the agony of watching her son die. Guards stand on either side of the Doge. He needs their protection more than ever, with the vultures circling. He looks pale and old. People are pushing forward now, and the row of uniformed men raises their shields, leaning their weight back into the crowd and looking over to their leader for instruction. Even the executioner looks impatient as he shifts his ax in his hand.

Something is wrong. I begin to move through the crowd, trying to get closer to the stage, Emilia's hand grasping my arm.

"Back, you!" a soldier orders and shoves me away. The Doge's eyes meet mine and widen in recognition. He gets to his feet, leaning heavily on the arm of his chair.

"Bring her to me!" he calls over. Now the murmurs and whispers that surround me become audible voices.

"It's the murderer's girl," says one woman.

"Have some manners!" I hear Emilia tell her.

My cheeks burn with humiliation. A soldier helps me onto the stage, taking my hand to pull me up. My wrists are still sore from Carina's bindings, but I brace my feet against the edge of the stage and lever myself up.

"Thank you," I say. I glance down at Emilia who watches me, wide-eyed. Then I brush down my skirts and approach the Doge. Despite his rich cloak and peaked cap, he looks frailer than I've ever seen him, and I can see that the fits have drained his strength.

"Come," he says as soon as I've drawn close. "We must visit the jail. I've heard . . . Well, come, let us go." He grasps my arm, and pulls me after him. As we vacate the stage, the crowd begins booing and jeering. They've been robbed of their morning's entertainment—for now. I can only hope that Emilia will get home safely.

"What's happening?" I ask as we hurry through the corridors of the palace, heading towards the secret passage. At last, we climb the wooden stairs that lead to the hidden entrance to the Piombi, the rings on the Doge's fingers now cutting into my skin. I pull my arm free, and he looks round at me, his face wretched.

"I don't know what we'll find," he admits. "But it sounds bad."

Horrible thoughts assail me. Has Roberto killed himself, finding suicide less humiliating than being executed as a criminal? I follow the Doge down the narrow corridor towards the cell where I last saw him, crumpled on the floor like a pile of rags. A group of men stand at the open door, their faces grim. Sweat streaks their shirts. The heat is still overwhelming up here, even at this time of day.

We come to stand before the cell and see a covered body being lifted off the stained floor by four men. The Doge lets out a cry of pain and reaches for me. I put an arm around his frail shoulders, feeling my own body drain of energy. My heart flutters in my chest.

"It can't be," I mutter.

The Doge stumbles forward and pulls away the bloody sheet. A gray face. Unseeing eyes. Smears of blood. Thick eyebrows and a smattering of warts.

It's the jailer who took me to visit Roberto.

"Where's my son?" asks the Doge. I look into the empty cell and then at Roberto's father.

"He's escaped!" I gasp. A flicker of joy passes across the Doge's face; then he quickly hides it from the men who watch us. His hands tremble as he reaches out to cover the dead man's face again.

"Tell the executioner he can go home," the Doge says. "There'll be no more death today."

"What happened here?" I ask the men. They share doubtful glances, their faces flushing.

"Tell us!" the Doge orders. I catch a glimpse of the man he was until recently—powerful, assured, ruthless.

"I'm not sure, I wasn't here when—" one guard begins.

"Well, bring us whoever was here!" The Doge's face is red with fury. The guard looks over his shoulder and motions to someone standing in the shadows. Another guard steps forward, his brow heavily bruised. He stands looking at his feet.

"Tell the Doge what happened," the first guard demands. He looks relieved that the attention is on someone else now.

"The prisoner escaped," the man mumbles.

"How?" I ask. Though already I think I know. The Segreta's vote, despite my worst fears, must have turned in Roberto's favor. But would they have killed a man?

The man shrugs. Behind him, other guards hurtle down the stairs and call out Roberto's name to each other, throwing doors open and kicking buckets out of the way. The guard we are questioning licks his lips nervously.

The Doge's face darkens. "If you don't tell us everything you know, you'll be in a cell yourself."

The heat makes my skin prickle. Now the corpse is being carried down the narrow stairs, men grunting with the exertion. One of them stumbles, and the body slips from their arms, its feet knocking against a wall. Hastily, they recover it and resume their descent. When they're out of earshot, the guard starts talking again.

"I was on duty, when an armed band broke into the prison during the night. I've no idea how. This palace is so full of secret corridors. . . . They killed the jailer and overwhelmed the others." His words come out in a rush now, as though he wants to be rid of them. "Then they freed Roberto and locked us up. It wasn't until the new guard arrived this morning that we were freed. We didn't have time to tell anyone!" His voice has turned pleading.

The Doge shakes his head. "Get out of my sight!" The two men clatter down the wooden stairs, and finally silence descends. Roberto's father casts me a glance.

"This is bad," he says. "Justice must be seen to be done. Especially as things stand. The power balance in Venice is . . . precarious." But he cannot hide the glint in his eyes. Neither of us says it out loud, but I know we are both thinking the same thing.

Roberto is free. He lives another day.

32

The Doge invites me to his private rooms for refreshment. Beyond the walls, we can hear the crowds calling angrily. A servant hastily goes to shut the window.

A marble table laden with fruit and jugs of water and wine stands at the far end of the room, and paintings line the wood-paneled walls. A couch upholstered in mulberry satin sits in the center of the room, beneath a chandelier, and the Doge indicates that I should sit. He nods curtly to a servant, who hastens over to the table and fills a plate, bringing it to us.

I reach out for a slice of melon, but as I lift it to my lips, nausea squirms in my stomach. Carefully, I place the fruit back on its plate.

"You must eat," the Doge tells me, smiling kindly. He's lost one son to death and now another has disappeared into the streets of Venice, yet he's concerned about my welfare. There is more to this man than power alone.

As I try to eat again, the Doge clears his throat.

"It is important you know the truth," he says, rubbing his brow. "I had nothing to do with Roberto's disappearance."

I'm sure he can't read my own dark suspicions about the Segreta's involvement. "But where could he be?"

There's a noise from the doorway, and a servant is standing there.

"You have a visitor," he announces, looking awkward. "Prince Halim requests an audience."

"Then you must show him in," the Doge says. I catch the merest tremble in his hand as he adjusts his doublet.

A moment later, Halim strides the room, his eyes sparking. Palace soldiers accompany him and station themselves around the room. The prince's own men follow him, empty scabbards at their sides, as they've had to relinquish their weapons. Halim's steps falter for a moment when he sees me, but he focuses on the Doge. "Justice has deserted Venice," he says.

The Doge gestures to the table. "Help yourself to refreshments."

Halim's eyes narrow. "I was promised that my sister's killer would meet his end today." The prince doesn't even look at me. "Roberto should have lost his head by now. Instead, I hear rumors of escape. It seems . . . convenient."

The Doge shakes his head. "Come. Sit down. No one here had anything to do with Roberto's disappearance. I'm as surprised as you are."

Halim begins pacing the room, turning in slow circles. Faruk has sidled into the room also, watching the Doge with a smirk of disdain. "You expect us to believe that the

206

most powerful man in Venice doesn't know how his prisoner escaped?" he says. "His son?"

Halim reaches down towards his boot and pulls out a knife. The soldiers in the corners of the room lurch to attention, but Halim picks a peach from a tray and begins to cut it into slices, allowing the juice to drip over the Doge's rugs.

"You should know," he says, all his attention on the fruit, "that fifty of my finest ships are stationed along the coast." He smiles coldly at the Doge, who listens, his face strained. Halim enunciates his next words carefully, as if placing chess pieces on a board. "If Roberto is not found and delivered to me within ten days, I will sail on Venice as an enemy." His voice turns as cold as the grave. "I will tear this city apart."

My gasp is the loudest sound in the room, and Halim's attention shifts. He sends me an almost imperceptible shake of the head, as if to say, *My vengeance is not meant for you.* Then he drops the remains of the fruit back onto the platter and walks out of the room, his men following.

When I look back at the Doge, he sinks down onto the bench, dropping his head in his hands. His voice comes out muffled. "Call an emergency council." The servants rush to do his bidding and the two of us are left alone, for a few moments at least.

"What can be done?" I ask.

The Doge looks up at me, a defeated old man. "I was going to ask you the same question."

Over the following hour, as the Doge's servants spread across the city, members of the Grand Council gather at the palace. I don't know what I should do, or where I should be, so I remain where I am. As the old men, my father included, fill the room, I notice they huddle roughly into two groups.

"She shouldn't be here," says one man, pointing at me.

"Let her stay," the Doge retorts. "There's nothing she doesn't already know, and she understands Roberto better than any of us."

I'm not sure the Doge is right. Over the past days, I've started to wonder if I know Roberto at all. So many are convinced of his guilt. And then there is the letter Halim produced, the secret escape. . . . It's like watching the actions of a stranger. But I'm glad I have the privilege of attending this meeting. If nothing else, I will be able to report back to the Segreta when the time is right.

The Doge quickly outlines Halim's threats. When he's finished, a Councilor speaks.

"We must find your son, at once. Guards must scour the city."

"And if we cannot find him?" says the Doge.

"We must ready ourselves for war, then."

"No," the Doge says. "On principle, I will not go to war over a prince's fury at not getting his own way. Venice is better than that!"

"Damn your principles!" the man argues. "We don't have time for them. Things are already out of control. I insist we take practical action, not sit around hoping that Roberto turns up."

The Doge sends him a smile that could cut through glass. "It is not for you or anyone else to insist on anything. I am still your leader."

The Councilor flushes. He darts a glance at the other men, and they in turn adjust their bodies until they all face one man standing just inside the door. I hadn't even spotted him before—the Admiral, the Bear.

"Massimo," the Doge says. "How much have you heard? We were just discussing—"

"I know what you were discussing," he says. He almost seems to fill the room as he steps inside. His broad shoulders and calloused hands speak of many wars fought and won. This is a man who doesn't like to lose. "We must prepare ourselves for the fight ahead."

"There will be no fight," says the Doge.

"At a time like this," Massimo says, "we need strong men to lead us. Men with vision." He leaves the rest unspoken, but his meaning is clear.

The Doge shakes his head and looks around the room, from one man to the next. Like a row of dominoes falling, each in turn drops his eyes to the floor.

"Soldiers!" the Doge says. "Escort Massimo from the palace!"

Silence poisons the air. Not a single man moves to follow the Doge's commands. The guards look only to the Admiral.

"See?" says Massimo. "The cards have already been played."

"I see treachery," says the Doge.

"It's nothing like that," says Massimo. "Every man in this room is loyal to Venice. The Council and I have reached an agreement. All we need now is for you to see our point of view. I will take control peacefully, until the threat to Venice's safety has passed. You're ill and you're sick with grief at all that's happened. Allow us to help you." He holds out a hand, inviting the Doge to shake it. "It will save face all round."

"And if I refuse?" the Doge asks, ignoring the extended hand.

Massimo spreads his palms like a reasonable man. "Then you're the biggest threat Venice has."

The Doge glances from man to man, in one last desperate appeal for support. No one says a word. I'm glad the Duchess Besina is not present to witness her husband's humiliation.

"So be it," the Doge says, his voice trembling. "But only for the good of Venice." He backs away from the men who were once his closest advisers. "Laura, accompany me."

Roberto's father leaning heavily on my arm, we cross the room.

"Goodbye, old man," one of the Councilors whispers to his back. A few of the others join in with low laughter.

I can't keep quiet any longer. "Who would have thought it?" I say as we pause in the doorway. "Snakes in the heart of Venice."

33

The crowds have dispersed from the square, and several hundred soldiers are stationed around the edges. It feels as though the city has been invaded by some foreign enemy. I peer into the faces of everyone I pass, half expecting one of them to be Roberto. But of course he can't risk showing himself. He's in hiding, and I know who can tell me where.

I head across the Rialto Bridge to the house of Allegreza. The last time I was here, my leader refused to even look at me, but she must still retain some affection. After all, who if not the Segreta could have masterminded Roberto's break out of jail?

I bring the sea serpent door knocker down hard and wait for the grumpy servant woman to let me in. She doesn't look surprised to see me and swings the door open wide, stepping back into the hallway.

"You do like turning up without an appointment, don't you?"

Allegreza sits framed in one of the open windows. Her

gray head bends over a tiny book that rests in her open palms, an illuminated letter glittering with gold foil.

"You're back," she says, without looking round. She closes the book slowly, and shifts in her chair, holding out a hand.

I take it. "I came to thank you," I say.

"And what are you thanking me for?" She pulls her hand free.

I examine her features, searching for a glint of playfulness. On the contrary, she looks only confused. "But Roberto is free . . . ," I say.

Allegreza gets to her feet. Now we stand face to face, and she shrugs. "I'm sorry to disappoint you, Laura, but the Segreta had nothing to do with his escape. He's a clever boy." She goes to a side table and reaches for a silver jug, pouring tea into two carved glasses. She passes one to me. "The Doge must have had a hand in it."

"I don't think so," I say. "He seemed as surprised as I was, and now he's paying the price."

"What do you mean?"

I tell her what I witnessed in the Doge's chamber. Allegreza is silent for some time, sipping her tea as she ponders my words.

"Massimo has always been ambitious," she says at last, "but the Doge is a fool. This is no time for nepotism."

"I told you, he had nothing to do with the escape."

"Perhaps not," she says. "You'd better go, Laura. And take care."

I'm relieved to hear her voice soften. I cannot yet be forgiven for going to the convent, but I have started to make amends. I curtsy and turn to go, when I hear the maid-servant shouting. "Get out, get out! What do you think you're doing? How dare you?"

Allegreza nods to me briskly and points towards the opposite door. I slip through a muslin curtain as a man's voice warns, "Move aside, old crone."

I look back through the curtain. Allegreza stands tall as a group of soldiers burst into the room and surround her.

"Can I help you, gentlemen?" she asks. Her politeness could freeze the Lido.

The men look uncertainly from one to the other; then one steps forward and grasps Allegreza's arm. The maid lets out a small scream of shock and hastily stuffs the hem of her apron into her mouth.

Allegreza calmly looks down at the man's hand. "Take your paws off me," she commands.

Slowly, awkwardly, he lets go of her. "You are to come with us, by order of the Grand Council," he says.

Allegreza smiles and nods. "And what have I done to offend anyone?"

"You're under arrest for the murder of a soldier."

Murder? Have they too linked the Segreta to the jailbreak?

"I don't know what you're talking about," says Allegreza.

"His name was Silvio."

Allegreza frowns.

Silvio is dead? Not the guard at the prison at all, but the man we humiliated. This makes no sense.

"I'm afraid I still don't understand," says Allegreza. "Why would I have anything to do with a common soldier?"

"One of your *secrets*, is it?" asks the guard. The way he says the word, with a sneer, makes the blood drain from Allegreza's face as it drains from mine.

They know of the Segreta. There have always been rumors, of course. But they know about Allegreza. They know who we are.

"Search the house," says the soldier.

I slip outside before any of the soldiers has the chance to notice that I was there. I race down the marble steps and turn into the first alley I come to. I wait, my heart thumping, then hurry away from the house. I know exactly where I'm going.

Grazia's apartments are down a small street just off the Calle dei Fabbri. But when I knock at the door, I discover that she's absent.

"I don't know where she is," the young servant tells me. "You can leave a message if you like."

I can't help the sigh of exasperation that escapes me. "Tell her that Laura della Scala needs to speak with her." I want to insist that it's urgent, but I have more sense than that. I've already risked the confidentiality of the Segreta, coming here in the first place. It's enough that Grazia knows I've called at her apartments. She'll be in touch.

In the meantime, I have nothing left to do but wait. I walk away from Grazia's home, towards the shoreline. I can barely think straight, so much has happened. Roberto is who knows where in Venice, the Doge is all but usurped, Allegreza arrested and . . . I spot three Turkish ships sailing away from our city, heading for the horizon. If Halim was telling the truth, a whole fleet waits somewhere out there.

He's promised to return in ten days.

I sink down on some dirt-stained steps and gaze out into the harbor. I don't care if I sully my skirts.

The seas will not be calm for long.

34

I spend the next few days at home, and each day I expect a note from Roberto, some hint that he's alive. I've asked Bella Donna to spread the word through her contacts, to tell me if anyone sees anything suspicious. The hope of news keeps me going, but nothing has come. How I long to see his face, or just hear his voice.

The curfew is still in place, following the action against the Doge. Faustina fusses and presses food on me, draws me baths and lays out my clothes. Even she has no homely wisdom to offer hope in these strange times. Father is deeply involved in the new revolutionary Council, and tells us that the Doge is confined to the palace. I treat him with the cold disdain he deserves, and this only makes his temper worse. Massimo insists the martial law is only temporary, but I know from this city's troubled history that the reins of power, once grasped, are all but impossible to relinquish.

My brother is trying to entertain Emilia as best he can—which is difficult. Venice is no place for a couple in love right now, its streets full of dissent and revolution since the foiled execution. The people think that justice has been snatched away from them, and they're angry. Bianca tells us that the guards who allowed Roberto to escape were later dragged out onto the stage and flogged almost to death.

This morning, Faustina has come to my bedroom to style my hair, twisting blonde locks into intricate braids. I reach over my shoulder and take the silver comb from her, drawing her hand down to rest against my cheek.

"Thank you for looking after me," I tell her.

She shakes her head and takes the comb back. "Stop being so sentimental," she chides, concentrating on a tangle of hair. She won't look at my reflection, and I know she's trying not to cry. We've both been doing a lot of that, these past days. I, for Roberto and everything that's happened. Faustina, because she cannot bear to see me distressed.

"It sounds far-fetched to me," Emilia's voice rings up the stairs.

"I wish I could say the same thing," says Lysander. "I've always wondered what women can gossip about for hours."

They pass my door, and I see Lysander rearrange his features from a smile to something more somber. He's clutching a pamphlet. "I'm sorry, Laura. I thought you were out."

"There's no need to apologize," I say as brightly as possible. "Life can't stop because of my troubles. What's that you have?"

Emilia smiles at me. "They were giving them out at a stall," she says. "Apparently, there's a secret society of women running Venice behind the scenes."

"A secret society!" says Faustina. She guffaws heartily. "Because women really have nothing better to do, what with all the laundry and cooking, housework, sewing. . . ."

"They say it's noblewomen," puts in Emilia. "But still, it seems absurd."

I keep my voice calm. "Can I see?"

Lysander holds the pamphlet out and I take in the silly woodcut print of a group of women in witches' caps, their faces twisted with ugly smiles as they huddle together. The drawing is rough and unsophisticated, clearly done in a rush. The words tell of a coven of she-demons intent on undermining the morals of our city. Silvio, it reports, was found dead in his bed, his throat cut. It asks for God's help in hunting down the black-hearted women. I stand up, knocking my stool back.

"Are you all right?" says Lysander, studying my face.

The pamphlet bears the mark of the Admiralty—it's Massimo's work.

"Quite all right," I reply, handing the pamphlet back. "How ridiculous."

"The city is troubled enough without secret societies meting out their own justice." He waves the pamphlet in the air. "They killed an innocent man!" He reads aloud from the bottom. "'Justice has turned her eyes from this cabal of women for too long. Now is the time to crack down!'" Lysander nods. "Lots of readers will agree with that."

"How do you know?" I ask. Lysander looks at me in surprise.

"Laura, darling. Do you need to ask? These women are making a fool of Venice. Do you know who they're led by? Allegreza, the Duchess's cousin. Can't you see? She's bringing shame on the Doge. This shouldn't be happening. Whatever you think of Massimo's tactics, this must be stopped."

I pace the room. "But how?"

Lysander peers at the writing. "We're being urged not to give shelter to any of these women or communicate with them. Apparently, Allegreza is in custody and being interrogated in the Piombi."

I gasp. "But the Piombi is a place for men."

"Massimo is making an example of her. Quite right too."

"I saw Roberto after he was mistreated," I say. "I can't bear to think of someone else suffering like that."

Lysander raises his eyebrows. "Perhaps she deserves it, little sister."

"Well, I for one hope she isn't suffering," says Emilia, shaking the shawl from around her shoulders. "I think there's more to it than the pamphlets suggest. Women don't go round stirring up trouble and murdering people for the sake of it."

"You're right," I say. "There's a reason this happened, surely. If it's even true."

"I don't care about reasons," Lysander says. "The law is the law! No one should take a life. If this is what women do to make their voices heard in Venice, then they should be silenced!"

I can't listen to him any longer. "Would you have me silenced?" I demand. "Or Emilia? Are you saying we don't deserve a voice because we wear dresses? For shame, brother. I thought better of you."

Emilia places a hand on Lysander's chest. "Really, darling, we should leave Laura alone."

But now Lysander's blood is up too. He shakes her off and points at me. "Don't twist my words," he says.

"I don't need to," I say. "You already sound just like Father."

A low blow, I know, but Lysander has made me so angry.

He seizes Emilia's arm and leads her with him from the room.

"Lysander!" Emilia tries to protest, but he isn't listening.

Faustina is gaping, still holding the comb to her chest. "Men!" she mutters.

From my brother's chamber, I hear raised voices behind the closed door. I hurry down the stairs, away from the angry sounds. At the bottom, I pause. Whether it was deliberate or not—I cannot tell—I find myself beneath the portrait Roberto painted of me.

That day he delivered it, before I knew who he really was, the work astounded me. He'd captured every detail of my face, and each brushstroke sang of his insight. He knew me so well, even then.

But I don't recognize that girl anymore. The glint in her eye, the promise that seems to linger about her, both have gone. All that remains of the girl I was is this portrait.

Roberto fooled me back then, when he was Giacomo the painter. Perhaps he's fooled me as Roberto too.

35

I can't live like this. Allegreza is being tortured and the Segreta are in more danger than I ever thought possible. Meanwhile, we each sit in our separate homes, gazing listlessly out of windows or picking at meals. *How can we call ourselves a society,* I think, *when not one of us is doing anything to help our leader?*

And just like that, my decision is made. I call to a servant boy to fetch my shawl. Before anyone else in the household can notice, I slip out and summon a gondola. Soon I am gliding down the liquid paths of the city and I emerge beside a small market where a beggar always sits in the shade of a stunted tree.

I drop a coin into her hat. Few would know that this toothless unfortunate, with her blind eye and hunched back, is a trusted messenger of the Segreta. I've learned never to underestimate anyone.

I kneel beside her. To onlookers, I'm a well-to-do lady with a soft heart. Little do they know that Margarita needs no one's pity.

"God bless you," she says.

"I need you to send the message out," I tell her. "To meet in the carpenter's basement."

Margarita raises an eyebrow. "These are dark times," she says. "I hear Allegreza is having her fingernails torn from their beds even as we speak."

I can't help wincing and Margarita notices, cackling with laughter.

"And who are you to make such a request?" She gives a gentle burp, staring brazenly into my face.

I reach into my velvet purse, pulling out a soft leather pouch that hangs heavy with coins.

"How many?" I ask.

Margarita grins, revealing black holes in her gums. "All of them," she says, snatching the pouch from me. She doesn't bother to count, stuffing the leather into her filthy cloak. She shifts herself on the ground. I straighten up and reach out a hand to help her, ignoring the creases of dirt in the wrinkles of her palm.

With a grunt, she's on her feet.

"By seven this evening, Margarita."

She's already moving away from me, leaning heavily on a crutch.

"Make way for the lady!" shouts a stallholder, and his friends break into laughter. I shake my head as I watch her depart the square.

A candle sputters in the draft as the carpenter's door opens for only the fifth time. Five of us, out of the whole of our number—dozens of women, perhaps more. The last of the five slips into the room, her face hidden behind her feline mask.

I look around. I remember the first time I encountered this small, damp room with its low ceiling. I thought I was coming to a music recital. Little did I know where the low doorway would lead. Back then, glittering masks crowded the room. Now I stand with four women only. None wears the silver ring of seniority, but what can I expect after my performance at the convent?

"Is this it?" I ask, despairing.

One of the faceless women shrugs. "I came against all my better instincts. There's a curfew, you know. Pamphlets spreading evil lies about the Segreta. We're risking our lives, just to be here."

"I've seen the pamphlets, but we cannot rest when our leader languishes in the Piombi. We must help her."

"She wouldn't want us to endanger ourselves," says another woman. "The society is greater than any one individual."

"So we should just leave her?" I say, my voice raised.

"All I'm saying is —"

Another woman pats the air. "We're on the same side, remember. Let's remain calm."

There's a sudden creak of wood and the stained door inches open. A slight woman steps into the room, glancing furtively over her shoulder. When she turns her face back to the room, I see a turquoise-lined mask. Paulina! Immediately, I feel my face flush. Last time we saw each other, she was cursing Roberto's name, clawing at my hair.

But before I can say a word, she rushes over to me and takes me by the shoulders, pulling me to her.

"I'm so sorry," she whispers into my hair. "For

everything I said. Everything!" She stands back and her eyes are rimmed with tears. "Please forgive me, Laura."

I pull her mask back, the better to see her face. She looks dreadful, her eyes bloodshot, her skin sallow. She's lost weight. "Of course I forgive you. Thank you for coming."

"What do you want us to do?" asks a woman from behind a fox's face, and her voice trembles.

I start walking around the room again, moving from one person to the next. I feel hopelessly unsuitable for the role of leader. How can they respect a woman not even eighteen years old? What if they laugh at my plan?

"God knows what they are doing to her," I say. "We have a power, and we must use it. Secrets!"

"What secret can free Allegreza?" says Paulina.

"Massimo is the key," I say. "He holds the power to release our leader. And think, what do we know about Massimo?"

"The gunpowder . . . ," the fox whispers. "Teresa's secret."

"That's right," I say, pleased to see my thinking is shared. "If the news of the ruined explosives gets out, Massimo will be shamed—publicly disgraced."

"It's a risky move," says the woman in the cat mask.

"If we were forced to make good on our threat to leak this information," says Paulina, "that would be treason. And with our enemies waiting, Venice's poor defenses are laid bare."

I incline my head. "True. But what is more important? Loyalty to the city or to the man who has usurped power? Who has fought harder for us, do you think?"

I watch the others carefully. It's impossible to read their

224

body language, and their expressions are hidden behind their masks. I don't even know if Allegreza would approve of this tactic. I could be casting my final die with the Segreta.

One by one, the other members nod.

"I'll do it," says Paulina quietly.

"Do what?" I ask.

"You'll need a volunteer to deliver this message. Someone you can trust."

"Are you sure?" I say. "I was going to do it myself."

My childhood friend shrugs. "I have access to the Doge's palace, don't I? Why not put it to good use? I can make sure a blackmail letter lands in the right hands."

I know she's underplaying things. She'll be putting herself in a position of extreme danger. If Massimo finds out who delivered the letter . . . He could lose his temper, drag her to the authorities or exact a colder revenge.

"Allegreza will thank you herself, one day soon," I say, reaching for my friend's hand. I squeeze her cold fingers.

36

I make my way back to the house and slip upstairs to hide in my room, picking up a half-finished piece of lace without much enthusiasm. How different are the two lives I lead.

We drafted the letter quickly, and Paulina has promised it will be delivered tomorrow. I urged her to be careful, but there was something so desperate about her this evening that I fear for her life.

Around ten o'clock, Faustina's face appears in the doorway. She's panting from climbing the stairs.

"Your father's back," she hisses, "and he has a guest with him. You're expected to dine with your brother and his wife."

I sigh and put down my lace. A guest—at this hour? "I'm not hungry," I say.

"Your father insisted," says Faustina.

She opens my closet and takes out a high-waisted mulberry velvet dress with ermine trim. I think about being stubborn, but I know this is a battle I can't win. Besides, perhaps the guest is one of the Council. If he's drunk, there may be information I can glean that could prove helpful to the Segreta.

Dressing quickly, I paint a smile on my face and rush downstairs.

But the moment I step into the room, the smile falls. I want to turn and run.

A man stands before me with a mouth of crooked teeth splitting into a grin. His shoulders are stooped, and his thin frame sags beneath clothes too large for him. Liver spots are scattered across his face like splotches of spilt ink.

Vincenzo.

"Good evening, Laura," he says, flecks of spittle gathering at the corners of his mouth. He gives a deep, mocking bow before straightening up again—or straightening up as much as his twisted body will allow. My father watches from a corner of the room, his eyes dark as coal. Emilia looks aghast and Lysander not a little troubled.

"I . . . I don't understand. How—"

"How is it that I'm back in Venice?" he says. "Let's just say that the injustices of the past have been rectified. The Council have recalled me."

But only one man had the authority to recall an exile—the Doge—and he would never have done so. The pieces fall into place. "Massimo must have summoned you weeks ago," I say. Which means the rebel faction must have been in contact for some time.

"Let's say our Admiral is a man of vision," says Vincenzo. "He knows my fleet is second to none. Venice needs her friends now."

This at least is true. I wonder if Massimo has already

shared details of the defective gunpowder with people he trusts. If war comes, then Venice requires all the ships and ammunition she can muster.

"I look forward to dining with old friends," says Vincenzo. He grins at me, and though he's no longer a threat, I struggle to feel anything other than revulsion for him.

"Welcome back," I say, lowering my body in a curtsy. Father smiles, and I know I have done well by him. It makes my insides churn.

Vincenzo steps closer, his robes rustling as he moves. Clearly, exile from his homeland has treated him well. His doublet is embroidered in gold thread and is deeply quilted. Sable lines his cloak, which he now throws over a shoulder, the better to reveal the heavy gold chain that sits on his chest. The Doge generously let him keep his fleet when he was banished, and business must have been good.

He takes my hand. Before I can snatch it back, he raises it to his lips and kisses my fingers. I feel the wet touch of his lips.

"Still no wedding band, I notice." He drops my hand, his face full of wicked delight. My whole body is rigid with tension. "So like a dove," he adds, his gaze traveling shamelessly over me. "Pure and white, cooing softly." He laughs.

I look over his shoulder at Father. A servant speaks quietly to him, and he begins to stride over to the dining room.

"Let us all catch up over dinner," Father says, leading us from the library. Emilia and Lysander follow, my new friend throwing me an alarmed glance.

I take my place at the long table. Of course Father has

arranged to have me seated beside his old ally. I feel a foot tap against my satin slipper and hastily tuck my feet under my skirts.

As the servants pass around soup plates, Vincenzo takes a wineglass and gulps noisily from it. Then he leans back in his chair.

"I thought I'd never see the city of my birth again," he tells us. "Despite what they said about me, I was always loyal."

I choke a little on my wine. Emilia and Lysander look confused. They weren't in Venice the day he was driven out of the city in disgrace, his machinations for the Duke of Milan exposed.

"I was honored when Massimo's representatives contacted me. Now the Doge is taking a . . ." He pauses. "As he is resting, I will do all I can to ensure the city is safe from the heathens who threaten our shores."

He bursts out laughing, the sound transforming into a hacking cough. We all wait in silence for the fit to end. Even Father looks a little discomfited. I see now that the challenges facing the Doge in his route back to power will be almost insurmountable. Too many are ranged against him.

Finally, Vincenzo draws a deep, ragged breath and continues as though he has not just made a fool of himself. "Of course, now that I'm here I can find out who was behind the trumped-up charges that saw me thrown out. I blame this conniving Segreta that everyone's talking about. Only a gaggle of women could concoct such a monstrous lie, wouldn't you agree?" He sends a long, meaningful glance around the table, his eyes landing at last on me.

"Quite so, Vincenzo," my father agrees, bowing his head. "They'll be ferretted out soon."

"I hear they do good too." Shy, gentle Emilia is standing up to this monster. "Haven't you heard about the charitable homes for destitute women? Rumor has it that they're funded by the Segreta."

Vincenzo shakes his head dismissively and raises a soupspoon to his lips, slurping noisily. "Destitute women! What do we care for them? Throw them in the canals!"

"My sister died of drowning in a canal," I say. "Surely you remember; after all, you were once engaged to be married to her."

"Laura!" mutters my father.

"I'm sorry," Vincenzo says, his eyes darting around the table as he realizes his mistake. "That was clumsy of me."

Father nods his head. "No matter," he says quietly.

Lysander is glaring at Vincenzo, anger narrowing his eyes. He turns to Emilia.

"I wouldn't talk about the Segreta," he advises her. "You know so little of Venice."

Emilia's face colors, and she suddenly stands up from her place at the table. "Please excuse me," she says. As the dining room doors close behind her, I feel certain I can hear a muffled sob.

I stare at my brother. *What's wrong with you?* I say with my eyes. I think of following Emilia, but I sense that she needs some time alone.

Dinner proceeds with dull conversation about shipping taxes. The bowls are taken away and the second course fetched in.

"Allegreza is close to cracking, I've heard," my father says, suddenly shifting the subject back to the Segreta. "She'll soon spill the names of her gaggle of harridans."

At this, my spine straightens. As gently as possible, I lower my cutlery beside my plate.

Vincenzo shovels veal into his mouth as he talks. "The Bear knows how to get answers."

"How can you talk of torture over dinner?" I say, my voice coming out high and strangled.

"Laura's right," says Lysander.

Vincenzo wheezes with laughter again, and taps his knife against his empty wineglass. A servant scurries to re-fill it. He stares at me, eyebrows raised in amusement, as though inspecting a fool. "We must do whatever it takes to keep our city safe."

His hand disappears beneath the table and grips my thigh. I push him off, resisting the urge to call him a lecher-ous traitor. Father at least has the decency to look uncom-fortable and clears his throat.

"And do you have a wife in your new home?" he asks.

Vincenzo rolls his eyes. "No wife, only lonely nights." He rubs his hands together, looking from Father to me and back again. "But who knows what could happen now. Back in Venice, a return to power, happily ensconced in my rightful place. A new bride by my side?" He grins at me. A servant dips between our bodies to clear the plates, but when she steps away, Vincenzo's leering smile is still there, waiting for my reply.

"I wish you good luck in finding a willing bride," I say coldly. "My father will have told you that I'm engaged, I'm sure."

"Indeed," says Vincenzo, looking uncertainly at my father. "Engaged to a . . ."

There's a cough in the doorway and when I look up, Emilia is standing there.

"Laura, could you come and help? There's a moss stitch that I just can't get right in this embroidery."

Vincenzo snorts. "Embroidery? Yes, yes—go and keep your soft little hands amused with skeins of silk."

For a moment, I picture his skull smashing against cobblestones. I drag a hand across my forehead, clearing the image from behind my eyes. I push my chair back roughly.

"Of course," I say, ignoring Vincenzo's insults. "Let me see what I can do to help."

Emilia holds out her hand to me as she waits in the doorway. I smile at her gratefully.

"Goodbye, sweet dove!" Vincenzo says as I leave the room.

In the doorway, I turn, my hands resting on the handles. "Good night, Vincenzo. May your return to Venice bring you everything you deserve."

His smile falters, and he seems uncertain how to respond to my words. But I don't give him the chance. I back out of the room, Emilia following, and shut the doors behind us.

37

In the days that follow, it feels as though Vincenzo's return has cast an even more somber cloud over Venice. Each morning Faustina whispers to me over breakfast about the latest rumors heard in the market.

"Vincenzo's ships are still docked in the harbor," she tells me on Sunday. "It's as if he's taken control there. His crew struts around the harbor as though they own it."

The curfew is still in place at night, but aside from the soldiers visible on the streets, Venice is returning to herself. The markets still trade, the gondolas still float down the canals and Allegreza is still in her stinking cell. Another pamphlet denouncing the Segreta has left the press, this one even more vitriolic than the last. It urges the men of Venice to question their wives, their sisters and their daughters, so that "we may cleanse this city of the stain in its heart."

Paulina sent word that the letter was delivered, but there has been no response. Does Massimo really mean to call our bluff? If so, can we carry out our threat to share his secret? One word is all it would take to spread like wildfire across the city. And what if word got out beyond? We could end up hurting Venice rather than protecting her.

And still there's no word from Roberto. There seems little doubt that he's fled the city, abandoning his father and mother to their fate. Abandoning me to loneliness and shame. Each time I hear the quick patter of a messenger's footsteps, I wonder if he will bring a letter — even a few lines to let me know he's safe. Each time I'm disappointed. More and more, I find myself thinking about how he lived for so long in disguise, posing as a lowly painter, and I wonder whether our engagement was simply another form of pretense. After all, Roberto's past is still a secret to me. Perhaps he fooled everyone.

"That's not all," Faustina says, shaking her head. "Massimo has scout ships roaming the waters. No one can come or leave on the seas without getting past him."

On my way to Mass, I go down to the harbor to see for myself. People move in nervous huddles, and soldiers stand guard, their hands resting on the hilts of their swords as they watch every face carefully. Vessels of all sizes are searched without ceremony, so paranoid is the Bear about spies and subterfuge. Vincenzo's ships, sails furled, sit at anchor, but his men move around the harbor like crows in their black doublets. His flagship, *Il Castigo,* is the most impressive craft in the harbor, and its side bristles with cannons.

As I step between coiled ropes, a man is dragged off a small boat and thrown to his knees. I shrink back behind a crate while soldiers surround him.

"Where have you come from?" demands one of them. The man looks up into his face, wide-eyed and terrified. He shakes his head; he doesn't understand. The soldier sends the back of his hand cracking across the man's face, and he falls back. "Who sent you here?"

The man gabbles in a language I don't understand and points to piles of burlap sacks in the bottom of his boat that have been torn open to reveal wooden carvings. It's clear he's a trader, come to sell his goods in the market. Utterly harmless. Yet with a vicious yank, the soldier drags the man to his feet and hurls him into the bottom of his boat. He props himself up on an elbow and wipes the trickle of blood from his mouth.

"If you don't have papers and can't explain your business here, you must leave Venice." The soldier unsheathes his sword and points the blade back out towards the ocean. The man stands, nodding, and begins to work on untying his mooring ropes.

As soon as the soldiers are busy harassing another captain, I step out from behind the crate and slip away towards the Church of St. John. I pass beneath the arched stone doorway into the cool and shade. I dip a hand into the holy water and make the sign of the cross. The service has already started, so I take a seat at the back of the church.

The Mass is well attended, a mixture of the wealthy merchant classes and the poor. A peasant woman sits alone across the aisle from me. I'm looking into space, barely concentrating on the priest's Latin chants, when I spot a familiar silhouette some rows in front. Paulina, her head bent and her lips moving. My friend looks floored by grief. A young woman, now a widow.

As the service ends, we are blessed and instructed to do God's will. I cross the flagstones swiftly and reach

Paulina. She turns when I whisper her name. Her eyes are ringed with the bruised circles of sleeplessness, and her irises themselves seem sunken, darting around with fraught anxiety.

"Laura," she says softly.

"How are you?" I ask, laying a hand on her arm. "Did you . . . ?" I daren't finish my question, but she knows what I mean.

"I think so," she begins, pulling her hand distractedly through her hair. "I left it where it could be found, marked with his name."

I draw her to one side, away from the departing worshippers. Her shrunken cheeks make her look half starved. "When was the last time you ate?"

She shrugs. "I have no appetite."

The two of us sit on wooden chairs in a side chapel off the main nave. No one will spot us here, and if they should, then we are just two friends talking.

She looks over a shoulder nervously. "I hardly know whom to trust." She turns back to me and then her gaze falls, guiltily. "There's something new. Have you seen this?" She slips a hand down the front of her bodice, and I see that there is a secret pocket hidden between the silk lining and the burlap stiffener. She quickly pulls out a fold of paper.

"More propaganda?" I ask, my voice thick with disgust.

In reply, Paulina unfurls the parchment and hands it to me. I scan its contents. It's another diatribe against the Segreta.

"I'm scared," says Paulina. She's the Segreta's newest

recruit, and the practical part of me realizes that she is our weakest too. She's already crumbling under the pressure of what she volunteered to do. I should have found someone else to run my dangerous errands for me.

"Don't be silly," I say, feigning lightheartedness. "You don't take things like this seriously, do you? The Segreta are too strong to be destroyed by printed words. *You're* strong."

Paulina doesn't look convinced. "I've heard they're doing awful things to Allegreza. Even worse than we thought. Oh, Laura, I've heard . . ." She lets out a sob and shakes her head vehemently. "I couldn't do it, I know I couldn't. I couldn't stay quiet under torture, and Massimo doesn't seem to be reacting at all to our . . . promise." She looks into my face, her eyes pleading for reassurance.

"You must be strong," I tell her. "The Segreta rely on us. Allegreza especially."

Paulina's face crumples, and she hides her head in her hands, her shoulders shaking as her body is wracked with sobs. Nearby, a woman with a broom glances towards the sound. I give her a minute shake of the head and smile patiently. She nods, and moves farther down the church, sweeping in wide strokes.

Paulina has managed to compose herself slightly, wiping away the tears with the hem of her sleeve. "Have you heard from Roberto?" she asks.

"No." I can hear the emotionless quality of my own voice. That's how he's left me. Not even a word.

"That's it, then," Paulina says, tucking the scroll back inside her secret pocket. "War will come to Venice. Even the Segreta can't do anything to stop this." She gets to her feet and turns to leave, pressing her hand into my shoulder. "Take care, Laura."

It feels as though she's bidding me goodbye for the last time. With a sweep of her skirts, she's gone, and I am left alone in the sparse little chapel.

When I arrive home, the villa is in chaos. Servants rush from room to room. One carries a pile of clothes while another heaves wicker baskets of food into a waiting carriage, luggage strapped to its roof. Faustina's voice can be heard from the bedrooms, crying orders to the servants, and Bianca bustles down the stairs, almost tripping over the gowns she carries. An open leather chest stands in the hallway, overspilling with skirts. Emilia kneels beside it, placing her silver-backed hairbrushes inside a vanity case that slots into the lid of the trunk. When she sees me, she smiles sadly.

"What's going on?" I ask.

"I hoped you would be back," Emilia tells me, climbing to her feet. "I wanted to say goodbye properly."

"Are you going?" I ask. "Already?"

Her eyes dart to the stairs, where my brother appears, his face set. Faustina hurries behind him, carrying Lysander's writing desk, and shakes her head at me as if to say, *Don't stir things up*.

"We're leaving now," Lysander tells me as he walks out to the coach. "We have to."

I leave Emilia in the hallway and follow him into the sunlight.

"So quickly? Why the rush?"

238

The servants are red-faced and sweating as they maneuver the heavy cases onto the coach's roof. The horses, already in their tack, hoof the gravel drive impatiently.

Lysander hands a sheaf of papers to a manservant and for the first time looks me in the face. He places a hand on my arm and squeezes. "War is coming. Venice isn't safe. I'm taking Emilia back to Bologna. As she's already told you, you are welcome to come with us."

I gently pull my arm free of his grasp. "Things will calm down," I say, though I can hear how hopeless my words sound. "I don't need to leave."

Lysander shakes his head. "Things are going to get worse before they get better. A lot worse. The Doge's power is stretched to its breaking point." He reaches out and strokes my cheek. "And Roberto isn't coming back. We can all see that."

He frowns and his glance flickers over to the doorway. I look over my shoulder and see Emilia following Faustina to the rear of the house. Lysander takes me to one side, farther away from the coach. "It's not just all the unrest. It's this damned secret society. I'm worried that Emilia will be vulnerable to their influence. We haven't been married long; I don't want her changing for the worse."

I groan. We've already argued about this once. "How can you be so close-minded?" I say.

"I've read the pamphlets. I know what the Segreta are capable of."

I can't contain the laugh that emerges. "I've already told you—those pamphlets are nothing more than rags circulating vicious lies. Only a fool would believe them!"

Lysander's face hardens. A wall has risen up between us.

"Lysander," I begin, drawing him to me. "I have enjoyed every moment of having you back, and Emilia already means so much to me. Let us not fall out during our last moments together. I cannot come with you, but I don't want you to leave as a stranger."

Something changes in his face, and he draws me to him in an embrace. When he releases me again, his eyes are fraught. "I worry about you, Laura. If I didn't know better, I'd think you were one of them."

"And what if I were?" I say. "Would you do what the pamphlets ask and hand me over to be tortured?"

He swallows. "Of course not."

I've taken a vow of loyalty to the Segreta, a vow I have already broken once before. This time it comes more easily. My brother's love is too important to lose.

"Lysander, listen. Without them, I would have been married to Vincenzo. I would have been forced to bear that man's children." I can see the emotions fighting in his face. He looks back to the house for a moment. "During my time with the Segreta, I have seen them do nothing but good. Truly! Hundreds of people in Venice owe their lives and health to these women. They help those with no power of their own."

"I should have guessed," he murmurs. "Laura, the city has laws to protect people. The Grand Council—"

"The Grand Council stands on the shifting sands of politics. But the Segreta's feet are braced on a bedrock of common decency."

Lysander shakes his head. He looks up at me, and his eyes are fearful. "Come with us, please. I'm begging you,

240

Laura. I don't care about the Segreta and I don't care about the Grand Council, I just want you to be safe! Massimo's men will kill you."

"My life is here."

"It will be no life if you are discovered."

He's my loving brother again, eyes soft with concern.

"I must take that chance."

I wait for him to tell me that I'm a fool, but instead he waves away a servant who stands over a chest. My brother goes to open the lid and reaches inside a case made of felt, bringing out a small glass vial filled with clear liquid. Cupping it in the palm of his hand so that it's concealed from view, he passes it to me.

"Hide it," he orders, "on your person, and never let it go." Forcing myself not to look down at my hand, I pocket the tiny vial.

"What is it?" I ask, my eyes fixed on his.

"An infusion of hemlock. It was given to me by a doctor friend. Small quantities can be a useful sedative, but he warned me that drunk whole it could kill a person." His eyes narrow. "Laura, if they discover that you're . . . Do what you must."

I understand, and lean in to kiss his cheek. By his ear, I whisper, "The death. Would it be a painful one?"

"It would not," he whispers back.

Our eyes meet. "Thank you," I murmur, struggling to contain the tremor in my voice.

"Tell Father goodbye."

Then I hear the crunch of gravel as my brother walks away from me. He calls out to Emilia, and I look up to see her run from the house. She goes to climb into the coach, then hesitates. She breaks away and races over to me, pulling my body to hers in a fierce hug.

"I love you like a sister," she whispers. Then she lets me go and I stumble slightly, watching her run lightly over to her husband, my brother. Now she does climb into the coach. She blows me a kiss through the air and Lysander waves a hand in farewell, before climbing in behind her and slamming the varnished door shut. There's a click of the driver's tongue and a snap of the reins and they're gone.

38

I kneel by my bed, but not to pray. I lift the lid on the box that holds the clothes from my past. Tucked away among mothballs and sheets of lavender-infused paper are my nun's habit and headdress. Faustina wanted to burn them, but I insisted on keeping some memento of that time. Now I'm glad I did.

I lift the robe and cowl and shake out the creased fabric as I go to stand before the mirror. On the dressing table is a small, stubby knife that I stole from the kitchen last night when Faustina was busy kneading bread. It's nowhere near as sharp as a sword, but it will do.

I dress in the musty clothes, pin my hair back tightly, then arrange the cowl over my head. Soon, I am all but hidden. I barely recognize the woman who gazes back at me in the mirror. The picture of innocence. At my bedroom door, I wait on the landing, listening for noises.

Nothing.

A short while later, I stand before the public door of the Piombi. The guard stares at me, frowning.

"What are you doing here, Sister? This is no place for you."

"I'm sorry," I say, ducking my head, "but I wish to give comfort to one of your prisoners. The lady Allegreza. She has been a faithful supporter of our convent and it would keep the Abbess—and God—happy if I could share a few words with her."

Perhaps the Abbess, if she knew, would call it the ultimate blasphemy, but God will surely forgive me.

The guard folds his arms and looks embarrassed. "I'm under orders to search everyone who enters. No exceptions." I gasp meekly, and see the tide of red travel up his cheeks.

Before I came, I dug out my Bible from beneath my bed. It was covered in dust, but I gave it a cleaning, and it looks for all the world like my dearest possession. I hold it out to the guard.

"I have nothing to declare but my faith," I say, smiling. "Feel free to search me, but this is all I carry. All I need."

The guard clears his throat and his eyes look up and down the street. It's thronged with people, too many to pay us much attention. He kicks the door behind him, and it opens a crack. Without shifting his stance, he jerks his head in its direction.

"Go on, then. Quickly, Sister."

In the darkness of the prison corridor, I see the shape of another guard, sleeping in his chair. He snorts and stirs as I draw near.

"I'm here to see Allegreza di Rocco," I say, keeping my head bowed in case he recognizes me from my previous visit. But he doesn't even spare me a glance.

"Up the stairs, first cell on the right," he grunts.

From the foot of the staircase I see a prisoner reach a skinny arm between the bars of his cell and paw the ground. "Help me!" he calls, his mouth frothing. I shudder and look away, running up the stairs. The heat is already oppressive, even this early in the morning. Beyond the turreted roof I can hear the noises of Venice. How horrible this must be for the prisoners, knowing they are so close to the life and energy of the city, yet so hidden from it.

Allegreza crouches at the rear of her cell on a bed of old straw. The acrid stench of urine stings my eyes. Through her torn dress I can see the nobs of her spine as she holds herself in a tight ball, protecting herself from whatever blow may come next. It is the same gown I last saw her wearing, the day that she was arrested. Now it is filthy, the silk covered in stains. A scattering of bruises decorates her arms and the skin exposed above the neckline of her gown. As she shifts, patches of baldness reveal themselves among her gray hair.

She shifts on her haunches and notices me for the first time. Her eyes widen in fear, and she scuttles back, pinning herself against the rear wall of the cell, until a second glance allows her to take in my cowl and Bible. Her face softens and she tries to smile, but her lips crack with dried blood.

"Prayers are no good to me," she says, her voice faint.

This is not the Allegreza I knew. For a moment, I want to race down the stairs and away from here, wiping this vision from my mind's eye. But then I remember what I've come to do.

"I'm not here to pray," I say.

The change in her is immediate. Her chin jerks up, and she narrows her eyes, as though testing to see if her vision deceives her. I smile and pull back part of my cowl so that she can see my face.

Allegreza braces her hands against the wooden floor and heaves herself up to standing. As she limps towards me, I notice for the first time what has happened to those beautiful hands of hers, once so adept at playing the spinet. Her fingers hang useless and gnarled, and where her polished nails should be are crescents of dried blood.

A sob emerges from me, despite myself. Allegreza shushes me as she used to. Up close, I see that what remains of her hair has matted into a solid, tangled blanket.

"How could they do this to you?" I ask.

"I suppose I could use some beauty sleep," Allegreza says, pressing her thin body against the bars. "You shouldn't be here. It's not safe." She looks down at her hands and gives an ironic laugh, which dies away, and she looks into my face. "You must go," she orders.

"Not yet. Allegreza, you need to know—we tried to get you out. A letter was delivered to Massimo, threatening to expose his secret about the useless gunpowder. Did anyone say anything to you? We hoped he'd release you, rather than risk his secret coming out, but . . ." I don't know what else to say. My plan has failed—like so many of my efforts on behalf of the Segreta.

A frown creases Allegreza's pale brow, and the look in her eyes is one I recognize—her mind turning over, calculating.

"What is it? Did they say something to you?"

She shakes her head. "Quite the opposite. Nothing has been said at all. You're sure Massimo received the letter?" Her voice has sudden life in it, as if her injuries are forgotten, at least for a moment.

"Paulina delivered it," I say.

"Paulina?" She frowns, as if considering the name. "She is an odd choice for such a mission."

Even now, in her sufferings, she has the power to make me feel small.

"She volunteered," I say. "She has access, and . . ."

"Yes, of course. You should go now, Laura."

"I came here for a reason," I say, remembering how this conversation was meant to go.

She gives me a wry glance that takes in my outfit. "To spread the word of God?"

"Better than that." I take my Bible and slip it between the bars of the cell.

Allegreza draws back. "I told you I have no need of prayers," she says, almost angry.

"Look inside," I tell her in a whisper.

Allegreza opens the thin pages. Last night I gouged out a coarse hole in their center with a knife. Inside it rests the vial my brother gave me.

The woman who saved me from a ruined life looks up into my face.

"What's this?" Though her eyes tell me that she already understands.

"Your escape."

A glossy sheen spreads in Allegreza's eyes, but the tears evaporate before they're shed.

"Thank you." With shaking hands, she starts to prise the cork out. "Now you must leave," she says firmly. "Let the others know — I have not spoken a word about us."

"I will."

I reach between the bars to retrieve my Bible. Then I wipe the tears from my cheeks, smooth down my skirts and straighten my back. As I walk down the stairs, I don't look back.

When I step outside, the light hurts my eyes, and they water. I take in a deep lungful of the salty air coming off the sea.

"Did the prisoner find her solace?" the guard asks gruffly.

"I think so," I say.

39

News of Allegreza's death leaks out by breakfast the following day. Emilia and Lysander are long gone, and Father is out of sorts. Cold silence fills the air between us as we eat soft-boiled eggs and warm bread. A man-servant comes in and whispers something in Father's ear. He grunts and scrapes back his chair.

"Halim has docked in the harbor," he announces, wiping his hands on a linen napkin. "The impudence of that man!" He throws the napkin on the floor and the servant has to bend to retrieve it, but Father is already striding around the room in agitation. He throws me an angry look, as though this is all my fault, forgetting that, not long ago, he was all too happy to throw his own daughter at the prince. "Your beloved fiancé has saved his own skin and served up Venice to the Turks." He turns and gazes out of the window, his hands behind his back.

"Is there no other way of appeasing Halim?" I ask.

Father scoffs. "Appeasement? No, my girl. Roberto may not care about Venice, but others do. We have Massimo and we have Vincenzo. We'll bury that Turkish upstart beneath the waves!" He grinds one fist into the other.

"Yes, but how many innocents will pay for victory with their lives?"

"Pah!" He waves a hand as if the matter is of little consequence. "You know, a resounding victory will make Vincenzo even more of a catch for a bride."

I wipe the corners of my mouth and stand up. "I'd rather die than marry that man," I say.

Father's smile fades. "Do you think I took you out of that convent to live as a spinster?"

"Of course not, but I could find a husband who isn't Vincenzo. He's older than you are."

"You've not done such a fine job husband-hunting, though, have you?"

I don't deign to respond to this remark. I make my exit.

A boat is soon taking me to the harbor, the gondolier's oar carving a path through the water. As we move across the lagoon, I see that the canals are busier than usual. Families are loading their possessions and heading towards the harbor too. Like my brother and his wife, people are vacating the city. I can only guess that they want to avoid the troubles that lie ahead.

Our boat passes the shuttered palace. At least with Allegreza's death, the Doge and his wife can hide their humiliations under a cowl in grief. The sun is out, and I carry a small parasol. I loosen the ribbon on my bodice. My upper chest and shoulders are bare, and I am wearing a saffron silk gown, hair snaking down my left shoulder in a bouncing curl that has been brushed and wound around warm irons until it sits just so. If I'm going to persuade Halim to call off a war, I have to look my best.

"Who are you trying to impress?" Faustina had asked when she'd poked her head into my room earlier.

I waved her away. "No one."

She raised her eyebrows at me. "Then 'No One'—whoever he is—will be grateful for all your efforts, I'm sure."

I raised the brush in my hand, and the threat was enough to send her ducking from the door, chortling.

Now I see that Halim's ship is a galley with rows of oars spearing its sides, withdrawn and lifted from the water. Red triangular flags decorated with gold brocade flutter from the mast poles. The stern of the ship is covered in a striped awning with three brass lamps sitting above it. At the prow is a figurehead carved in the shape of an eagle.

As I approach, men on the ship share startled glances, and one breaks off from tying a rope and runs down the plank. He throws a volley of words at me that I don't understand, pointing back to the city. The message is clear: *You're not welcome here.*

I stand my ground, and smile as seductively as I can. "I'd like to see Halim."

The man folds his arms, and calls up the plank behind him. Another barks an answer, and disappears out of sight.

As I wait on the harborside, more deckhands come to the rails to watch, fixing me with their greedy eyes. From behind them emerges Faruk. He looks down his nose at me.

"You shouldn't have come!" he shouts down. "Let men deal with men's business."

He's like a guard dog, jealously keeping watch over his master. But like all dogs, he can surely be tamed.

"I only ask for a few minutes of your master's time."

"Time is running out for Venice," says Faruk.

The men on deck suddenly scatter back to their work as Halim reaches Faruk's side. His head is covered by a sparkling white turban and he wears loose-fitting trousers, a red tunic with gold buttons and, over that, a black waistcoat. He looks immaculate — ready to entertain guests rather than go to battle. But then I spot the sword that hangs from a leather belt by his hip. The hilt is shaped in the form of an eagle's head, just like the figurehead.

"I was just telling this young lady to go home," sneers Faruk.

Halim ignores him and stares at me. I hold his powerful gaze.

"Please," he says, "come aboard."

Faruk grunts and disappears from sight. I lift my skirts and begin walking up the gangplank. Halim reaches out a hand to me and I accept it.

"Thank you," I say.

"Come to my pavilion," says Halim, "if your reputation can stand it."

I force a laugh. "My reputation isn't much, these days." My father would never forgive me if he knew what I was about to do. "People can think what they like," I say, "I came here to talk."

Halim leads me onto the ship. I've never seen anything like this before. We move down the narrow galley, past clusters of men, making our way back towards the stern. Halim leads me under the awning of his pavilion, where embroidered cushions are arranged along wooden benches.

"Would you like some refreshment?" he asks.

"Yes, please."

As I sit, Halim moves to a low table, on which there is a brass jug and crystal glasses. He pours me a goblet of wine. "You are brave coming here," he says. "But I fear your visit will be a waste."

I take the glass and sip. The wine is nothing like our own. It's sweeter, with a background of light spice. I notice he doesn't partake.

"You aren't having any?"

"My religion forbids me," he says. "But, please, my beliefs should not ruin your enjoyment."

But I haven't come here to enjoy Halim's hospitality. We sit in silence for a minute or two, interrupted only by the occasional bellowed cry from belowdecks and the creaking and clanking of the rigging. Now that I'm here, I wonder what I can possibly say. How can one girl succeed where the Grand Council have failed?

"Venice grieves for two of her children," I say at last. "Just as you grieve for your sister."

He stiffens. "Venice is a city," he says. "My heart is a human one."

"Nicolo has a family. Allegreza had one too."

Halim sighs, sinking back against the cushions. "You think I want war?" he says.

"The power to prevent it is in your hands," I reply.

"And if I do as you ask? If I turn my fleet around and sail away, will my sister's ghost find her rest?"

Pain is etched across Halim's face, and I feel the urge to

place my arm around his shoulders. But words will have to suffice. "Your sister would not want more bloodshed."

His head snaps up, and his eyes flare with sudden anger. "What do you know of her wishes?" he demands.

As soon as he's said it, the fury passes from his face. "I apologize," he says. "I am not myself at the moment. For the first time in my life . . ." He looks at me almost tenderly. "I'm confused, Laura."

The pavilion suddenly seems small.

"Your argument is with Roberto," I say. "Not with Venice. And he has disappeared."

"He was allowed to escape," Halim retorts. "Who bears responsibility? Whoever it is must pay."

"Then ask the Doge for some financial reparation."

"I have no need of money." For a moment, silence settles between us. Then he says, "He was to be your husband. How does that make you feel?"

I gaze into the dark liquid, then into his eyes. "I'm disappointed," I say. "Angry too."

He suddenly buries his face in his hands, and utters a groan of despair. Is he weeping? I put down my wine and move closer.

He draws his hands away, but I see his eyes are dry. "Sometimes my anger overwhelms me," he says. "My sister was the dearest person in the world to me. Without her, my days are darkness. Do you understand?"

I think of my own sister. Poor, beautiful Beatrice, so full of life's joys. "I understand." I place a hand over his. He looks down at it, then lifts my fingertips to press his lips against them. I should pull my hand away, but I don't. Halim notices this, and before I know it, he's turned my hand over to plant another kiss on the inside of my wrist. I have to bite my lip to contain the moan that threatens to escape me. I shouldn't let . . .

"I love you, Laura," he says.

My blood feels hot in my veins. I wasn't expecting this.

"How can you—"

"Come away with me," he says. "You are better than these people. I can make you happy. You'll have more riches than this city can ever give you. You won't have to worry ever again, and these silly politics will seem like a bad dream."

His lips move towards mine.

"This is my home, Halim."

His face clouds, and he moves away. "You have to understand, Laura. I will be victorious here. Soon, Venice will not be a good place to live. With me, you'll be queen of an empire."

The intensity of his gaze makes every part of my skin tingle at once. The conviction of his words almost sways me. He might well be right. Even if the combined might of Vincenzo's fleet and the Venetian ships manages to hold firm, what will I have here? My brother has fled back to Bologna. Roberto—he could be dead or alive for all I know. My father is trying to marry me to a monster, and Allegreza, the woman I held in the highest regard, is dead.

"If . . ." I am not sure I can get the words out.

"Go on," Halim urges.

"I will consider it, but you must not attack the city."

I know from the flash in his eyes that this bald offer is not what he wants to hear. Halim reaches under his tunic and pulls out a pendant that hangs on a golden chain around his neck. He holds it out in the flat of his palm. "She is the reason I cannot do as you ask." He takes the chain from around his neck and hands the pendant to me. It is heavy and warm from where it's been pressed against his skin. There's a hinged lock on it, and I press the crescent of my fingernail into a groove. The lock clicks, and the panels of the locket spring open. Inside is a miniature painting in oils. It's of a woman.

"Her death must be avenged. What sort of brother would I be if I walked away now?"

As I peer closer, the warmth from the locket seems to drain away. The warmth of the pavilion too, as if a cold winter breeze has slipped in.

I try to make sense of what I see. For the portrait is not of the woman I saw lying on Roberto's floor in a pool of blood. It is of the girl who fled the convent. The one whose knees buckled when I mentioned Halim.

Almost instantly, I understand that I cannot allow him to see my shock. I need time to order my thoughts. His sister is alive, somewhere in Venice. But, but . . . My brain feels as though it's going to explode. Halim gazed on the dead woman in her coffin. He must have known it was not his sister.

I look up at him, carefully composing a sympathetic smile. Am I seeing things, or does his face carry the tiniest shadow of suspicion?

"She was very beautiful," I tell him. She still is, I think. "I can see why you fight for her honor."

If he knows the victim wasn't his sister, why is he pretending? Unless . . .

"I would lay down my life for yours too," he says.

Hastily, I get to my feet, feeling a little unsteady. Halim leaps up to help me. Whatever intimacy I felt is gone, but I must keep up a pretense. I take his hand and press my lips against them. A chaste kiss.

"Will you think about what I said?" he asks as I give him his pendant back.

"I will, of course."

He strokes a hand down my face. "I'll come for you once all this is over. I hope you understand, Laura. I have to do what I came here to do."

"I understand," I say. "I understand everything."

40

I ignore the ship's crew and disembark with quick, sure steps.

My mind is swirling. A street entertainer wearing a harlequin's outfit prances before me, hoping to earn a few coins. I shake my head and storm past him, nearly oblivious to the low curses he sends after me.

I find myself in a small piazza and sit on a fountain ledge to think. I imagine that Allegreza is by my side, probing me with questions to tease out the truth and its significance.

Perhaps he was mistaken?

But no. I remember the sight of my own poor sister in her coffin. Despite the ravages of death, I still knew her face. There's no way Halim could have made such an error. He was so sure. And why did he ask to see the body in the first place, unless he already had an idea about what he would find? How is it that no one wondered about this before? The implications are almost too horrifying to contemplate. It would mean that all he's said is part of a ruse.

He's not declaring war on Venice in the name of Aysim's honor—he's doing it to suit his own ends. He's trying to sow discord among his enemy by blaming an innocent man. When I think how carefully the Doge has tried to placate him, how the whole of Venice has been besmirched by his claims that we are a heartless nation, how Roberto has fled and politicians have flourished. How I . . . how I allowed myself . . . And Massimo and the rebels are playing into his hands—

"Laura!"

I swivel round and see Paulina. She's much changed since our encounter in the church. She's freshened herself up and tidied her hair and it looks as though she has managed to eat something, judging by the color in her cheeks. I'm glad—but confused to see her here. As we sat in the chapel, she seemed terrified of all that was afoot in Venice and keen to hide away, even to cut herself free of the Segreta.

"I'm glad to see you looking so well," I tell her.

"Did I see you coming from Halim's ship?" she asks.

I nod. "I was hoping to dissuade him from his plans." Guiltily, I rearrange the ribbons on my dress, covering myself up. But Paulina doesn't seem to notice. She shakes her head bitterly.

"Sometimes I think Venice deserves to suffer for all its pride."

Her words startle me. Partly because they could be construed as treasonous in these times, but also . . .

"I have to be going," she says. "My mother is expecting me at home. Take care of yourself, Laura."

As I watch her leave, stepping out of the square, her words still echo within me. I realize why they've left me ice-cold.

I've heard them before.

That, and her polished appearance, are making my pulse quicken. And why is she heading the wrong way? Her mother's home is in the northwest of the city, while she took the eastern path.

In an instant, I decide to follow her.

Yes, those words — Venice and her pride. Carina said something similar — months ago — just before she tried to kill me on the boat.

It could be a coincidence, but it could be something far worse. . . .

A traitor in the Segreta.

Paulina picks up her pace as she winds through the streets and alleys, and I move after her, pausing at turnings to give her space. This is definitely not the direction of Paulina's home. As we travel farther from the harbor, the cobbles become loose, and paint peels at the shuttered windows. Rats chase each other down the open drains. We're entering the poorer part of the city — a place where young noblewomen are advised not to travel alone. I can't think what business my friend might have here. This does not strike me as the behavior of the fearful woman I met a few days ago, driven to distraction after delivering a blackmail letter to Massimo.

The blackmail letter . . .

Waves of fear wash over me. I see Allegreza again in her cell. Her strange tone when I tell her who it was that delivered the letter.

Paulina? She is an odd choice for such a mission.

Did she too suspect? Has she always? She wouldn't let Paulina go to Murano—why?

Paulina pauses to pull a threadbare shawl out of an embroidered bag at her wrist. She wraps the shawl tightly around her shoulders, transforming herself into a peasant woman. She looks over her shoulder, and I duck behind a crumbling wall just in time. I wait, pressing my body against the bricks, until I judge it's safe to peer around the corner. She's walking away again. I've no time to buy a simple shawl of my own. We move deeper into the slums of the city.

She arrives at a tall building with a series of arched windows. Several of the panes of glass are broken. The gates are rusty and hanging from their hinges, and there are chips in the fleur-de-lis that decorate the grids over some of the windows. This is a beautiful building, left to rot.

Paulina slips through the open doorway, stepping over discarded bundles of rags. I wait a moment, then follow. As soon as I step inside, the smell of damp and decay hits me. I hear the creak and groan of floorboards above my head, and, peering through the slits, I see a shadow pass overhead. Paulina must already be on the floor above. I climb the stairs after her, testing each one before placing my full weight on it. It's still impossible to climb without making a noise, and I'm glad that, farther ahead, Paulina has disturbed a flock of pigeons that take to the air, screeching.

I walk down a corridor lined with hanging rags. Was this once a cloth-dyer's? A larger rag hangs over a doorway to form a curtain, kept in place by a nail in each corner.

Beyond it, I hear voices and can just make out the shadows of two people moving about a room. I creep closer until I can hear what they're saying, pressing my body against the wall. A mouse scuttles over my slippers, but I keep my nerve.

"I've done everything you asked." Paulina sounds frightened.

"Stop whimpering!" replies another voice. Carina. "You chose to follow this path with me. Allegreza is dead, thanks to you!" She laughs.

I can hear the quiet sound of Paulina's desperate sobbing. Any anger I have quickly vanishes. She's in over her head, fit to drown.

"I just want to go now," she says. "Please let me go!"

There's the sudden sound of their footsteps beyond the curtain, and I slip behind one of the rags hanging from a line near the ceiling. Fortunately, it's so crumpled with age that I can hide in its folds. I watch their feet walk past me along the corridor. A stride or two to the left, and they would brush my skirts. I'm about to breathe out with relief when Paulina stops.

"What about him?" she asks.

"I haven't decided yet. I may let the rats have him."

Him? I wait until the creaks of the stairs have died away before coming out of my hiding place, brushing the cobwebs from my skirts. *Him?* Oh, God, how my heart is beating. I creep on light feet to the room they've left, parting the curtain.

It's small and dark inside. Unlit candles are ranged across the fireplace, leaning in pools of melted wax. A single chair sits in the center of the room, and tied to it is Roberto.

He strains against the ropes, his eyes bulging as he sees me. Muffled sounds emerge from behind the filthy rag tied over his mouth. He is bare-chested, his skin slick with sweat. I throw myself towards him, grappling at the ropes, and all my doubts take flight.

41

I fall to my knees and cover his face with kisses.

"My darling," I whisper. I don't care if he's streaked with dirt and sweat; he has never been dearer to me. I crane around the back of the chair and untie the knots in the rope. His wrists are bloody and the skin chafed from where he has strained to free himself. As the ropes fall into a pile around the feet of the chair, Roberto's body slumps forward, and I have to push him back to prevent him from collapsing on the floor. His eyes roll back in his head as unconsciousness threatens to overcome him.

"Laura . . . Laura." He says my name over and over again. I hook an arm around his waist and help him to his feet. "I thought you were . . . She told me . . ." His knees buckle beneath his weight.

"You must try to walk," I say gently. He nods in understanding and licks his cracked lips. He takes a tentative step forward, and another, while I support him. So, we make our way slowly out of the abandoned building. I pause near the doorway, just in case Carina and Paulina are waiting, but no one is there.

We take a different route back to the shoreline. After a few turns, Roberto spots a brimming water butt beneath a broken drainpipe. He staggers towards it and leans over the edge, submerging his arms up to his shoulders. He cups great handfuls of rainwater and brings them up to his mouth. He plunges his head in the water and flings it back again so that sparkling droplets arc through the air. I wait as he drinks more and more, rivulets of water running down his chest, his body slumped against the butt. Finally, he braces himself against the side and rolls his body around so that he's facing me. He grins with pure joy and I laugh with relief, running to him.

A sodden arm falls around my shoulders but I don't pull away. He can ruin my dress. I care for nothing but him.

"I never thought I'd see you again," he says, his voice croaky. He drags me to him and kisses me passionately. "Carina told me you were dead. She even brought a lock of your hair and held it beneath my nose."

"It's a long story," I tell him. "Stay here."

From a stall near the harbor I buy a pot of pickled fish and a twist of sweetened bread. From another I find a simple hooded cloak. We make an odd couple. Me with my yellow silk dress, Roberto looking like a vagrant, cloaked on a warm day. Luckily, people are used to eccentrics in this part of the city.

I don't think I've ever felt happier than I do now, feasting my eyes upon this filthy man cramming food into his mouth. "You saved my life," he says.

"How did you escape from the jail?" I ask.

"I didn't. A group of men attacked the guards and kidnapped me. They dragged me to that building and delivered me to Carina. I was just left to starve, with no food or water. From time to time she'd come to me. She'd taunt me. She said she had cut your throat. I thought I'd go mad—or die. Death seemed a better option."

I feel the flush of guilt. I had let myself believe the worst, that he'd abandoned Venice and myself. And all that time he was suffering alone.

"But where did she find the men?" I ask.

"Ruffians can be bought, can't they?"

"But these men must have been trained," I insist. "They overpowered the guards."

Roberto shrugs. "I couldn't believe Carina was alive," he goes on. "For a moment or two, I even felt sorry for her."

There's no time to talk about Carina now. I tell Roberto what's been happening with Halim and the fleet. About the deception that has brought Venice to the brink of war, about the missing girl who looks just like the portrait of Halim's sister, who could be the key to exposing it. I tell him about Allegreza, and he pulls me to him.

"I know how much you admired her," he says.

When I talk of Massimo, and the rebellion within the Council, his features darken. "What shall we do?" he asks.

"For now, we hide. We need to weigh our options."

I hold my hand out to him and, gratefully, he takes it. Then I lead him to a canal, where we find a gondola, and the two of us climb aboard.

Roberto settles in beneath his hood as the boatman pushes off.

"Where are we going?" Roberto asks. His eyelids are already drooping with fatigue.

"Home," I say.

Through the gate, I can see some of the servants on stepladders in the courtyard, painting a section of the wall. Faustina is snoozing in a chair by the kitchen steps. I lead Roberto through a side entrance, and then upstairs. He's as weak as a kitten and I must be patient as he slowly climbs the steps to my room.

"I shouldn't be here," he protests. "We're not yet married."

"Wedding vows can wait," I tell him.

Roberto smiles. "You never did like being told what to do."

I lean past him to open my bedroom door and usher him inside. He sinks onto my sheets, and within moments he's asleep.

I slip out of the bedroom and go to the kitchens for a pitcher of hot water.

Fresh sheets of pasta hang from a line above the counter and—there!—a copper urn of water is steaming on the stove. Bianca is leaning over the deep sink, up to her elbows in suds and steaming water.

"I'll just help myself to some water," I whisper, not wanting to disturb Faustina, whose chair is visible through the open door. But as I step towards the urn, I trip over a coal scuttle. Faustina stirs in her chair.

"Is everything all right?" she asks. Her eyes fall on my dress. "Oh, Laura, you're filthy!"

"I tripped," I say. "I'm going to bathe."

Faustina bursts out laughing. "That's right! A lady

drawing her own bath. As if Bianca or I would allow that! The household might survive many scandals, but not that!"

"Faustina, no, really . . ."

But it's too late. She's already cutting through the courtyard, into the main doorway and up the stairs.

"Stop!" I call after her. "Faustina, please . . ."

She bustles straight past the bathing chamber and turns the handle of my bedroom door. I rush in just as she shrieks, "Get out, get out, or have your filthy hands chopped off!" As she tries to run from the room, I seize her arm.

"Will you calm down," I whisper, dragging her aside.

"Calm down? Venice is soon to be at war and there's one of . . . one of . . . *them* in your bedroom!"

I give a deep, exasperated sigh. "That man isn't a Turk," I say.

"You've seen him!" Faustina does a rapid sign of the cross.

"Yes, I've seen him. I'm engaged to be married to him."

I wait for my words to find their mark. Faustina blinks once, twice—then understanding dawns.

"That's Roberto?" she whispers. I nod, but she still looks doubtful. "He's losing his looks, Laura."

"He's half starved. He was kidnapped. I need your help to return him to health. And Father must not know."

Faustina's lined face is wracked with indecision. She looks at me, then back at my bedroom door, then at me once more. "I'll get you some hot water," she says.

I smile as she scuttles back to the kitchens, and I know that Roberto is in the best possible hands.

When I poke my head around the door, Roberto looks

solemn. I sit beside him on the bed, and he reaches to stroke my hair.

"Each day I was tied up there, I would close my eyes and try to summon your face," he says. "But you're much more beautiful than my imaginings."

I nestle my cheek against the warmth of his palm. "It must have been horrible."

Roberto grimaces. "Carina . . . she didn't just torture me with words. She kissed me too. She said we could be together now you were gone. I tried to get away, but . . ."

"Don't punish yourself," I say, feeling sick and guilty at the same time. How could I ever have doubted him? I think of telling him about Halim, not that anything really happened between us, but it would only cause him pain, and he is too weak to bear it. Perhaps one day I will reveal to him all that went on while we were apart. "It's over now," I tell him. "Your father will be reinstated and honor returned to Venice. Carina cannot touch us."

Roberto's hand drops from my face, and he gazes out of the open window. "I hope so."

42

From below, the dinner gong rings a second time.

"Laura!" Father calls gruffly. "Get down here, before the food turns cold."

Faustina is sworn to secrecy, but I shouldn't keep my father waiting and force her to make a suspicious excuse for my tardiness. After his bath, Roberto crawled into my bed and fell into a deep slumber. I tuck a blanket around him and kiss his forehead. "Sleep well, my love," I whisper.

Over a plate of grilled sardines, Father is full of excitement. "Two days!" he declares. "Then we will sink Halim and his filthy crew. Our men will make Venice proud."

Easy for him to say. Father won't be carrying a sword or musket; he won't have to risk spilling his own blood. Members of the Grand Council are too important to lay their lives on the line. It will be new recruits or loyal soldiers—sons and brothers and young fathers—who will leave families grieving.

Ever since my reunion with Roberto, my mind has been

constantly turning over. Even if Halim were to discover that he's in Venice, it would not avert the battle. He would accuse us of giving him shelter and seek retribution before we had time to reveal his lies. It's clear that our visiting prince doesn't set much store by honor. He's determined this war will go ahead, whatever the stakes. Venice is too great a prize, and Carina's meddling has played right into his hands.

My thoughts are interrupted by a polite cough from the doorway.

"There's a visitor with a message for the lady of the house," a manservant says, looking at me. He appears to be nervous.

"Show him in, show him in!" cries my father. "Pour him a glass."

"Are you sure?" the servant begins to say, but Father slams a fist on the table, making the crystal decanter shudder.

"Do as I say!"

The servant's nerves have made my own senses heighten. I hear stately steps. Then Father gasps and pushes his chair back. I lift a napkin to hide my smile.

Bella Donna hasn't even bothered to discard the yellow scarf that marks her as a prostitute. Her hair has been curled around her face, and she wears a low-cut maroon bodice embroidered with gold thread, the sleeves slashed so that clouds of white linen poke through. She sports no gold or pearls, but there is heavy rouge on her cheeks and she carries a gaudy peacock feather fan in one hand. A black veil spills from the crown of her head, but does nothing to cover her chest or arms, and she moves towards us on high-platformed shoes. She does her best to ignore Father's shocked expression, and her best is very good.

"Calm down, Father," I say. "This is a friend of mine."

"She's a . . . a . . . in my home!"

"Won't you take a seat?" I ask her.

Bella Donna sashays into the room, going to sit next to Father. He shakes his head with disgust.

"Whatever you have to say, you can say it standing!"

Bella Donna smiles sweetly. "Don't worry," she tells me. "I simply came here to tell you that the gloves you left in the convent have been found."

Aysim. Bella Donna has found her.

"Thank you so much," I say. "I thought I'd lost them forever." I get to my feet to follow Bella Donna from the room. "Take me to find them."

"What's this? Gloves! You come into my home and talk to my daughter about a wretched pair of gloves? Get out—both of you! Laura, have you not brought enough shame on this family?"

I don't hear what else he has to say; we're already out in the hallway.

"Where is she?" I hiss.

"At my place of work," Bella Donna tells me.

I swallow hard. The idea of returning to the unseemly place where we trapped Silvio makes my stomach clench. But our needs are of the utmost importance. I must go where Bella Donna leads. For Venice, for Roberto. "Take me to her."

"You're sure about this?" she asks. "You, an ex–convent girl?"

"Don't be silly," I joke. "How much difference can there be between a brothel and a convent?"

Bella Donna raises her eyebrows.

We arrive at a low, discreet doorway in a tiny alley off the Calle Bressana.

"The House of Provocation," Bella Donna murmurs, cocking her head to the sounds of laughter that emerge from a window set high in the wall. "Ready?"

I draw my cloak closer around my shoulders and nod. Bella Donna pulls back the hood of her cape to show her face to the man at the door, and he grunts in acknowledgment, stepping aside to let us in.

"The girl was caught trying to steal food from a stall," Bella Donna explains as we walk past an open salon where a group of men and women chat in low voices. "She fell and sprained her ankle trying to escape. We took her in to save her from being beaten by the stallholder."

We duck down a narrow corridor lined with gilt-framed paintings. Beside each painting is a closed doorway, hung with tasseled curtains. I can hear more laughter and the sound of a spinet being played. Bella Donna shows me into a kitchen with a table in the center, along which are ranged decanters of wine ready for customers' refreshment. At one end sits a young woman, her head in her arms as she sleeps. I recognize her instantly—the golden skin, slight frame and the frown lines that crease her brow even in her dreams. The room is lit by lamps that hang from the ceiling, casting golden circles over the furniture.

Bella Donna steps forward and gently places a hand

on the girl's arm. She wakes with a jolt. When she sees me, she leaps up, knocking her stool to the ground. She scrambles away towards the back door, grappling with the iron bolt.

"Calm yourself," Bella Donna says, going after her. "This is a friend."

"I'm not here to harm you," I say in French. "I know who you are, who your brother is. Halim." The girl lets out a whimper of fear, looking wildly from me to Bella Donna. "I'm here as a member of the Segreta. You were looking for us, weren't you? Seeking our help? My fiancé, Roberto, is charged with your murder, held accountable by Halim. We have a shared enemy, you and I. You can trust me."

Aysim's face is softening, and slowly, cautiously, she steps away from the door and stands behind Bella Donna. She clears her throat.

"I'm sorry," she begins in swift, fluent French. "For so long, I haven't known whom to trust."

I straighten the stool that she kicked over, and the three of us come to sit around the kitchen table. Bella Donna pours us all tumblers of water, and Aysim begins her story. We hear how she arrived in Venice with her loyal maid-servant, Emen. How they were wearing each other's clothes as disguises, fleeing from Halim's violence. They were attacked, and Aysim managed to escape, but Emen did not.

Aysim's voice breaks. "My faithful servant, the only person to show me loyalty. I let her die." Her dark eyes brim with tears.

"She was the girl in Roberto's apartments, wasn't she?" I whisper.

Aysim nods, tears coursing down her cheeks. Bella Donna hands her a linen handkerchief.

"It was me they meant to kill!"

I feel sick to my stomach. Gales of loud male laughter spill from one of the rooms down the corridor, as though mocking me. Through the kitchen doorway I see a member of the Grand Council emerge, straightening his tunic. I quickly turn my face away, and Bella Donna hurries to shut the door.

Aysim tells me of her brother's lust for power, his hatred of Venice.

"He's been planning this moment for over two years," she says. "At first it was just a fantasy. His advisers told him it couldn't be achieved."

"So what changed?"

"He sought new counsel—a witch who covers her face with a silver mask."

I swallow hard. "Why does she wear a mask?" I ask. Though I suspect I already know the answer.

Aysim waves a hand before her own face. "A terrible disfigurement."

My mind fizzes as a spiderweb of connections starts to take form. Prince Halim and Carina are working together? So Roberto's kidnapping wasn't a coincidence—it was orchestrated with Halim's knowledge. Can my dead sister's old friend be behind everything that's happened?

The scale of the plot is almost too great to believe, and I try to see its many facets. One other point also bothers me. "Roberto?" I ask her. "Have you ever . . . met him?"

Aysim shakes her head. "I saw him from a distance in

Constantinople. After I tried to dissuade my brother from his mad plans, he shut me out of everything."

"But Halim showed us a letter, in Roberto's hand-writing," Even now, those words of affection sting me— they seem so real, so true. "A love letter."

Aysim laughs bitterly. "My brother has a forger. A cunning man called Faruk. It must have been his work."

The plan is almost perfect. Paint Roberto as the cause for a war, sow discord among your enemies. But what sort of monster would try to kill his own sister?

"What can we do?" asks Bella Donna. "Is it too late?"

Not if I can present this girl to Massimo and the Council—if I can show them Roberto too. Then they'll have to believe me. Roberto will be pardoned, and the Doge's authority restored. As much as I dislike Massimo and the new leaders of Venice, they do care for their city. They are not heartless, like Halim. They will do what is best for Venice, when they are shown all the facts.

I hold out my hand to Aysim. "You must come with me," I say.

She's quaking again, and shakes her head. "Why? I've told you all I know."

"To make men listen."

43

Getting Roberto out of the house is easier than I expected. Father is asleep, and with Faustina keeping an eye on his door, I go to wake my fiancé. He looks so peaceful, his curls resting on the pillow. I kiss his lips, and he stirs.

"We must go to your father," I say. "I have the key to your freedom."

He dresses quickly in clothes Faustina has borrowed from the laundry, and we are soon outside in the predawn twilight. Aysim waits in a gondola, her shawl drawn over her head. Roberto nods politely to her, and she responds in kind.

"This is the woman you're supposed to have killed," I tell him. "Halim's sister."

"I recognize you," he says. "You were there—when I visited Constantinople."

"My brother likes to keep me close," she replies, "but not too close."

We disembark a few streets from the palace, and the gondolier slides off silently.

"Don't you need to pay him?" asks Roberto.

He hasn't seen the mark of the key subtly inscribed on the outside of the gondolier's oar. Nor does he see that, beneath the scarf, the pilot is a woman. "It's fine," I tell him. "I paid in advance."

As we approach the palace, Aysim takes my arm. "There's something I meant to tell you," she says. Her brow creases in concentration. "Halim has another accomplice in Venice — someone who used to send him secret messages."

I share a look with Roberto. "Do you know who?" I ask. "Carina?"

Aysim shakes her head. "I think it would be a man. Halim doesn't trust women. He thinks they're too emotional."

Another Venetian in league with Halim. How many traitors can one city hold to its bosom?

I push my thoughts aside as we enter the palace through a servants' doorway. We pass unhindered up a stairwell until an old man crosses our path. He's one of the many older grooms who wait on the Doge, and when he sees us he looks so startled I wonder if he might fall over. "Roberto?" he says.

"It is I, Carlo," Roberto replies. "Please, not a word of this to anyone."

The old man nods, and Roberto leads us on through the palace, creeping along the narrow, low-ceilinged corridors normally used by staff alone. Finally, after following the convoluted channels, we emerge from behind a curtain into a gallery within the Doge's private apartments. The golden ceiling and marble floors no longer intimidate me. The three of us walk to the set of double doors that leads to the Doge's office. Two uniformed guards see our approach, but although they gape with shock, they don't question Roberto's authority, and they throw open the doors. "Wait outside," I say to Aysim gently.

The Doge sits at a large desk with a small group of men, the faithful few who have stuck by him. He looks up at our appearance, and the scroll he is holding falls from his hands.

"My son!"

Roberto is already striding across the room, and within moments he is in his father's arms. The older man sobs with relief, rocking Roberto as he squeezes his eyes shut. No one says a word; we wait for the Doge to compose himself again. He holds Roberto at arm's length and shakes his head in amazement. "Where have you been?"

"We don't have much time," I interrupt. "Can we speak in private?"

There are low grumbles of protest from around the room.

"Do as she says," Roberto tells them. "If it weren't for Laura, I'd be dead."

After the men have shuffled out to an anteroom, I clear my throat. I tell the Doge that Halim's pretext for war is a lie. His sister isn't dead at all. The Doge shakes his head in disbelief.

"But I saw his face," he says. "He almost tore out his hair with grief."

"My brother—he is good actor," says a voice in faltering Italian. All eyes turn to see Aysim step into the room, drawing her scarf away to reveal black locks. "For years he fooled even me."

"You are his sister?" asks the Doge.

"The girl who is killed—she is my servant," says Aysim. "My friend, also."

The Doge's face darkens as he looks from Aysim to Roberto. "You'd better explain what's really happening."

"My brother wants war to . . . to make himself a man," says Aysim. "He use tricks."

"And why are you helping us?" asks the Doge. "You are no daughter of Venice."

His tone is hard. Too hard, I fear, but Aysim lifts her chin to answer him.

"My mother come from Venice," she says. "When I am small girl, she tell me of it, at night before I sleep. So I am part Venice, see?"

The Doge nods, and his hand falls heavily onto his desk. "And to think that villain would have taken my son's life. . . . We will blow his ships out of the water!"

"There's no need for bloodshed," I say.

"No need!" shouts the Doge. "Halim and his plotting almost cost us everything. My own Council turned against me."

"Laura's right," puts in Roberto. "We should expose them publicly. That way you can win back the support of the Council."

The Doge turns away from us and walks towards the west-facing window that opens onto St. Mark's. I can tell that he's thinking, measuring up one course of action against another. "This girl is wiser than most of my Council," he murmurs. When he turns again, a smile has crept over his lips. "Noon is the time when Prince Halim's ultimatum is due. Perhaps we can deliver more than he expects. Summon my messengers!"

44

When the time is close to midday, the main hall of the palace is crowded with men from the Grand Council and their retinues of clerks. The Doge has sent out word that his errant son has returned, and it's as much because of curiosity as anger that the men gather.

Aysim and I sit half hidden in a gallery above. We watch the Councilors flock into the chamber with their attendants. They preen and strut like exotic birds. Massimo is the last to appear, escorted by a dozen soldiers.

"Where is he?" he bellows. "Where is the murderer?"

The Doge, dressed in his officiating robes at the other end of the hall, looks calm. "He will be handed over when the Ottoman delegation arrives."

Massimo bristles. "If this is some trickery—"

"It's almost as if you're looking forward to battle," says the Doge.

From the look on Massimo's face, I rather suspect he is.

As the clock strikes noon, Faruk arrives at the head of several fearsome-looking footmen with their bare chests oiled. He strides into the heart of the chamber with his chin raised haughtily until he stands before the Doge's dais. I wonder if Massimo does not wish the Turks to know of his grab for power, as he did nothing to prevent the Doge from taking his usual place, nor did he ever expel him from the palace.

Ranged before the Doge are the men of the Grand Council. Behind them crowd lesser officials and scribes clutching parchment and quills. The room falls silent at last as they listen carefully to everything that's being said.

"I hear that your son Roberto has reappeared. I am pleased for you, Alfonso," Faruk says. "Pleased for Venice also."

There's a gasp—how dare he call the Doge by his first name! Faruk sends a quick, nervous smile around the court, realizing his mistake.

"Where is your master?" asks the Doge.

Faruk grins, and shrugs. "My master is not a fool. In this city, he trusts no one."

"Is that right?" asks the Doge. "We are men of honor."

Faruk's grin falls away. "I mean no disrespect to Your Honor," he says, "but now that your son is back, we'd like him to be handed over. As you are aware, Prince Halim wants to see justice done. If he can deal directly with Roberto, Venice will be saved"—he waves a hand through the air—"from a most unfortunate set of events."

The Doge gets to his feet. There is nothing of the frail old man about him now.

"I'm afraid that won't be possible," he says, maintaining his politeness despite all that's happened. "New information has come to light."

Angry muttering breaks out in the chamber, and the Doge waits for it to die away. He looks over the top of Faruk's head and snaps his fingers at us. I press gently at Aysim's back, and she stands, moving forward to the edge of the balcony. Her head is bowed modestly, and she is dressed in the latest Venetian fashion. But then she lifts her head to look into Faruk's eyes, and energy crackles through the room.

Faruk staggers back in recognition. He licks his lips nervously, his glance darting from the Doge back to his master's sister.

"Who is this woman?" he asks, his voice faltering. "I don't understand."

The Doge's eyes narrow. "Oh, I think you do."

Faruk seems to see that there's no denying Aysim's existence and switches his tactic. He gives a cry and lifts his hands towards the balcony. "Princess Aysim! You're alive!"

The assembled Councilors burst out in exclamations. Aysim's glare doesn't shift from Faruk.

"It's a miracle," he continues. "Prince Halim will be saying prayers of thanks all night!"

"It's not a miracle, Faruk," she replies in Italian. "Your killing men found Emen in my place. By her death, your crime is seen."

The Doge motions his head, and several soldiers, sensing the shift in power once more, draw their swords. Faruk's attendants do the same. Most of the Councilors, my father included, huddle around the perimeter of the chamber.

"You would not harm an ambassador?" asks Faruk.

The Doge points at him, taking a step nearer. "I would not," he says. "I will show you more respect than you have shown us. Go back to your cowardly master. Tell him that if he has not left my harbor within the hour, I will smash his ships under the iron fist of Venice. Do you understand?"

Faruk looks to his men, then backs away, before turning and retreating to the door through which he entered. Aysim takes her seat beside me once again and smiles.

"Did I perform well?" she asks in French.

"Perfectly," I say. "It's time for us to go down and tell our story."

The Councilors are stunned into silence, and Massimo's face burns red with shame. The Doge stands before them.

"We were all taken in by Halim's deception," he says, "but now we must stand together again. Swear loyalty to me, and the past will be forgotten."

One by one, the members of the Council line up to kneel at the Doge's feet and kiss the ring on his right hand. I hear my father muttering something about "never doubting you, my lord"; loyalty is as fickle as the winds of the sea.

Massimo, I notice, is last in line. "Forgive me," he says, bowing obsequiously.

The Doge's jaw is set hard. "Of all those who turned against me, your actions were the most disappointing."

"My lord, I—"

"But you are a good soldier, and Venice needs you more than ever," he says. "Halim may still risk a fight. Can I trust you, Massimo?"

"I will do everything in my power to serve you," says the soldier.

The Doge's face relaxes into a smile. "Then go. Keep the fleet on alert."

Massimo steps down from the dais and summons his

men around him. They process out of the chamber, leaving only the Doge, Aysim and me.

"Come here, child," the Doge tells me. He takes my hand and brings me to sit beside him. "I owe you everything."

"Our fight is not over yet," I warn him. "It has only just begun."

45

My limbs feel heavy with tiredness, yet my mind is awash with a hundred thoughts. I kiss Roberto farewell and make my way back home with Faustina. Aysim has been given a room in the palace, and the parties are already under way as news of Faruk's departure spreads. Apparently his oarsmen rowed him from the harbor at quite a pace. Musicians sprinkle the alleys with their melodies, and laughter, so long absent from our city, seems to have returned. I hear snatches of a conversation between two laborers in the doorway of a tavern. "I always knew the Doge had it in him!" one says.

I can't help a rueful smile. Only a few days ago, people were saying that the Doge's days were numbered. Now they clamor to pour praise on his head.

Father is already at home. As I walk into his library, accompanied by Faustina, he twists round in his tall armchair to look at me.

"I suppose I owe you an apology," he says, closing his book.

"That's up to you," I reply. "You're the master of this house, after all."

His face softens, but he drops his gaze. "I was wrong about Roberto," he says. "He will make a fine husband."

"Better than Vincenzo?" I ask.

Faustina snorts with derision, but Father silences her with a glare. A smile plays on his lips. "Perhaps," he mutters. "Although he will surely be a hero when his fleet helps defeat those wretched Turks."

"Surely Halim will not fight now," I say.

"He'd be a fool to do so," my father agrees. "Massimo has stockpiled enough gunpowder to sink Halim's fleet of ships—to sink ten fleets!"

Not if Teresa's information is correct, he hasn't. But there's no reason my father would know this. "Then let us hope there's no bloodshed at all," I say.

"At any rate, this is men's work now," Father says, turning back to his book.

After I've left the room, Faustina begins to climb the stairs. "Would you like me to take the pins out of your hair?" she asks.

Something is troubling me, and it's not just my father's brash confidence in a Venetian victory. I shake my head, trying not to let my face betray the turmoil of my emotions. "No, thank you."

When I hear Faustina's door close on the upper level, I stand for a moment on the stairs, letting my thoughts lead me. Something about the gunpowder doesn't add up. If it's useless, and there was no reason for Silvio to make up such a lie to his wife, Massimo can't possibly be so sure of himself. He must know the battle is far from won.

I head straight back out the front door. My suspicion is building like an unstoppable flood. It's a conspiracy grander than anything the Segreta could achieve, but it's possible.

For if the Segreta didn't murder Silvio—and I'm sure they did not—then who did? Could it have been the man who knows that the barrels of gunpowder stored in the Arsenal are useless? Could he be Silvio's murderer?

I know my mind is getting ahead of itself, that I'm seeing treason where perhaps there is none. But Aysim said that her brother had a fellow plotter in Venice. What if that person is the very man Venice expects will save them? Massimo was quick enough to depose the Doge when he had the chance. His loyalty is only to himself.

Enough gunpowder to sink ten fleets.

Or not even enough for a fireworks party.

Could the Bear of Venice be about to turn his claws upon us?

It's dark when I reach the palace, and all the way I've been turning over the possibilities. There's a chance, of course, that Silvio was wrong about the powder, but if he wasn't . . .

It's easy enough to gain access to Roberto's quarters. The guard at the gate can hardly suppress his grin. I find Roberto asleep in a chair. After so many days in captivity, he's still exhausted. He smiles lazily as I wake him. "Am I dreaming?"

"I need to ask you something," I say, perching on the edge of his chair. "Did Massimo accompany the delegation to Constantinople earlier this year?"

Roberto's grin fades as he catches the seriousness of my

tone. He rubs his head. "Yes. He was there as an escort with a small detachment of men. They were rude and loud, and he was told not to attend the evening banquet."

My simmering suspicions begin to boil over. "I think he's a traitor."

"Well, he all but usurped my father—"

"No," I interrupt, "a traitor to Venice."

"What do you mean?" asks Roberto. "He commands our fleet against the Ottomans."

"If I'm right," I say, "it's our fleet he means to send beneath the waves."

Roberto's eyes widen. "How?"

I explain to him what I know about the gunpowder. "What if he's sending the ships out unarmed? They'd be sitting ducks in the water."

Roberto frowns. "Where did you come by this information?"

"You cannot ask me that, but I think my source is reliable."

Roberto shakes his head, and strokes my cheek. "But I've seen the plans. Vincenzo has plenty of gunpowder of his own."

"Vincenzo's ships may not be enough to defeat Prince Halim. Think about it. If the Turks were to conquer us, they'd need a strong leader here. Massimo would be the obvious candidate. And what about the men who kidnapped you? They must have been soldiers too. Perhaps they were working for the Bear."

I can tell that Roberto isn't convinced. "You're seeing conspiracy where it doesn't exist," he says. "This soldier who was killed, he probably tried to swindle the wrong man in a game of dice."

Something about his earnest eyes in the candlelight soothes me. He's right. I've spent too long in the presence of the Segreta, seeing secrets knotting themselves together.

"Massimo may be ambitious, but he's a soldier through and through," Roberto says. "My father trusts his loyalty to Venice, if not to the Doge. Venice is Massimo's city too. Do you think he would risk his men and his home to become an Ottoman puppet? I'm sure the gunpowder must have been replaced by now."

I smile weakly. "You must think I'm stupid."

"I think you're beautiful," he replies, leaning forward to kiss me. "I also think the servants will start talking if you stay much longer."

I ease myself from his chair and wish him good night.

"Sleep well," he says.

I do sleep well, for the first time in a long while. I don't even hear the rain that must have poured throughout the night, for the garden's washed bright green, and puddles stand in the lanes beside the house. The blue sky is trailed with wisps of cloud, and the air smells clean.

Soldiers are patrolling the city, Bianca tells me, just in case of a surprise attack, but by noon we receive word that all but a handful of ships from the Ottoman fleet have vanished from the horizon.

"The upstart has fled!" my father announces.

I think of Halim on board his ship, brooding on his foiled plans. I can't help but smirk, imagining his fury.

Shortly after our conversation, we receive an invitation

to the palace. There's to be a celebration in honor of the Doge and the power of Venice. My father can't stop smiling as he hums a naval song.

"I've never seen him so happy," mutters Faustina. "He actually kissed me on the cheek this morning."

I grin, and dispatch a note to Roberto. It contains only three words, but what else matters?

46

That night, I'm back at the palace, wearing a dress that once belonged to Beatrice. It has a girdle of woven gold, with white silk tassels hanging from the waist. The skirt hangs around me in heavy black folds with gold thread running through the velvet. Gold satin slippers peek out from beneath the hem, while against the perfumed curls of my hair, I wear a light veil with crystals embroidered into the net. I feel my cheeks flush in the warmth. My arm is linked through Roberto's, and he keeps me close by his side. He wears an ivory padded doublet, slashed in the shape of stars and crosses to reveal the taffeta lining. Over the top he wears a short, gold-embroidered cape. His beard is trimmed and his bruises have almost faded away. I have my fiancé back.

Father saunters alongside us, then hurries to slap a friend on the back.

"I told you, Luca. We sent those Turks running!"

Along with the other noble men and women, I stroll beneath the oil paintings that line the Doge's palace and step inside the ballroom. The first face I recognize is that of Aysim, who throws herself into my arms. She is resplendent in a dress of mulberry silk, with rows of glass buttons down the bodice. Her hair is plaited with flowers. This is a far cry from the frightened girl I first found cowering in a nun's cell.

"Thank you, thank you!" she cries. Around us, people look startled. I hold a finger to my lips to hush her.

"Most people here don't know how much I am responsible for the turn of events, and they must never know," I tell her, glancing up at Roberto. "That's how Venice works."

Aysim frowns. "Will I ever understand your city?" she asks in French.

"If you stay here long enough." The voice echoes with authority. Turning round, we see the Doge in his white peaked cap and ermine robes. He extends his gnarled hands, and we each place a palm in his. Roberto gives his father a small bow.

"You'll have asylum in Venice as long as you need it," he tells Aysim. "For life, if you wish. You've been through many trials."

Aysim's eyes brim with tears. "I will like that," she manages in Italian, dipping in a curtsy.

"You'll be treated like the princess you are as long as you stay," he adds.

The Doge's wife, Besina, arrives by his side. This is the first time I've seen her since Nicolo's funeral. There's some color in her cheeks and, although she's lost weight, she's still taking great care over her appearance; her hair is coiled neatly and her jewels are sparkling.

"We would be proud to have you continue to stay with us," she says.

The Doge lets our hands fall and puts an arm around his wife's shoulders. It's the most informal thing I've ever seen him do. Roberto comes to stand on the other side of his mother.

"My son," she whispers. Then she looks at me. "We owe you our deepest gratitude," she says.

"You owe me nothing," I tell her. "I only did what any woman would, for Venice and the man she loves."

The Duchess nods. "If you'll excuse us." She strokes Roberto's cheek; then she takes Aysim and leads her around the room, introducing her to the guests as men of state crowd around the Doge. It feels as if things are returning to their natural balance. Then, as Roberto talks to a group of men, and the Doge converses with his Councilors, the unwelcome face of Vincenzo appears.

"Laura," he says, his stale breath washing over me. "May I speak to you in private?" His glance flickers towards Roberto, hostile.

"We have nothing to say to each other," I tell him.

"Now, now," Vincenzo replies. "Can't we both be happy?"

I'm actually grateful when Massimo comes to our side. The Bear is wearing a puffed-up velvet jacket. He motions to a passing servant, who holds out glasses of wine on a tray. Massimo hands one to me. "Could you excuse us?" he says to Vincenzo.

The old man looks disappointed, but he bows. "Of course."

When he's gone, Massimo smiles. "You looked like you needed rescuing."

I take a few polite sips of wine. We make small talk about the good fortune of the city, and he even says how foolish he felt on learning of Halim's deception. But his cold eyes watch me carefully, searching for my reaction to his words. I cast my eyes around for Roberto, and can't see him anywhere. I can hear my father laughing from across the room—deep, drunken guffaws.

"Tell me, Laura," says Massimo suddenly, "what do you think of these women called the Segreta?"

The air suddenly feels hotter, and I quickly swallow a mouthful of wine. Does he know? Could he?

"I'm sure their malign influence has been blown out of proportion," I say.

"They tell me you were close to Allegreza."

I hold his gaze. "I was," I say, "which is why I have such doubts about the power or even existence of any secret society. I feel she would not have kept it from me. At any rate, it sounds rather far-fetched."

Massimo raises his own goblet, grinning. "Quite right!" he says. "Here's to the future—whatever it may hold." We clink glasses, and I take another sip.

Roberto arrives at last and holds out a hand. "May I have this dance?" he asks.

Placing my wine on a passing tray, I turn to Massimo. "It was a pleasure speaking with you."

"Perhaps we shall do so again," he replies.

When we've walked away to where others are dancing, Roberto asks, "What was that all about?"

"I still don't trust that man," I say.

We link the crooks of our arms and circle one another. "Can't you forget about it?" says Roberto. "Tonight's supposed to be a celebration. Just enjoy yourself."

The steps of the dance are simple, but as we turn on the spot, I feel a little dizzy and stumble. Roberto catches me. "Are you all right?"

"I think so," I say. There's a dull pain building across the front of my head. "Too much wine, maybe."

"Perhaps I should take you home?"

I hold a hand to my brow as Roberto steers me through the crowds. From the edge of my blurred vision, I see him gesturing to someone; then suddenly my old nurse is beside me, holding me up.

"Child, what's happened to you?" Faustina asks. I find I can't answer; my lips won't work.

She and Roberto help me into a coach stationed beneath an archway, safely away from prying eyes.

"I'll be fine in a moment," I say, but I can hear my own voice slurring.

Roberto presses a hand against my shoulder, forcing me to sink back on the cushioned seats of the coach. The look of concern on his face frightens me. "You need rest. Driver, take her home."

I don't have the energy to protest. It has been such an anxious few days. Perhaps all I need is sleep.

When I wake, the tang of salty air stirs in my nostrils. I sit up, my body lurching to one side. The pain in my head is still there, worse than before. Cautiously, I squint out from behind my eyelashes and see the darting points of waves. Where am I?

I snap my eyes open, dim sunlight making them water. My tongue sticks to the roof of my mouth, and I gaze down at my black velvet skirt. Wasn't I wearing this in the ballroom? Where am I now? How long have I been sleeping in my gown?

"I don't understand," I mumble, glancing around me.

We're in a white-painted rowing boat. Faustina huddles in the prow, weeping softly, while two men stand, each maneuvering an oar through the water. "I tried to stop them," she says, seeming to plead for my forgiveness.

Beyond Faustina's shoulders, Venice recedes out of sight. The pointed tower of St. Mark's has grown so small that I can barely see the gilded angel that sits on top of the belfry. The boat swings on the choppy waves beyond our city's harbor, and nausea squirms in my stomach.

I hear a cruel laugh behind me. I twist round on the bench I'm slumped on and see Faruk watching me.

"Welcome aboard," he says.

"Where are you taking me?" My thoughts can barely keep up with what's happening, but one realization slams into me: The wine last night. It was drugged.

Massimo.

"Haven't you guessed?" Faruk asks. He points towards a large ship, squatting among others farther out beyond the harbor. "Halim is waiting for his concubine."

47

"What will happen to us?" Faustina sobs. "These brutes are capable of terrible things!" She wraps her shawl more tightly around her bosom. Despite the pain in my head and my parched throat, I give her a reassuring smile. "We'll be fine," I tell her, wishing I could believe my own words.

I shift myself awkwardly across the boat, trying to anticipate each lunge and swell of the sea. I stumble, falling like a toddler at my old wet nurse's feet. She helps me up onto the bench, and we sit side by side, my arm around her shoulders as she turns her face into the crook of my neck.

"What shall we do?" she asks softly. Faruk is gazing out to sea, his eyes fixed on Halim's ship. All around is water.

"You have to trust me," I whisper into her hair, "I'll get us out of here."

"Here?" Faustina pulls away to reveal a tearstained face, and looks out at the ocean that surrounds us. "It's hopeless. I can't even swim!"

Our little boat draws up beside Halim's ship. Canvas

299

sails are rolled tightly. Cannons bristle from its lower decks. It's as impressive as I remember, the awning over Halim's pavilion decorated with golden tassels. Smaller ships are ranged around it. Their shallow keels mean that Halim's crew can sail in close to Venice's harbor, should cannons not be enough and they want to use swords too.

Halim appears on the deck. He's wearing scarlet robes with a sash of gold, and on his head is a blue turban. In one hand he carries a golden staff, and in the other a drooping chrysanthemum. Even from this distance, his dark eyes glimmer. He gives us a deep bow.

"Lower the gangplank," he orders, straightening up.

Faustina grabs my hands, crushing them in her terrified grip. "They'll slit our throats!" she murmurs.

One by one, I prise my fingers free. I need her to calm down. "The Turks are civilized people. They'll do no such thing." I know she won't really believe this, so I turn to whisper in her ear. "And Halim has a soft spot for me."

She gasps, and her mouth opens as if to protest. Even dear old Faustina catches my meaning. "You can't!" she hisses.

Faruk prods us to stand, and we climb stiffly up the gangplank. It isn't wide, and as the ship and boat sway in the water, the narrow length of wood shifts so that we move in shuffling steps. This is not the most graceful entrance I've ever made. Finally, I jump to the deck and reach down to help Faustina. Beside Halim, clutching a curved sword, is one of the men who guarded his apartments in Venice.

"What an unexpected surprise," Halim says, looking sharply at Faruk. The older man's cheeks color.

"A gift from our friends," he says.

"I'm no gift," Faustina says, turning her face away.

Faruk laughs cruelly. "I wasn't talking about you, old crone!" He shoves me rudely in the small of my back, and I stagger forward. My hand slaps across his face before I can stop myself. The snake only grins as he touches his cheek. "You'll be tamed," he says. "In time."

Halim smiles at me, his teeth sparkling white against the mahogany of his skin. He's still handsome. A handsome monster.

I shake my head in disgust and all thoughts of reasoning with this despicable man vanish. "You murderer. To think I almost kissed you!"

Faustina lets out a small, scandalized gasp but Halim ignores her, arching an eyebrow.

"You make me sound so devious, when you put it like that," he says. "I assure you, I only ever pursued justice. But I see that my plans have been exposed." He pauses. Placing his staff in the crook of his arm, he starts to pluck petals from the chrysanthemum, allowing them to flutter down one by one to the wooden planks of the deck. "A shame, because the game isn't over yet."

The sun comes out from behind a cloud, and the light sparkles off the sea, forcing me to shield my face with a hand. It's almost impossible to read the expression on Halim's face.

He gives a short laugh. "Venice will be mine by nightfall."

"Roberto is safe," I tell him, "and your sister will never have to see your face again. Venice will resist you."

For a moment, his brow creases. "We'll see," he says. He casts out a hand and sweeps it through the air, taking in my body from the topmost curl on my head to the satin slippers on my feet. "Anyway, I already have Venice's most precious jewel."

"It's lost, all lost!" Faustina cries, sinking to her knees.

Faruk comes to stand beside his master, and the two of them look out at the shores of Venice. "Are you ready to see your city aflame?" Faruk sneers.

I send him an icy glare. "You may have bought Massimo, but Vincenzo's fleet —"

Halim gives a bark of laughter and hurls away the bare stalk of the chrysanthemum. "Oh, Vincenzo! Savior of Venice! If only it were so."

Faruk is grinning too. The breeze around us stiffens, and I understand. *A gift from our friends,* Faruk said. More than one.

I shake my head. "No — he wouldn't —"

"Will someone explain to me what is going on?" wails Faustina.

Halim smiles. "That's right. The man your father would have you marry, the person you dismissed as an old fool? When I raise a flag from my mast, he'll be waiting for the signal. He'll turn his cannons on the Venetian fleet. The Doge's ships, armed with nothing but useless powder, will be aflame within moments." He brings his face close to mine; I have to force myself not to cringe away. "And there's nothing you can do, my Laura."

So Massimo and Vincenzo were in league all along. That's why the Bear summoned him back. They worked together at the party last night, Vincenzo drawing me to one side while Massimo applied the tainted wine. It is no secret how much I despise Vincenzo. But to be capable of something like this? It is unthinkable.

The attendant guards us at swordpoint while Halim strides across the decks, organizing his men. Flags are raised, giving signals to other ships in the fleet. Men scurry this way and that, readying themselves for battle. When Halim passes close to me, I can't help but call to him.

"Your sister meant nothing to you, did she?"

He smiles, but only anger lights up behind his eyes. "You're wrong. She betrayed our plans. I loved her until that moment."

"She sought to uphold the honor of both our countries," I say.

Halim scoffs. "This is war. Honor is an abstract concept. There is only victory, or defeat."

"Then I hope you taste the latter."

Halim jerks his chin at something beyond my shoulder, and I twist round to take in the sight of Venice's fleet sailing towards us, ready to chase the Ottomans out of sight.

"We shall soon find out," he says.

The long Venetian galleys sit low in the water. Their sails bulge as gold flags flutter at the top of the masts, and the decks are crowded with men—officers, soldiers and sailors.

I spot Vincenzo's ships. Each has three masts; sails bearing his crest snap in the wind. The sea swells, and water foams as they carve a path through the water. They're gaining on the Venetian ships by the moment.

My mouth turns dry. The Doge's men are trapped between a traitor and a madman. As I watch the ships moving through the water in formation, my stomach knots. Vincenzo might be easily bought, but I will never give in to men like Halim. I must find a way to fight back.

I turn around, careful to erase the expression of anger from my face. I needn't have worried; Halim is not thinking about me anymore.

"Raise the red flag!" he shouts, pushing me out of the way. He goes to stand at the edge of the ship, braced between two swivel-mounted guns. Men are sponging the barrels and carrying the iron balls into position.

"Are we going to die, Laura?" Faustina asks in a quavering voice.

"Not if I can help it," I tell her.

A man pulls on a rope, craning his head back to gaze at the sky. Halim's flag unfurls and flutters out, then begins to rise slowly up the mast.

This is it, I think. *The battle begins.*

As ropes are tightened and tied off, the sails catch the wind, and the ship begins to move through the water. The whole fleet stirs. We slice through swells as men scramble to and fro through hatches. From below deck I hear pounding feet and shouted instructions as the well-drilled crew go about their loading.

As we sail to within a hundred yards, Halim offers his arm. "Better hold on to something," he says.

I don't take it, and he bellows an order. Suddenly the sails snap, and the ship's prow jerks to one side. I'm thrown into Faustina, and we both stagger across deck. As I climb to my feet and help my old nurse, I see we're floating parallel with the first Venetian ship. Halim shouts again and men angle the cannon barrels towards my countrymen.

"Please!" I hear myself shout. "Don't do this!"

In turn, Venetian seamen line the side of their vessel, staring over the barrels of muskets or crouched beside their cannons.

"I don't believe it," Halim murmurs.

His face is white with shock. Faruk is backing away, towards some steps leading down into the pit of the ship, terror writ large over his face.

Then I spot what they've already seen. Beneath the crest of Vincenzo's ship, on the deck of *Il Castigo,* a man strides towards the stern of the vessel. He moves confidently, with youth and strength. Where are Vincenzo's stooped shoulders and limp? The stranger climbs up to hold on to the forward-facing mast of the ship and waves a sword in the air, his legs braced.

"That's not Vincenzo," Faustina says, her voice cracking.

"No, it's not," I say.

It's Roberto!

48

Cannons bristle from the side of Vincenzo's ships as they steer round, trained on the Ottoman fleet. On us.

Halim's men look to their leader. "What are you waiting for?" he shouts. "Attack positions!"

A faint shout of command from Roberto carries on the air. Instantly, his ship lurches in the water to bring itself side-on, and the first cannon muzzle flares from *Il Castigo*. A second later, a boom cracks through the air, and the water beside our ship explodes, showering us all in spray. Faustina and I fall to our knees. Low clouds of smoke billow upwards, making us cough and our eyes water. Immediately, there's another forceful boom and our ship heaves dangerously to one side. For a moment, our deck slopes as steeply as a cliff face and I grasp the railings with one hand, my other fist holding on to Faustina's collar to stop her from sliding down. She's sobbing with terror.

"Save me, Laura. Save me!"

The ship levels out, water spilling over the deck. Halim has run to the other side, and is braced behind the second mast. He shouts back what can only be an order for his own men to fire. The ship shakes and roars as a volley of cannonballs replies. I can barely look as the rounds howl away, smashing into the water just short of *Il Castigo*.

Gunfire fills the air as more cannonballs fly towards us. Halim's men are struggling to return fire—one of their guns goes careening across the deck as if it weighs nothing. Young men race down below deck and come up hauling fresh supplies of powder as the crew hastily wipes down the cannon.

Halim shouts more orders, and the ship steers tightly in the water. The sails lull and snap tight once more, but we're heading away from the fight. Away from Venice.

I grab hold of Faustina and drag her back under the canvas awning, poking our heads out to watch.

Faruk emerges from belowdecks, keeping his body low as he scuttles across to his master. There's a thin whistling sound and another iron ball crashes into the deck. Planks of wood splinter and explode. Faruk's body is there one moment, whipped away the next. My eyes find him on the other side of the ship, lying still. One side of his skull is dented and a trickle of blood emerges from the corner of his mouth. His legs are twisted beneath him, and he groans with pain as a shard of white bone breaks through the fabric of his tunic, blood blossoming around it. His eyes seem to fix on mine, then narrow, until they roll back and he stills.

Low groans emerge from other injured men like a terrible choir of pain. Blood circles out around the body of a sailor lying prone on the deck, reaching out pathetically, calling a word over and over. It might be for water, it might be for his mother—I can't tell. At a short distance from him, another crew member clutches his head in his hands, where the powder from his gun has exploded in his face. Others are still trying to load the guns. They suddenly look hopeless; nothing like the battle-hungry men sending out war cries only a few moments ago. The whole of the Venetian fleet is turning as one.

Halim staggers over to his old servant and kneels beside him, passing a palm over his eyes to close them. Faustina maintains a low wailing, and flames flicker at the corner of one of the sails, from sparks sent out by the gunpowder. The ship leans heavily as we cut our retreat. *Il Castigo* is already lagging.

Halim seizes a passing soldier by the collar, and shouts at him while pointing to us. He looks at me. "I can't listen to that noise a moment longer."

Faustina's cheeks are wet with tears as we're roughly pulled to our feet. "They'll throw us overboard!" she screams.

But our guard jostles us belowdecks instead. It seems incredible, but Halim must want us out of harm's way. We pass behind more rows of cannons, through bitter smoke and heat, men struggling to maneuver them into the gunports. I step over a dead man's body.

"Hurry up!" Our captor takes us around a corner, along a short corridor, and then pushes us into a cabin. He smiles grimly, his face shiny with sweat. "Enjoy yourselves," he says, before slamming the small door shut.

We listen to the lock sliding into place. Faustina clings to me. "This will be our tomb," she says.

We're surrounded by wooden boxes. There's some

navigational equipment on a low table, and I recognize a sextant. Rolls of charts are tucked into a shelf. I wonder if Faustina is right. One direct hit, and this ship will be blown to splinters. I prise the lid from one of the crates with the edge of a compass. It contains what looks like spare sail-cloth. I try the next, a smaller box, and find what I was hoping for. An unmistakable fine black powder. If a flame reaches this room, at least our death will be quick. It would be far worse to drown slowly, pulled into the depths by the sodden weight of my clothes.

The noises of battle continue beyond. Explosions, muffled thumps, the singing cannonballs and above it all the screams of the raging and the dying.

As I see it, we have two choices. Either Halim is defeated and goes down with the ship, or he makes his escape and we never see Venice again. Either way, we lose.

"I can't go to Constantinople," says Faustina. "The food will never agree with me."

Despite everything, I laugh. "We won't be going to Constantinople." Then I see there's a third choice, and at once I have a plan.

I grab the sextant lying on a side—its angle-arc, eye-pieces and handle are all solid brass, and it's heavier than it looks. I throw myself against the door. "I'll do anything if you'll let us out!" I cry desperately. "Please! Anything!" I can only hope that the sailor understands the full meaning of my words.

"What are you doing?" Faustina asks, frowning at the sextant in my hand.

"Getting us out of here," I hiss. I bang the door again. "Please. Help us!"

There's the sound of the lock being drawn back. I wait behind the door, standing on a crate, and put a finger to my lips. Faustina nods uncertainly.

The door creaks open. The same sweat-smeared sailor pokes his head into the room, and I bring the sextant down on his temple with a thud. Faustina yelps as he falls, a dead weight at my feet. "Help me with him," I say. We bend over, taking an armpit each, and drag his body aside. I check that the corridor beyond is empty, then grab the hem of my skirt and begin tearing at it with my teeth and nails.

"What are you doing?" Faustina protests. "For heaven's sake, do you know how much that dress cost?"

"I think the dress is ruined already," I say. Faustina hesitates, then comes beside me and shows me how to find the warp and weft of the fabric, tearing easily along the line of the weave. The two of us rip my skirts into lengths of fabric. Soon, there's nothing left to guard my modesty but my underskirt.

"Twist them into ropes," I instruct Faustina. We work quickly, knotting the silk until it resembles a rope of sorts — enough to carry a flame along its length. I take the box of gunpowder down and pour it in the far corner of the room, then carefully lay one end of the silk rope in the powder and trail the rope towards the open door. Finally, I feel through the sailor's pockets, rifling through his clothes until I find what I'm looking for — a flint box.

"Wait outside," I tell Faustina.

She finally understands, and her eyes widen. "You're going to blow up the ship?" she asks.

"Yes, and unless you want to go up with it, I'd move."

Faustina gathers her skirts, and I kneel beside the end

of the rope and light a spark, bringing it down in cupped hands. The silk sets alight easily and the flame fizzes and hisses slowly along its length.

"Time to go!" I drag Faustina after me. Above our heads the cannons are quiet for a moment. We must be maneuvering into position. Voices call out desperate commands.

We head in the opposite direction, not towards the lower gun deck, but towards a leaning stepladder. Through an open hatch, I see smoke in great drifting swathes overhead. I go first, poking my head through. Dead and injured men lie everywhere, the planks slick with blood. A mast hangs at an awkward angle, the sail in shreds. One man rushes past, missing an arm, but hardly seeming to care. For the first time since this battle began, I feel a well of horror swell in my chest.

"Come on!" I hiss to Faustina. My limbs are trembling as I climb into the open. The deck pitches and judders as the keel smashes through rolling waves. There is one remaining mast at full sail, but still she's fast. I run to the railings, over an injured man whispering a prayer, and see another ship — yes, *Il Castigo* — in pursuit.

"You!" cries a voice filled with fury. I swivel round to see Halim glaring at me. "Do you know what you've cost me?" He lunges and I shrink back. At the same moment, the ship gives a massive shudder. An explosion rips through the air. The gunpowder.

Halim staggers to one side, his mouth hanging open with terror. Splinters of wood erupt into the air, and I cower, shielding my head with my hands. The ship lurches heavily to one side and water swells over my feet. I grab the mast and cling to it as a man slides past me, crying out. His body plunges through the broken railings and disappears over the side of the ship, flailing into the waves.

There's the hiss and roil of water gushing into the lower quarters. It's as though the sea is sinking its jaws into our ship. Faustina cries out in terror, clinging to a barrel that's slipping down the deck. I reach out and just manage to pull her to me as the barrel crashes through the railings and goes the same way as the sailor, into the watery depths.

"Here. Hold on." I wrap her arms around the mast and grab her chin, forcing her to look into my eyes. "You have to be strong. You have to save yourself."

The glint of metal catches my eye. Halim has drawn his sword and is climbing slowly to his feet. "It should not have been this way!" he shouts, staring at me, his nostrils flaring. His turban is streaked with blood and the gold sash has been torn from his body so that his tunic hangs in rags.

"Your fate is no one's fault but your own," I hiss back.

I spring away, past the main mast, and try to pick my way up the sloping deck. I can hear his grunts of effort as he climbs and slides after me. I clamber over a fallen mast and find myself trapped between the ship's wheel and a rearing section of the broken deck. Any other men still here ignore me, too busy trying to save their own lives. They hang on to smashed rigging or leap into the water.

I twist round on my backside and come face to face with Halim. He's been scrambling on his hands and knees, but now he straightens up. His mouth twists in a jubilant smile as he raises his sword in a bloody hand above me. There's no way out, but I'm not scared anymore.

"Just do it!" I shout.

As I brace myself, there's a soft thud, and something

happens to Halim's face. The smile of victory softens and slides. His brow creases in confusion. His sword hand falls, and the weapon clatters to the deck; then Halim follows it. He crashes onto the planks at my feet, face-first. A huge splinter of wood emerges from between his shoulder blades, blood spreading over his tunic. And behind Halim, gasping for breath, stands Faustina. She's soaked through from lying in the water that floods over the deck. "I wasn't going to let him kill you," Faustina pants.

We both stare down at the prone figure of an Ottoman prince.

I manage to get to my feet and hug my savior close to me as the ship jerks and shifts beneath us. If this is the end, I want us to face it together. "Thank you," I say. "Thank you."

A hand grasps my ankle, and I stumble to my knees. Faustina falls backwards with a cry, cracking her head on the wheel. Halim's face, twisted with anger, grimaces through bloodstained teeth. The wood still protrudes from his back, and he's mad with rage. I kick, catching his shoulder, then clamber on top of him. His hands flail at me, and his throat gives out a bloodcurdling cackle. I push his arms aside and find his throat with my fingers. I press tighter and tighter, watching his eyes bulge in their sockets as the seawater froths around his shoulders and over my knees. He tries to speak, but nothing comes out. I squeeze with all my strength, pushing his face beneath the welling water. His hands scrabble at my arms, but I push harder, gritting my teeth.

At last, slowly, the fight leaves him. His arms slacken. A trickle of bubbles escapes between his gnashing teeth, and his face is suddenly peaceful once more. This time there is no doubt that his life is over.

I drag myself back up to standing. Faustina is seated against the wheel, her face dazed, blood leaking from a cut under her hairline. The ship sinks farther with each second that passes.

"He won't be bothering us again," I tell her. For once, Faustina is too shocked even to cry.

I crouch beside her and throw her arm over my shoulder. My God, she's heavy! The water climbs up to our knees as the sea starts to swallow Halim's ship. The sails billow on the water, and the rest of the ship's carcass turns ghostly as it sinks beneath the surface. I feel my feet leave the deck below, and I struggle to tread water. Faustina throws her arms over a floating piece of timber.

Then the shadow of another ship looms over us, and I look up to see Roberto standing at the gunwale.

He rushes across the deck of his ship. "Hold on!"

He climbs onto the rail and dives off, entering the water like a graceful dart among the floating bodies and detritus. His head breaks the water a few yards away and he swims towards us with powerful strokes.

I hold tight to Faustina with one hand. What's left of my dress is soaked and heavy. "We're going to be all right," I tell her.

As we sail back to the shore, I want nothing more than to fall asleep, but even though I have a blanket wrapped around me, a violent shivering keeps me from slumber. Faustina is muttering her discomforts to the poor young sailor trying to dress her wound.

"How did you find us?" I ask.

"It's Bianca you should thank," Roberto says, stroking my hair. "She noticed you hadn't come home, and told your father. He in turn came to the palace."

Roberto tells me he was wild with concern, and realized that only one person might know my whereabouts.

"I remembered what you said about Massimo. You were right, and I should have trusted your judgment all along. My father sent soldiers to the barracks, and they arrested him. At first he played innocent, but when we asked about the gunpowder, he couldn't deny it. The interrogators only had to show him the thumbscrews for him to start blabbing about the rest. He named Vincenzo as his coconspirator, and laid out all the plans that Halim had put in place."

"So Vincenzo has been found too?"

Roberto shakes his head. "He must have gotten wind of Massimo's arrest. They found his apartments empty. They've put a watch on the harbor, but he's a wealthy man. He's probably slipped through the net."

As long as he's gone, I'm too tired to care anymore. I find a smile, despite everything. "I wonder if my father still thinks of him as a good suitor," I say.

Laughter makes Roberto's chest shake beneath my head. Finally, I let my eyes drift closed.

49

I stand in the center of St. Mark's Cathedral. The domed roof with its tiny windows casts a buttery light over the people below, reflected off the gold leaf.

Roberto stands beside me, looking more handsome than I've ever seen him, even with a bandage still tied around his right hand. I wear a dress of green velvet, stamped with gold. My hair cascades over my shoulders, and my head is crowned with a woven circle of flowers that Faustina picked from our gardens this morning. I wear a shawl to hide the last of my bruises, but in a day or so no one will ever be able to tell that I was once on a ship bound for Constantinople, fighting for my life.

My husband gazes down into my face. "I love you," he says gently, bringing a hand round to stroke my cheek. I bend my head to meet his touch, and grab his hand to bring his fingers to my lips, kissing them.

I am a married woman now. Roberto and I have said our final vows before the priest and we turn, hand in hand, to our guests. Smiling faces are everywhere, and beyond the open doors at the rear of the cathedral there are more people, spilling out onto the streets. Even with its high ceilings, the cathedral is warm with the press of bodies. Everyone in Venice has gathered to celebrate the marriage of a man once spurned by the city and a woman almost lost at sea.

The Doge and the Duchess Besina sit in the front row, beside my father. The Doge, imperious in his robes of office, nods his head, and the Duchess beams with delight. Once, she thought she'd lost both sons. Now, Roberto is returned to her. Not only that, but he has helped save Venice.

Roberto leads me down the main nave of the cathedral, towards the sunlight that pours through the open doors. As we pass, people get to their feet, applauding. Young children give chase, scattering flower petals for us to walk through. The Basilica becomes heavy with the scent of roses.

There's only one person missing — Paulina. She has disappeared from her mother's house, and there has been no word of her through any of the Segreta's contacts. I wonder if our friendship could ever have been repaired, after a betrayal such as hers.

I squeeze Roberto's hand, and try to push the thoughts away. I cast a glance upwards, but no one lurks in the galleries today. There's been no sign of Carina either, and a warrant issued across the city means there's nowhere she can hide. Has she taken Paulina with her, I wonder, abandoning Venice for good? Will I ever see her again? I hope not, for, in her case, I know forgiveness would be impossible.

It takes a friendly face to banish Carina from my mind.

Aysim steps forward from the crowd. She dips in a low curtsy, her hair braided and arranged in the latest Venetian fashion. It's almost as if she grew up here.

"May your marriage be a long and happy one," she says in French, her eyes brimming with happiness.

"Thank you," I respond in the same tongue. "May you too find such happiness."

As Roberto and I pass the last of the Grand Councilors and emerge into the sunlight, the waiting crowd of spectators outside erupts in applause. Scanning the celebrants, I spot various faces that I recognize but cannot acknowledge. These women of the Segreta stand with their husbands, or with their children or parents, or even alone—widows and spinsters of the city. No outsider could guess the invisible web that binds us, the threads of which stretch all over Venice. Teresa's secret was just one tiny tug on the web. When I introduced her to our number, I could never have guessed how crucial her secret would prove.

We have survived them—Vincenzo, Halim and Carina—although we have lost the most powerful of our number. Allegreza's death is the only cloud in the clear sky today. *Thank you,* I tell the women silently.

Other women in the crowd aren't as restrained. I spot Bella Donna and her friends, being held back by guards. Their dresses are outrageously gaudy, as are their wigs and the bright spots of rouge on their cheeks. Their yellow scarves flutter in the wind. I wave to them.

"Laura!" A young girl presses forward from the crowd, reaching past a guard's staff.

"Oh, let her out, let her out!" I gasp, rushing towards

her. The guard reluctantly lets my old friend through, and Annalena falls into my arms. "What are you doing here?" I ask.

She's even prettier without her cowl, and it's a delight to see her slim waist and the curve of her shoulders for the first time, liberated from the shapeless convent robes.

"A mysterious benefactor purchased my freedom," she says, arching her eyebrows at me. "I wonder who that could have been?"

I smile at Roberto as he arrives by our side.

"I've heard much about you," he says. He takes Annalena's hand and kisses it, making her cheeks blush furiously. I wonder if those are the first lips she's ever felt.

"Come and see me at the palace," I say, hugging my friend. "I'm sure we can find work worthy of a former *conversa*. A lady-in-waiting, perhaps?"

Annalena gasps with delight, but Roberto is already gently steering me away. There are so many people to see and thank.

"Thank you!" she calls after me, and I smile to myself. I know what it is to have one's first taste of freedom.

Roberto and I arrive in the center of the square. The palace looms before us, and up above it, the Piombi. Despite the sunshine and the happiness of the day, I shudder. Somewhere, up there, in the heat and stench, Massimo languishes. His trial is to take place in a month's time. A whole month of enduring those cells beneath the leaded roof. He won't be exiled like Vincenzo; his fate will be far worse. I take no joy in his suffering.

The crowd presses around us, cheering and throwing

more flower petals over our heads. My eyes linger on Roberto's face as I press my body close to his.

"Happy?" he asks.

"Never more so," I say. I wish that I could stay in this moment forever, all our troubles behind us and who knows what joy in the future.

I look around me. At the palace, the canals and their gondolas, the people in their ornate outfits and the shifting colors of Venice's buildings.

The city I love is safe. The man I adore is by my side.

The Segreta remains. There will be other trials to face. But when Venice calls, we will be ready, of that I am sure.

All we need is a secret.

50

That night, I brush the last of the flower petals from my hair as I gaze at Roberto's sleeping figure. He's draped across the bed, his arms thrown wide, his face buried in the pillows. I draw a satin-edged blanket across him and lightly kiss his brow. He shifts his body a little and buries himself deeper into the mattress. I smile and tiptoe out of the room, my silk stockings silent on the marble tiles. From my dressing table, I take out a black velvet sack.

I pull the door gently behind me and smile at the servant who waits outside.

"You can retire for the night," I tell him. He throws me a grateful smile and goes up the stone stairs that lead to the servants' quarters in the palace attic. I need to be alone for what happens next.

I follow the double stairway down to the ground floor of the palace. Candles burn low in the gold sconces that line the walls. The eyes of men in oil paintings watch me as I walk down a wide corridor towards the dining room. On the way, I take out the mask and place it over my face.

I open the varnished door, leaning on the ornate handle, and slip inside.

My friends are waiting for me. I catch the glimmer of a cat's eye, a peacock feather rising high above a head, the white feathers of a swan's visage.

Masks are everywhere, and there's the rustle of silk as people rise to greet me. I pat the air, sending them the message to sit back down, and the women of the Segreta lean back in their seats, waiting for me to take my place at the table.

Silence.

Then an older voice speaks: Grazia.

"You missed the initiation," she tells me. I look around and see that a woman has a bandaged hand. I remember my own initiation and the drag of a knife's point across my palm. Her wound will heal soon enough.

She's wearing a mask I haven't seen before: the hooked beak of an owl, tawny feathers sewn over the surface of the mask. But I know who hides behind it, taking her rightful place at last.

"I am honored to join you," says Aysim.

"I'm sorry," I say, "it was difficult to get away." Gentle laughter fills the room and my cheeks blush.

"So, to business," says Grazia. "We have word that—"

There's a sudden glow of light as the door opens a second time and someone else enters the room. I recognize the proud stance, but the unmasked face is timid. My whole body tenses.

"What are you doing here?" I ask.

"I invited her," says Grazia, placing a hand on my arm. "We must hear her out."

Paulina bobs in a hasty half curtsy, not moving from the doorway. She wears a simple black mourning dress and holds a small purse. "I'm sorry," she says. The women watch her solemnly. "I'm so sorry for everything. You must understand—I was led astray. I let Carina pour her poison into my ear. I—"

"Please!" I say. "Don't try and pretend you were enchanted. You've always known your own mind, Paulina."

She begins to cry, a sad, lonely figure. No one goes to her. She looks like a little girl, abandoned. Despite everything, I feel a pang of sympathy, but it's not enough.

"You betrayed us," I say. "You betrayed my friendship. You betrayed Venice."

"Please." She sniffs. "I have no one."

"What about Carina?" asks Grazia.

Paulina dries her eyes, reaching inside the purse clutched at her waist. She approaches the table and slips a sealed creamy envelope towards me across its surface. "She has gone. This is for you, Laura."

Grazia stands and seizes her arm. "You must come with us, Paulina," she says.

The girl's face is afraid. "Why? What will you do to me?"

Grazia sighs. "We need to speak with you, that is all. Have no fear, you will not be harmed."

While Grazia and the other elders take Paulina into another room, I go to the fireside and hook my thumb under the wax seal on the back of the envelope. It pops open and I tug out a thick piece of paper. The brown ink flickers in the light from the fire as I read the note.

Dearest Laura,

    This is not over. I swear to always be a plague on your happiness. One day Venice will spit you out and I will be there to erase every last memory of you. You may have married a prince, but you will die a bride to grief and pain.

    That is my promise.

Carina

I watch the paper tremble in my grasp. I take a breath and focus my mind until I am calm and my hand is steady. Such threats are easy to make, but I refuse to live my life in fear. I lean over the flames to hold the corner of the note against a glowing orange coal. Instantly, it catches fire, sending a column of smoke swirling up the chimney. I drop the note and envelope and watch the red wax seal melt as the paper shrivels and chars. Soon, nothing is left.

"What was that?" asks a member wearing a dove's mask.

I shake my head. "Nothing of any merit," I say.

Ten minutes or more pass before the elders and Paulina return. Grazia addresses the room.

"Some of our group would like to allow Paulina another chance," she says. "But the voice that will decide is that of our new leader."

New leader? We haven't discussed this at all. Grazia slips a hand into her sleeve and pulls out a pouch. She shakes its contents into her open palm and I spot a glimmer of dull silver. Then she approaches me and holds out a ring I know well, mounted with a small ruby.

"I d-don't understand," I stutter. I look about the room and see the other members of the Segreta watching me. I can sense their smiles.

"It was a unanimous vote," Grazia says. She takes my hand and slips the ring on it, the silver cool against my skin. It fits perfectly. I hold my hand up in the candlelight and turn my wrist. The ring looks as if it was made for me, even though I remember seeing it on the papery skin of the woman I helped to die. "It's as Allegreza would have wanted," Grazia adds softly.

Is this really true? Am I to be the new leader of the Segreta?

"I'm not sure. . . . I don't think I—"

Grazia tuts. "Don't insult us," she says quickly. "Do you not think that these women—the most powerful and influential in Venice—know best? Without you, we would be no more. Allegreza always thought so much of you. She may have been harsh at times, but it was only because she wanted you to be prepared when this day arrived."

Truly, I am honored. I take off my mask, and the other women do the same. I gaze from face to face.

"I will be your servant as long as you will have me," I promise my friends. The last face my eyes come to rest on is Paulina's. She is staring at the ground.

I think about everything I've been through. Incarceration, betrayal, death and marriage. I'm still here, aren't I? Paulina has been weak, but she has returned to face the consequences. She has lost a husband, while mine was saved. She has broken her vows, but then, so have I.

I nod. "You are welcome to join us again," I say.

The smile that breaks out as Paulina lifts her head is filled with such hope and relief I cannot help myself. I take my old friend in my arms and feel her sobbing into my shoulders. She mutters, "Thank you, thank you," again and again.

After a time, I take my place at the head of the table. The fire is dying in the grate and soon it will be time to separate again.

"The Segreta are a force for good," I say. "We have been sorely tested, but we have prevailed. A city cannot stand proud without a strong backbone. You are the reason that Venice remains intact."

I turn to one of the curtained windows. Beyond it, beneath the blanket of night, lies the city. What secrets are unfolding, even now? I stroke the ring on my finger and feel its weight on my hand.

"Ladies, our work has only just begun."

About the Author

Sasha Gould lived in Venice until she was nine years old. She later studied fashion in London. Her favorite things are opera, ballet, and romantic movies. She lives in the Lake District of England with her cat, Tosca, and writes about Venice, the beautiful city she knows and loves.